I0768220

THE CATALYST

THE CATALYST

A Novel

Nat Bickel

The Catalyst by Nat Bickel

Identifiers: LCCN 2024911481 | ISBN: 979-8-9907828-0-8 (hardcover) | 979-8-9907828-2-2 (paperback) | 979-8-9907828-1-5 (ebook)

Library of Congress Cataloging-in-Publication Data is available on file.

Cover Design by Gwen Galeza
Typesetting by Nicole Frail Edits
Printed in the United States of America

One

THE THREE-WEEK-OLD ELECTRIC blue nail polish distracted her for the moment. She fiddled with the misshapen remnants, her thumbnail tracing over a piece that resembled a crescent moon, scraping at the edge until it was set free. It fluttered down toward her feet as the lights above pulsated in the reflection of the laminate tiles. The flickering fluorescent bulbs threatened to burn out with a high-pitched whine, mocking the relentless throbbing in her head.

"Looks like my favorite patient is finally awake," Dr. Roski said, leaning against the door to her hospital room.

"It happened again, didn't it?" she asked, sure of another blackout.

"Yes, this is the fifth time. You don't recall *anything*?" Dr. Roski asked, a fatherly look of concern across his face, which was fitting as Kelynn viewed him as much after her many visits.

"I remember sitting in the library thinking about my class load this semester. I looked around at everyone else studying, too, and wondered what careers they were working toward. Then my thoughts shifted to a fire." She paused. "Something about if there were a fire right then, whose future careers would matter most and who should survive. From there, everything started to feel heavy. I couldn't stop looking from one person to the next, wondering and contemplating." She took a deep breath, her muted headache now chanting. "That's all I got, Doc," she said, shifting her eyes to his.

"It sounds like you had an anxiety attack, but I rarely see someone fall unconscious for this long."

"How long was I out?"

"About four hours. Have you been sleeping well?"

"The best I can as a college student," she said, rubbing her forehead.

Dr. Roski prescribed her a higher dose of medication to help prevent anxiety. She'd taken it regularly as requested, but it never seemed to work. Kelynn had been experiencing blackouts since her senior year of high school, triggered by a multitude of thoughts about her uncertain future. She looked down at the opal necklace clasped around her neck and thumbed the semitransparent gem; the only thing that made it better. A gift from her dad, who promised it would help if she pushed her thoughts into it instead of holding them in. It didn't make sense, but an opal blessed by a Romani traveler made her life easier. However, keeping it a secret as her father requested weighed heavily on her, making her feel crazy at times and forcing doubt to intrude. It was when she stopped believing in that magic that she ended up in hospital beds. She wondered how many more times she was going to wake up somewhere she didn't know, unsure of what got her there, unable to stop the darkness from consuming her.

Three Years Later

"You're going."

"I don't know, Preston. I've had a lot going on, job hunting while already working two jobs. I'm just ready for some 'me' time." Kelynn rolled her eyes.

"He's a friend of a friend, though. I promised him you'd show. Don't be such a buzzkill," Preston insisted, filing her nails to a point pretty enough to catch your eye but sharp enough to hurt if you got too close.

Kelynn sighed and reached for her favorite sweater.

"Oh, no you don't," Preston said as she grabbed it out of her hands. "This is way too safe. It literally covers half of your neck. How is Hastings ever going to fall in love with you if he can't even get a glimpse of you?"

Preston Willimby thrived at parties, always grabbing the attention of guys—who were drastically different from Kelynn's type.

"Maybe he'll learn to appreciate a woman's mind," Kelynn said as she snatched the sweater back.

On the drive to the restaurant, she fiddled with the radio while fidgeting in her five-inch heels. The boots Preston picked out were taller than she would've normally worn, but it was the only way Preston would let her wear the sweater.

As Kelynn walked into the Lantern, she was immediately aware of how slowly she was moving in her heels. She could hardly breathe. Situations like this always made her uncomfortable. Her motto was always, "You can't force love," and this felt undoubtedly forced. She had met Hastings Caldwell once, at a party three years ago with the glue that held it all together, Preston. At the time, he was on an athletic scholarship with the University of North Carolina, which ended as soon as he blew a whopping 0.20 into a breathalyzer at the ripe age of twenty, but Preston promised he'd matured.

"Hey, good-lookin'."

Kelynn jumped at the low voice. If this was Hastings, he wasn't how she remembered. He leaned against the gate out front of the restaurant smoking a cigarette. His brown hair was wavy with loose curls, giving him an effortless attractiveness.

"Hey . . . Hastings?" Kelynn guessed, as she held out her hand. Hastings's handshake was a little too tight for her preference.

"I've got a table outside in the garden. Just thought I'd wait for you out here so you didn't get lost."

As if looking through that small restaurant would have been so hard, thought Kelynn.

He guided her into the garden area with an elevated roof that let in the night breeze. She was thankful she had won the sweater debate.

Normally, Kelynn wouldn't go for Asian fusion cuisine, but with this ambiance, she was down to try anything.

Well, almost anything.

Something about Hastings left her with her guard up. Maybe it was his cocky demeanor or the way he dragged her through the restaurant, never letting up his tight grip on her hand.

You've been single for almost a year. Just push it aside and try, Kelynn thought as she sat down across from him.

"You've graduated already, right? Must be some super genius," Hastings chuckled.

"Right," Kelynn said, squinting at Hastings, trying to figure out if he was being sarcastic. "I only graduated a semester early because I took summer classes. When are you finishing your degree? You've probably broken a record by now. Trying to get into the Tar Heels hall of fame?"

Hastings's smug look proved she'd hit a sore spot. "I'm almost done. Just one more semester in the spring, and then I'm off to a real job. Don't you still work two jobs?"

Clearly, the conversation had quickly turned from friendly banter to pointed jabs.

Thank God, Kelynn thought as the waiter stepped in with the champagne Hastings had clearly ordered in advance.

She wasn't impressed, but she was grateful for a break from the conversation, and champagne *was* her adult beverage of choice. Although, she usually couldn't afford it, and if she couldn't afford it, *she* didn't know how Hastings could either.

Regardless, the alcohol eased the tension, and Kelynn started thinking this wasn't that bad after all. She actually laughed hard enough to cry from his stories about Preston. Turns out he knew her pretty well—like how Preston claimed to be vegan but always ordered her coffee with skim milk, thinking they took out the dairy instead of the fat. After taking another sip of bubbly, she looked up from her glass, past Hastings, and noticed a rather tall man walking by. He was staring at her, hidden mostly by the shadows in between street lights. She couldn't fully make out his face, but she could see his eyes fixed on her, suddenly feeling like he was peering into her soul and rummaging through all of her thoughts. Everything melted away.

"Hey, you gonna finish off the bottle?" Hastings broke her gaze.

"No, I'm good. You can have it," Kelynn said, a little shaken up.

When she looked over Hastings's shoulder again, the man was gone, but something about him stuck with her. She wished she had more time to memorize the rest of his face.

When the check came, Hastings opened the leather pocket it was nestled in and nonchalantly reached for his wallet. "I don't want to insult your 'womanness,' but I was planning on paying. Is that cool? Or should I also start taking feminism classes?"

With a glare, Kelynn said, "Go right ahead." He paid and they walked outside together, the date undoubtedly over. She gave him a side hug, and as she walked away, he grabbed her hand and pulled her close.

"Aren't you gonna kiss me? I wined and dined you. It's the least I deserve," Hastings whispered.

"Not tonight, Hastings. I've got to go."

But he wouldn't let her.

"Come on now. I thought we had a good time tonight. I had you laughing all evening."

"Hastings, let me go. I need to leave."

He didn't. As she raised her voice and said it one more time he replied, "Fine. I don't get you. You think you're better than everyone."

Once he released his grip, she swiftly headed to her car and didn't look back, doubling the pace from when she approached the restaurant at the beginning of the night despite her heels.

Damn it, Preston, she thought. *From now on I pick my own dates and my own shoes. No more being set up.*

When Kelynn got home, her roommate, Indi, was asleep on the couch with their dog, Roscoe. She tiptoed past them to her bedroom and wiped off the excessive makeup Preston had applied, then put on her favorite worn-out T-shirt and climbed into bed.

As Kelynn drifted off to sleep, she couldn't help but think of that mysterious guy outside the Lantern that made time stop. She hoped she would dream of him, but it was more likely she'd have nightmares involving Hastings.

Clay.

IT WAS A bet. I was supposed to show up and wreck the date. Did I do that? No, I couldn't—because of her. I thought back to Tuesday when it started. It was poker night, a night full of distraction. I tried to relax as my mind traveled back, replaying everything that went down, trying to find a nonexistent loophole.

"Where's Gunner tonight? Doesn't he usually catch a ride with you, Hastings?" I asked, fully invested in our fifth round of Texas hold 'em.

"He couldn't make it. Had business to attend to or something. It doesn't matter though, because I'm totally _gunner_ score big time, and I don't just mean in poker," he said.

"Dude, another girl? She must not have met you yet," I said playfully.

"She hasn't. At least, not that I remember. It's a blind date. Preston set me up." Hastings rolled up the sleeves of his flannel, studying his hand.

"Why are you talking to Preston? So help me if you got with her . . ." Lliam trailed off.

"Don't worry, Lliam. Your precious little ex doesn't interest me. Too easy in my opinion."

"Shut up," Lliam said.

"Oh. Do you love her now?" Hastings asked.

"Can we just get back to the game?" I sighed. "And who is this girl?"

"Some girl named Kelynn. Apparently, she's a hot friend of Preston's," Hastings said.

"Did she go to UNC?" I asked.

"Yeah, like three years ago," Hastings said as he threw down his royal flush and grabbed the large pile of change we'd been betting with.

"Thanks, guys. At least try to make it harder. I can get Kaitlyn nice and tipsy with this. I'm told she is way more fun when she's drunk."

"Isn't her name Kelynn?" I asked.

"Yeah, whatever." And with that, Hastings left.

Lliam let out a sigh of frustration. "I think he's lying about not going out with Preston. What do you say we make this interesting?"

"How so?" I responded, raising my eyebrow.

"What if you were there?" Lliam grinned.

"How am I supposed to tag along? I'm not third-wheeling, dude."

"No, just see if Preston is actually his date, and if she is, you say you happened to be there and break it up," Lliam insisted.

"Did you even hear where they are going?" I asked, exasperated with the Lliam and Preston saga.

"I'm pretty sure he told me before we got here. The Lantern, I think. Knowing him, he'll get a table outside under the moonlight," Lliam said, disgusted.

"Fine. I'll go check and see if he's there." I hesitated. "I'm not sure I can break it up, though."

"I'll bet you a hundred bucks you can," Lliam said, a little too aggressively.

"Lliam," I said with a sly grin while rubbing my forehead, "you know I can't turn down a good bet. It's a deal."

When I got to Franklin Street, the sun had disappeared, but a soft glow lingered on the horizon. The breeze was just right. If Hastings was going to jump in and steal Preston, tonight was perfect for it. When I made it to the Lantern, Lliam was right, Hastings had reserved a table on the patio. Except, he wasn't with Preston. As I stood on the street, my eyes froze on *her* and refused to budge. I couldn't help but stare at her dirty-blonde hair that turned lighter when the breeze gently blew it. Even her distant laugh drew me in. I never wanted to hear it end. I rubbed my hand over my beard, studying her. Then her gaze met mine over her champagne glass. That's when I realized *she* was Hastings's date. He always bought the cheapest champagne to get girls relaxed. She was definitely no Preston, in the best ways. She seemed sophisticated but hesitant, until she looked at me—any uncertainty fading away. The connection was like an electric wave of something. I couldn't put my finger on it. Who was she? Why had I never seen her? I suddenly remembered why I was there. It was all for a bet that I wasn't even going to cash in on. None of that mattered, but I knew my friendship with Hastings was about to get as rocky as the Blue Ridge Mountains.

Two

IT WAS THE beginning of Kelynn's shift at La Vita Dolce café, a quaint, modern coffee and gelato shop where the drinks speak for themselves. Located in the heart of an up and coming residential community of well-off dog owners, Kelynn couldn't have picked a better job. No matter the time of day, there was bound to be at least one dog walker strolling past. It also wasn't unusual for the place to be swarmed with women sporting Lululemon leggings when the barre class across the street let out, which was the case today. Kelynn was just starting to get a handle on the rush when Blakely and Preston walked in.

Great, Kelynn thought, *I just want to get through this shift so I can sleep, and now Preston is going to prod about my date.*

"So tell me everything. Did you shack with him?" Preston started as she leaned over the counter, clearly unaware of the spandex clad group.

"Oh my gosh. Definitely not. Literally one of the worst dates, no, THE worst date I've ever been on, Pres. I mean it. No more setups. I'd rather drown myself in espresso than go out with him again," Kel replied.

"Hastings is hot. What happened?" Blakely asked. Blakely O'Donnell had been Kelynn's friend since her freshman year of college when they happened to sit next to each other in Art History 101. She just so happened to get along with Preston, more so than Kelynn did. Those two were practically inseparable now. Kelynn knew to keep them at bay, that they were more of the casual, party-type friends, not the kind she would tell all her secrets to.

Kelynn's tone shifted as she quieted her voice, "He kind of got pushy with me."

"No way. You're probably overreacting," Preston said.

"I bet he leaned in for a kiss and you weren't in the mood, like always," Blakely said as she and Preston laughed in unison, like sorority sisters from hell.

"Maybe if you would relax a little, some guy would ask you on a second date," Preston continued, shoving off a ponytail of one of the barre class attendees that kept brushing her shoulder.

"The fact that you automatically take his side shows how much you truly care about me. I'm telling you I said no, and he wouldn't let me leave. He was holding me so tight," Kelynn insisted.

"Sounds like role play to me," Blakely mocked.

Preston rolled her eyes. "Geez. Relax. Of course I care about you. Why do you think I set you up?"

"Whatever, guys. I have milk to steam," Kelynn said, turning her back to her so-called friends.

Clay.

I HAD AN unusually large amount of work to do. It sounds nerdy, but software is my home away from home, which is why AnaScape, a modern technology company focused on app development and the latest and greatest devices, is a perfect fit for my job. Thankfully, my boss approves of getting out of the office to get into a creative head space. I was headed to a new spot to get some original ideas flowing, enjoying the fresh air when Gunner texted me.

Hey, man. Sorry I couldn't make it to poker. Had to go to dinner with a client.

No problem, man, I replied.

I heard Hastings had a big date. Lliam told me about the bet, but I never heard what went down.

Well, he wasn't out with Preston, so nothing too crazy happened, but I think I'm in trouble.

Oh, no. What is it this time? Gunner texted back.

Hastings saw my car after his date ended and pulled it out of me. He said I owed him. So, since Hastings couldn't get a second date, I bet him I could. With the same girl.

As soon as I hit send, I looked up to catch the door for a group leaving La Vita Dolce. I watched my phone as Gunner typed, with the three little dots moving back and forth on my screen.

"Welcome to Vita. What can I get started for you?"

Holding my breath for Gunner's reply without looking up, I responded, "Cold brew with an extra shot."

"It's $2.75. Would you like to join our loyalty club?"

The three dots went away. In frustration, I put my phone in my pocket. Holy shit. There she was. Hastings's date was standing directly in front of me.

"Hi," I barely got out.

"Hi. Did you want to?" she asked, seeming a little stunned herself.

Did I want to? Did I want to stare at her for hours? Ask her why she went out with scum like Hastings? Touch her perfectly disheveled hair?

"I'm sorry. What's your name?" I asked, running my hand over my beard.

She hesitated, looking confused as she said, "My name is Kelynn. Your total is $2.75, and I'm assuming you don't want to join the rewards club?"

"Kelynn, that's no way to address a customer," an artsy woman who I assumed was her boss with the name tag, Gwen, corrected.

"It's my fault, ma'am. I would love to join the loyalty club." I put my cash on the counter and walked away.

Kelynn shouted after me, "Sir, I need your name."

Amused, I smiled and said, "Clayton."

Then I saw it in her eyes. The electric wave I felt the first time. She looked at me like she'd just been told the world was ending. I could see the same yearning I was feeling reflected back at me. I set up camp at a corner table near the window. I had three hours allotted outside the office, and when she called my name signifying my drink was ready, I didn't know how I was ever going to leave.

"So, party at your place tonight?" Gunner asked over the phone. I'd called to distract myself from *her*.

Nat Bickel

"Yeah, I haven't had a big one since the summer. Bring whoever you want," I said.

Gunner Chapman is my best friend who I met while studying at UNC. He's the kind of person you can hang out with and not have to fill the air with constant conversation but still gets you regardless.

"I hear Hastings is coming. Who knows what's going to happen," Gunner said.

"I know. I'm getting tired of his bullshit. He always causes problems, but whatever. Is Preston coming?" I asked.

"Lliam invited her, so probably. She'll show up and not talk to him, as usual."

"Well, hopefully we get some new faces and no drama," I replied, optimistic.

"Amen to that," Gunner agreed.

"I've got to get back to the office. I got stuck at a coffee shop for over four hours today working. Well, trying to anyway," I said.

"Cool. See you later," Gunner said as he hung up.

After I got off work, I went to grab all the party essentials: ice, liquor, chasers, and snacks. You never want to be out of snacks when you have a bunch of drunk people over, especially girls who don't eat beforehand trying to look skinny and then don't know their limit. My place had become the designated party house since I moved to a nicer locale, and tonight was going to be another one for the books. I could feel it.

Three

"DOES THIS DRESS look slutty?" Preston asked.

"It's a little short," Indi started, "but you look great—not slutty, just like an empowered woman who is proud of her body."

"Perfect. The sluttier the better!" Preston giggled.

"Preston, you're sure Hastings isn't going, right?" Kelynn asked.

"Yes, for the millionth time, it's not his party. Lliam invited me. I'm pretty sure he thinks I'm trying to hook up with Hastings, so I doubt he would invite him."

"Okay. I really don't want to see him again," Kelynn said with an undertone of worry and doubt, practically shivering in disgust.

"I know. You're traumatized or whatever," Preston said, pushing Kelynn's concern aside.

Kelynn rolled her eyes as she threw on a jean jacket over her black dress and slipped on a pair of black boots. Her white-blonde ends popped against the blue denim.

"I approve, for once," Preston said, sizing up her friend.

Kelynn laughed, "Thanks. Let's go have fun. I could definitely use a drink after this week."

Indi, the DD for the night, drove the squad to the party with Beyoncé playing in the background. As they pulled up to the house, the street was already lined with cars.

"Let's go!" Blakely yelled. The four walked in unison, a lame tradition they did entering all parties, dating back to sorority days.

Lliam saw them from the window and greeted them as they entered.

"Hey, babe," he said to Preston, casually grabbing her backside.

"Lliam, don't call me that. We aren't together, remember? Go find Becky with the good hair," she said with a hair flip and walked into the dimly lit house.

As they continued past the entryway, they were greeted with high energy, "Hey! Welcome! The real party is out back. Our guest DJ, Feverish Haste, is out there mixing it up real nice and, more importantly, the bartender is, too. I'm Gunner by the way."

Feverish Haste? Interesting name choice, Kelynn thought, wondering if she'd heard him right. *Did he say Feverish Taste? Gosh, why am I so paranoid?*

Gunner was right; the backyard *was* where the party lived. Kelynn immediately noticed the crisp smell of a bonfire brewing, its warmth teasing her. Strung lights hung above, but the stars were still visible in the night sky. A bar cart was set up with every type of drink imaginable. This was one of the classier parties Kel had been to. Normally, there were cups everywhere, people puking in the bushes, and definitely no Edison bulbs or art-deco patio furniture. Though, the night was still young in reference to the puke situation. As they made their way to the bar, a familiar face approached them. Kelynn searched her memory for his name.

"Hey, I've seen you before. At La Vita Dolce, I think. Kelynn, right?" he asked.

"Yeah . . . you were the guy who didn't want a loyalty card," she said, trying to play it cool.

"If I remember right, I only have nine more stamps to go before I get a free drink." He smirked, amused. "What's your last name?"

"Sanders."

"Sanders," he repeated. "I like that."

"And who are you?" she asked, her expression calm.

"I'm Clayton Fogerty, but I go by Clay most of the time. This is my house."

"Clayton. That's right. I feel like we've met before," she said, his eyes feeling as though they were grounding her rather than gravity. "Like before you came to the café." A feeling of deja vu suddenly overcame her.

"What do you want to drink? Shall I dare say shots?" Blakely broke in, quickly ending the conversation with Clay.

"I think I'll start a little slower," Kelynn said.

"Yeah, me, too," Preston agreed.

"How about . . ." Kelynn started.

"How about more champagne for my girl?" Hastings broke in, putting his arm around Kelynn.

Shit. What was he doing here? I knew I wasn't paranoid! Kelynn thought.

"Feverish Haste, I should've known," she said aloud, briskly brushing his arm off.

"So? More bubbly, miss?"

"I'll just grab a beer, but thanks." Kelynn pushed him aside as she grabbed a Heineken and went to the opposite end of the yard. As she walked away, she could hear Hastings confronting Clayton.

"What the hell were you doing with my date?" Hastings asked, angry and drunk, clearly a common combination for him.

"*Your* date? Didn't she turn you down?" Clay replied.

"Hey, man. Back off." Hastings pushed him.

"Dude, knock it off. Enjoy the party. Do you even remember what happened that night?"

"Bro code, dude. Bro code," Hastings said.

Their voices faded as Kelynn found a secluded spot by a big cypress tree near the back of the yard. As she stood there, the breeze brushed past her, intertwining in her hair. She sat down under the protection of the pine tree, able to drink her Heineken in peace as she forced her thoughts elsewhere from Hastings. Instead, they shifted to the idea of serious relationships. She didn't have one, nor had she ever felt "in love," but love was never meant to be a part of her plan. Unexpected fear started to creep in and then she sensed it—that feeling she got over and over again, the one she could never control. Without warning, all of her dreams, wants, and aspirations overtook her mind. They swallowed her whole. The twinkling lights began to fade as an all-consuming dizziness rushed in.

Clay.

GUNNER AND I had just started a game of pool when I saw Preston walk up to Lliam. It was hard not to eavesdrop when they were just a few feet away.

"Haven't seen you at these parties before. I'm Preston," she played.

"Preston … what're you doing?" Lliam asked.

"Oh, come on, Lliam. Don't you wanna have some fun? Pretend with me." Preston continued, "So, what's your story? Grow up around here?"

I rolled my eyes and tried to focus on the game as Preston teased Lliam.

"Fine," Lliam said, amusing Preston. "As a matter of fact, I grew up just one town away."

"You seem mysterious, like you have a record, and you know how to make troubled girls fall in love with you," Preston said, pouting her lips in a way she knew Lliam couldn't resist.

"As a matter of fact, I have had a couple of intense relationships. I guess I attract that type of girl," he said.

"Oh yeah? What about now?"

Lliam began to move his hand to Preston's midriff, where her dress cut out to reveal glimpses of her skin.

"I don't know. I've got a couple things going on, but I'm not sure if any of them will materialize," he said, moving closer.

"Hmm," Preston hummed into Lliam's ear as her hand touched his chest. "We should change that, Kapoor," she said.

Lliam was so weak when she called him by his last name. "Oh yeah?" he played back.

"Mhmm," Preston giggled.

"Aw shit, Clay," Gunner said as he saw them kiss.

Before I could respond, I heard someone yelling in the distance. "KELYNN! KELYNN! WAKE UP! DAMN IT!"

"Preston, get over here!" the same girl shouted, her eyes darting at each of us.

Preston looked at Lliam, then walked past us as she reassuringly said, "Don't worry guys, this has happened before. It's fine."

I started to walk over, but a girl named Indi stopped me. I tried to look past her to see Sanders, but her friends were blocking her. She told me they could handle it, but I hung back so I could hear what was going on. For some reason, I already felt protective of her.

"It'll be fine, Indi," Preston said. "I'll stay here with her to make sure no one touches her, especially Hastings. I don't have anywhere to be tomorrow anyway." She was eyeing Lliam.

I could barely hear Indi say, "Let's just take her home now. I'm not leaving her here, and neither are you."

I went back to my game of pool with Gunner, after several attempts of trying to help and Indi telling me to go away. I couldn't even see what was happening. I turned back over my shoulder after a few turns, but they were gone. A glint of something dangling from a low-hanging tree branch caught my eye. I squinted, trying to make it clearer in the dark.

I started to walk towards it when Gunner said, "Hey, man. Your turn," as he handed me the chalk.

Four

"KELYNN, YOU'RE UP already!?" Indi asked, apparently startled to find her in the kitchen making breakfast the next morning with Roscoe begging at her feet.

"Yeah, sorry that happened again."

"Maybe you should go to the doctor," Indi said, rubbing her hands together, a clear sign she was worried.

"I've been. I don't know what else they would do for it," Kelynn sighed. "It's the weirdest sensation. I'm calm, then all of a sudden, my thoughts about life are overwhelming. They're all fighting for space, for the spotlight. Then I can't function anymore, and I black out. I know you know all of this, but I just wish I could make it make sense. I'm not sure what other medicine would help, but clearly my anxiety medicine doesn't," Kel explained.

"Maybe it would help if you slowed down a bit. You're constantly working, going to the gym, or working on a project. Maybe you should just 'be' for a while," Indi said.

"It's hard to slow down. When I do just take a moment for myself, a lot of times that's when my thoughts multiply, like at the party. I think juggling so many different things in my life distracts me from my thoughts."

"Well, you can't be the only one that happens to, right? I can go with you to a doctor or specialist sometime, if you want," Indi suggested.

"Do you know Clayton?" Kel asked, eager to change the subject.

"The guy whose house we were at?" Indi asked, confusion lining her voice.

"Yeah, did you notice his eyes?"

"His eyes? No, I remember him introducing himself, but I didn't get a good look at him."

"They're the kind of eyes that see right through you. You know, like the kind that peer into your soul? They're so blue I could just swim in them for days."

"Damn. You got that from two minutes of talking to him?"

"Yeah, I guess so. It felt like he could be . . ." Kelynn trailed off.

"He could be what?"

"I don't know. I just felt something when I looked into his eyes."

"Like he's your *soulmate*?" Indi taunted, dragging out the word.

"Well, no, not that. I don't even want that. Indi, I can't explain it, but it feels intense. It scared me. I can't tell if he's good or bad yet."

"Good or bad? You make him sound like fruit you're scared to eat. What is going on with you? Why are you even up? Normally, you have to sleep for a day when you black out like that."

"I know. That's what I'm trying to say. I saw Clay at the party right before I blacked out. I think that's what made me okay afterwards. But it's not okay, you know?" Kel tried to explain, while Indi's brows furrowed deeper in confusion. "Does he know I blacked out?"

"No, at least, I don't think so. We blocked you as best we could from everyone, and he was nowhere in sight when we moved you to the car. We looked ridiculous, Kel, like we were trying to move a dead body through a sea of people."

Kel let out a breath of relief. "Wow. I owe you breakfast for that one!"

"Hell yes. I could go for some scrambled eggs and potatoes. What are you making?"

"Huevos con patatas!" Kelynn winked.

"I knew you were my best friend for a reason!" Indi said with a cautious smile.

I WOKE UP to a trashed house, which was to be expected. That's the price you pay when you host a party, I guess. I was used to it, but it didn't feel the same this time. I was usually exhausted after a shindig like that, but today I almost felt inspired. What the hell did I drink last night? Then I remembered Sanders staring into my eyes like they were giving her life, like they were her air. Kelynn Sanders. Her name burned in my head like a hot brand had been freshly pressed against my skull.

"You're going crazy," I said to myself as I grabbed a trash bag and began shoving red plastic cups into it. I had a weird rush of energy today. I was already outside and about to start on the yard when something caught my eye in the sunlight. A tiny necklace that could have easily been destroyed by the lawn mower glimmered on the ground next to the tree in the yard. It was so delicate, radiant. What do they call the gemstone that reflects the colors of the rainbow? An opal? It looked like it belonged to a goddess. I carefully picked it up, and suddenly I wasn't in my backyard anymore but in Times Square, walking into a white-walled building with giant windows that towered above. I blinked a few times to make sure it was real. Several people greeted me as I entered, wearing a suit. I took an escalator up to the third floor and found my desk. I was a journalist, writing a story about animal shelters partnering with thrift shops to provide donated recliners and lounge chairs as a more comfortable living space for cats and dogs waiting to be rescued. A tunnel opened up behind my desk, and I was quickly shoved through. Pictures and thoughts rushed past me. There were polaroid pictures of faces I'd never seen—people yelling at me to do more and do better, people handing me coffee, homeless people asking for money, friends hugging me. The tunnel closed and I moved onto a movie set, finding myself behind a camera, yelling *"Cut!"* My own voice startled me. I was directing a movie, coordinating all the moving pieces into one fluid motion picture. This was my job? I thought I was a journalist. What was going on? I looked down at my feet. They started moving faster. The ground became steeper and rougher. I looked up at the glorious mountain I was suddenly climbing. I could feel the fresh air fill my lungs as I smelled the cypress pines surrounding me. I started to feel at ease when something began jumping on me, pushing against my legs.

"Hey! Hey, bud!" I was in my backyard again. Willie, my black Labrador, jolted me back to reality as she jumped on my legs, almost knocking me down. "Hey, Willie! Are you glad the party's over? I missed you! Sorry you were in your crate most of the night! I couldn't risk someone taking you home."

As I reached down to pet her, I saw the opal necklace on the ground. I had a weird feeling that hours had gone by. Was I daydreaming?

"Did you knock that out of my pocket, girl?" I questioned, feeling a little dazed. Willie just wagged her tail and licked my face as we sat outside in the sunshine.

Five

IT WAS TIME for her shift at La Vita Dolce, and Kelynn was ready for some normalcy. She didn't know what to think of her interaction with Clayton, or "Clay" as his friends called him, but she knew it was more than she could handle right now. As she headed into work, a homeless man was sitting in the alley by the back door where she normally entered using her key card. As she walked past, he looked up at her, his eyes lacking a spark, lips turned downward in a seemingly permanent frown.

"Ma'am," he started. "I don't even know what to ask for anymore." His eyes were downcast.

"What's your name, sir?" Kel asked.

"Roger," he mumbled.

"Roger! I didn't recognize you. You were here a few months ago. We used to get lunch together, remember?"

"Kel, is that you?" He looked at her quizzically, a small trace of recognition dancing across his face.

"Yes! Wow, I've missed you. I have to start my shift, but if you want, I can join you for lunch in a couple of hours?" Kelynn offered.

"Sure. I have nowhere to be," Roger obliged.

"Roger that," she said, winking at him. Roger nodded, the sadness leaving his eyes for a brief moment. She shut the back door and grabbed an apron. Kelynn's shift started in disillusion. For a moment, she thought she was going crazy. Clay was here.

Seriously, he's here again? she thought. *Why do I feel like I can't trust myself around him? I can't decide if I even want to. I'm not sure I like how he makes me feel, invading my space like this.*

"Hey . . ." Clayton said as he approached the counter.

She refused to make eye contact.

"Hi. What can I get started for you?" Kelynn asked, busying herself with organizing the mugs.

"I'll take a cold brew with an extra shot, Sanders," Clay said playfully.

She couldn't help it. The way he said her name forced her to look up. "Want me to stamp your loyalty card?"

"Damn it. I misplaced it," he said, shuffling through his pocket.

"You lost it already?"

"Kelynn, come on. We can get you another one, sir," her supervisor Gwen warned, once again.

"We're old friends. It's okay, really," Clayton defended.

He lowered his voice so only Kelynn could hear, "I just came here to work, and also to make sure you're cool. I saw your friends freaking out at the party. Are you okay?"

"What do you mean?" Kel asked, avoiding eye contact again. She knew very well what he was referring to.

"They were shouting at you to wake up. I didn't know if you passed out or something," he said, now leaning on the counter.

"I'm fine, really. Thanks for stalking me at work for evidence of that."

"Hey ... can we start over?" he asked, seeming to have sensed her irritation.

"I don't have time right now," Kel said, grabbing a pitcher of cold brew, holding a cup that read 'Clay' across the front in her hand.

"How about lunch?" Clay pressed.

"I have plans."

"Sanders, come on. Give me a chance to talk. Don't make fake plans just to avoid me."

"Fine. We can talk tomorrow night, and I'm not making them up. Swear," Kel said, raising an eyebrow.

"Alright. Well, I better get to work before my boss checks in," Clay said, grabbing the cup of coffee as he turned to find a table.

"I guess you'd better," Kelynn said, with the corners of her mouth fighting back a grin.

C. lay.

I WORKED FOR a couple of hours in the café but kept getting distracted by two things. One, the dead leaves bustling by the entrance felt extra loud and enticing. I loved when someone's foot crunched one. Today, it was like they were cracking me open with each step, unearthing deep, buried thoughts.

The second was Sanders. The way she made coffee was mesmerizing. I didn't know something like that could be so beautiful. Her ashy blonde hair that was tied back in a loose ponytail sashayed across her back as she moved from the cash register to the espresso machine with a whitewashed brick backdrop. One strand gently brushed her cheek as she moved swiftly back and forth. I could write a book about that one strand of hair.

I did my best to force my thoughts back to work. I started a list of prospective clients and went to take another sip of cold brew. Shit. It was empty. I usually only allowed myself to drink one to avoid the caffeine jitters, but I didn't care today. I couldn't feel more at ease. As I went up to the counter, I was thinking of a witty way to order another when I was suddenly face-to-face with Sanders's boss.

"Another cold brew?" she asked, reading my mind.

"Yes . . ." I answered as I looked around.

"She's on break. Sorry for how she spoke to you earlier. She doesn't realize how she comes across sometimes."

"She's fine, really. We're friends; it's no big deal." As I finished paying, she handed me my liquid energy. "Is it cool if I step outside for a moment and leave my laptop?" I asked.

"Sure thing."

I needed some air. I exited through the grand glass doors and made my way down the sidewalk, purposefully stepping on every crunchy leaf in my path. It was like opening a present with each step I took. A cover band began to play at the amphitheater across the street, making my steps feel even lighter. Then I heard voices, *her* voice. I looked to my left and found her sitting on the ground, eating lunch with what looked like a homeless man from his dirty beanie and tattered boots. They were both laughing so hard I saw tears fall down his face. She was so casual and relaxed with him. I normally avoided homeless people, but she acted as though they were best friends. I watched for a bit longer and saw her hand him a bag of food I assumed was meant to last him a few more meals. I moved on. I didn't want her to see me. Who was this girl and why did she make me question everything? Something was weird, but I didn't know what. All I knew was that it was definitely a good weird.

Six

THE LIGHT FROM her phone illuminated her bedroom, waking her. It buzzed twice. Kelynn squinted as she sleepily rolled over to check it. It was a Facebook message from Clay.

Seriously. He's not only stalking me at work but on Facebook, too? she thought.

See you tonight. I'll pick you up at 7:00 p.m.

Aggravated about his intrusion in the middle of the night, Kelynn's eyes glanced from his message to the time on her phone.

Damn. 5:00 a.m.

She only had two more hours of sleep before she had to be up for her second job.

She rolled over to go back to sleep, but her mind was now fully awake.

Why did he have to message me right now?

Clay seemed nice, different, but something about him scared her and made her want to keep her distance. For example, he didn't give her a choice about tonight. What if she wasn't home at 7:00 p.m.? Would he wait outside? Would he ask Indi to let him inside?

Ugh! Why did I have to say tomorrow night when we were at the café? she thought, wishing she hadn't agreed to anything.

Kelynn decided to make use of the time she would normally be sleeping. She threw on some leggings and headed to the gym. Instead of replying to Clayton, she took her frustration out on the treadmill. Three breaths in, four breaths out. She repeated her breathing pattern for the entire three miles. She felt like she could run for days. The sweat dripping down felt so invigorating, like all her stress demons were leaving her for good. As she headed towards the showers, she caught a glimpse of herself in the mirror. She paused; something about her reflection was off. She looked herself up and down three times before it hit her. Her necklace was gone. In a panic, she scoured her gym bag. No luck. She tried her best to brush it off as she got ready for work.

It has to be at home somewhere, she thought, trying to convince herself. *Take a deep breath.*

She showed up to work that morning surprisingly refreshed, even with the lack of sleep and subsiding panic over her lost necklace.

"Good morning, Kel."

"Morning, Joe," she said to her boss. "What department am I with today?"

Three days a week, Kel worked for an entertainment agency, the only thing truly keeping her in Chapel Hill. They deal with record labels, concert venues, and film companies. Her main duty was to fill in the gaps for whichever department needed extra help that day. She never knew what the day would bring, which she loved. It was a spontaneous adventure every day. If only they would hire her full-time, however they required a master's degree, and since she couldn't afford that with her combined paychecks from both La Vita Dolce and Radical Entertainment, she took what she could get.

"It looks like the film crew could use an extra set of hands. Are you up for it today?"

"Sure!" Kelynn responded excitedly. The film department was one of her favorites.

"They're prepping on the fifteenth floor if you want to start there."

"On my way," she said beaming, walking backwards towards the entry door. Once inside the elevator, she pushed fifteen, only five flights up to go. The doors opened at one.

Crap. This one was going down, Kelynn thought as she glanced through the doors to see the one and only Ben Stiller standing in front of her.

She was no longer upset about waiting on the elevator as a giant smile made its way across her starstruck face.

I BARELY MADE it to my desk when my boss pulled me aside.

"Your work last week was by far the best work you've turned in all quarter. What's gotten into you?" Mr. Maté asked curiously.

"Thank you, sir. I've felt more in tune with our consumers' expectations, and I've been hyper-focused. Not sure what's changed, but I'm glad you liked it."

"Your new app ideas are great. I'm pitching at least three of them to corporate tomorrow. If you want to come and comment on the specifics, I could use the help."

"I'll be there."

"Be there at 9:00 a.m. sharp," he said, turning to go into his next meeting.

"Got it. Thanks, Mr. Maté."

He winked as he walked away. Last week I worked mainly at the café. How could I have possibly done great work? I felt so distracted. I started towards my office cube when I remembered I hadn't seen a reply from Sanders. I pulled out my phone to check Facebook. Nothing. Maybe she hadn't seen it. I felt weird looking her up, but I had to learn more about her. She wasn't telling me much at La Vita Dolce. Her pictures were with shelter dogs, her family, college friends, and at a nursing home with someone who I'm guessing was her grandmother. She only had one picture of her by herself, in a Jeep with her arms spread wide, smiling big, wind blowing her hair everywhere. She looked truly free. My phone buzzed, pulling me out of my thoughts. It was Gunner.

Hey, you left me hanging. How much is this bet Hastings has going with you? Anything I can do to help? You know how much I love to see Hastings lose.

Bing!

Before I had the chance to respond to Gunner, I got another message.

I looked at the screen in disbelief. It was from Sanders.

Make it 7:30. And I prefer to drive.

Seven

HE WAS NOT going to have all the control, Kelynn thought as she replied to Clayton.

She honestly thought he would argue, but all his next message said was, *Deal.*

Great. I didn't scare him away, she thought sarcastically.

At work she felt like a golf caddy, but it was worth it getting to watch Ben Stiller in his element. Kel carried equipment from one set to the next, moving props from one location to another, all day. The producer couldn't make up his mind on the feng shui.

She checked her watch.

Shit. It's 7:15, she thought.

She had worked late without realizing it. She darted out of the office, but the elevator took its sweet time, stopping on almost every floor. Everyone was on their way home. She had ten minutes to make it home. Clay would most likely be there. She'd have to somehow run past him, get inside to freshen up, and then act casual.

She pushed the gas pedal about an inch from the floorboard as she raced down the highway. She finally turned onto her street. It was three minutes before they said they'd meet. She could see her house. A truck was parked outside, the bed of it facing her. Assuming it was Clayton's, she parked around the block and cut through her neighbor's yard.

"Hi, Betsy," she whispered to the Golden Retriever that lived there.

Betsy was so excited to see her that she nearly knocked Kelynn down. "Down, girl. I've got to go."

Bety's owner, Wanda, came outside. "Everything alright, sweetheart?"

"Yes, sorry to cut through your yard. I've got a guy parked outside my house who can't know I'm just now getting home."

"Sounds like love to me, girly!" her neighbor said whimsically.

"Yeah right!" Kel yelled back. "I'll bring Betsy some treats to make up for it."

"Don't worry about it. Just go get ready for your 'date,'" she said, using her fingers to make quotation marks.

Kel winked as she ran inside.

"Someone's parked outside our house, and why are you coming in the back door?" Indi asked as Kelynn rushed upstairs to her room as Roscoe tumbled after her, anxious to greet her.

"It's Clay. He's picking me up. I'm late!" she yelled.

"Okay, so you're seeing him now?" Indi asked, confused.

"No, I don't know."

"Why are you hurrying?"

"I look like shit. I was on set all day dragging equipment around."

"Meet anyone cool?"

Kelynn had a shirt halfway over her head as she came to the top of the stairs. "Ben Stiller," she said, grinning so wide her cheeks hurt.

"No freaking way! Please tell me you guys discussed *Walter Mitty*," Indi replied in disbelief.

"We talked all day about it, Indi! Literally a dream. I love my job!"

"I'm so jealous, but also so incredibly happy for you! You deserve that after obsessing over that movie for years."

Kelynn laughed as she ran into the bathroom. She quickly threw on some lipstick as the doorbell rang.

This is as good as it's going to get, she thought, checking her reflection in the mirror.

She grabbed her denim jacket and answered the door with a chill, "Hey."

"Ready to go? I didn't see a car outside, so I didn't know if you were home," Clay said, looking back at the driveway.

"Yeah, well, I'm driving yours," she said, trying to avoid the truth.

"Okay, cool," Clay half laughed, his expression unsure as she walked past him and straight to the driver's side door.

"Are we heading toward your house?" she asked.

"No, that's why I was planning on driving. It's a surprise," he said, still standing outside the truck.

"Are you going to get in or what?" At that, Clay climbed in on the passenger side. "Guess you'll have to direct me," she said, flashing a satisfied grin as she put the truck in drive.

Clay.

"TURN LEFT AT the next light," I said nervously as Sanders drove my dent-free Dodge truck. It's not that she was a bad driver; I just didn't have the control, and that scared me.

"Next time we should try this blindfolded," Sanders said.

I tried not to look directly at her, but it was hard not to. Her black jeans hugged her in a way that showed off her strong legs. Plus, there was something about a girl in flannel that made me stare.

"If we do that," I said, "it better be in your car."

She shot me a playful look as we continued down the road toward the annual street fair.

"Where are we going?" she asked.

"We're almost there," I answered back. "Go ahead and park on the street on the next block."

Once the truck was in park, I looked over, taking her in. Her wavy hair framed her face, hiding her in its shadows, making me want to lean closer.

"What?" she asked.

"Nothing. I'm just glad we made it safely," I said, trying not to stare.

She smiled smugly and jumped out of the truck. "So, you took me to a virtually abandoned street? Seems a little sketch."

"We're not staying here, if that helps. I just knew there wouldn't be parking any closer."

We were walking down the street in silence when she stopped dead in her tracks.

"Clayton, I'm sorry. I forgot my jean jacket in your truck."

"No worries. I'll run back and get it."

"You sure?"

"Yeah, it's no big deal. Just wait here, and by the way, you can call me Clay."

Eight

KELYNN SAT ON the sidewalk, rubbing her arms to keep warm.

Where are we going? she thought, feeling oddly comfortable. *I feel like I already know him and that scares me. I don't trust anyone this quickly, especially not on a first date . . . although, this wasn't technically a date. He just wanted to talk to me about his party. That's the only reason we're hanging out.*

"Well, hello there," a voice that didn't match Clayton's came from behind her.

"Hi," Kelynn said sternly as she shot up to her feet.

"I'm Sam. What's your name?"

Kelynn started backing away, but he swiftly closed the gap.

"What's a pretty little dollface like you doing all alone on an empty street?" the stocky man asked as he stroked her arm.

He was about the same height as Kel, but much broader. She took him in, measuring his build, contemplating how much force she would have to use to try and escape him, if she could escape him.

"What do you want?" she asked, hoping he didn't hear the fear in her voice.

"Come on now. That's not very polite of you," he replied, tightening his grip. "Let's get out of here," he said, pulling her closer. He started to move his other hand to cover Kelynn's mouth.

"Get the hell off of me!" she yelled, kneeing him in the groin and running.

She started screaming hoping to alert anyone around. She didn't care how crazy she sounded. She kept screaming as she sprinted, not realizing she'd ran right past the truck until someone grabbed her by the hand.

"LET ME GO!" she yelled as she turned around and started clawing at their face.

"Sanders! Sanders! Kelynn! It's me, Clay! Stop!"

She sank into his arms and started crying.

"What in the hell is going on?"

She couldn't catch her breath. "I can't. I need to go home," was all she could sputter out.

Clay wrapped her jean jacket around her and got her into the passenger side of the truck. Locking the doors, he turned and looked at her. The color had drained from her face.

"Sanders, you've got to talk to me."

"A man just tried to attack me!"

"What? Where?" he asked in shock. "This is my fault. We should have gone together to get the jacket."

"It's not your fault. If I hadn't left my jacket . . ."

He cut her off. "I left you alone."

"I'm not some helpless little child, Clay. I was obviously able to fight him off by myself. It just scared the shit out of me."

"What did he try to do?"

"He was stroking my arm, asking me why I was alone. I kneed him in the balls and ran. Thank God for those self-defense classes."

"Martial arts?"

"No, I took a self-defense class once I started working downtown. I didn't want to encounter some creep in my parking garage and not know the basics."

"Did they teach you to claw like an animal?" Clay said with a chuckle, lightening the mood ever so slightly.

"Yeah, sorry about that. Is your face okay?"

"I mean, I was a little stunned. I think I have a few scratches, but yeah, I'm okay." He paused. "I'll just drive around until I find a spot on another street."

"No," she said. "I don't want to be around here, knowing *he's* here somewhere. Where were we going, anyway?"

"The annual autumn street fair. I thought we could walk around."

"Clay, I can't. He's probably headed that direction looking for his next victim. Can you just take me home?"

"What if we go somewhere else, far away from here? Somewhere in-doors, in public."

"Okay," she said softly, laying her head against the seat, grateful to no longer be driving.

Kelynn stared out the window, her body language reflecting her post-adrenaline rush exhaustion. Clay took Exit 39, the change in speed causing her to perk up a little.

"We're almost there," he said quietly to avoid startling her.

She gave him a side grin and nodded. He was looking at her like she was a bewildered child. She had just kicked someone's ass, but Clay seemed scared he'd break her simply by talking to her.

Clay pulled into the parking lot of a Starbucks. "I know it's no La Vita Dolce, but . . ."

"It's perfect. Thank you."

They got out of the truck, and Clay followed her into the surprisingly busy coffee shop.

"What's your drink?"

"Latte," she responded.

"That's it? Just a latte? You work at a café. How could you not have a specific drink like half-caff, coconut milk, a dash of honey, or a pinch of cinnamon?"

"As flattering as that is, there's something about a simple latte. Warm, steamed milk in the shape of a leaf. Its simplicity is beautiful and . . ." She trailed off as Clay caught her glance, and their eyes locked. "And I'm gonna go grab a table before they're all gone," she said, turning away from his magnetic gaze.

"Sounds good," Clay said and got in line to order.

Clay.

"WAIT, WAIT, WAIT. *The* Ben Stiller?" I asked a second time to be sure I heard her correctly.

"I know," Sanders said with a wide smile as she snuggled up to her latte.

"How? Just how?"

"I never know what I'm going to get into at my job or who I might meet. That's why I love it."

"Why don't you do it full-time? Why work at the café?"

"I would if I could. Since I don't have a master's, they won't let me. It's a requirement for all employees at Radical, but I'm working on it."

"Oh, really? Where do you study?"

"Well, I'm working on saving enough to get my master's, but at this rate, who knows when I'll be able to start it, let alone get hired full-time."

"You could moonlight as a karate instructor?" I suggested, raising my eyebrows.

"Right," she said. "A little too soon to joke, don't you think?"

"Sorry." I tried to hide my smile, but failed.

"I can explain, if you really want to know."

I nodded, releasing any humor that was present in my expression before.

"I was attacked once before. I had just graduated from high school, and my friends got me into a frat party. One of the guys was taking people on tours of the house, so I joined in, not knowing it was a ploy to get girls into the bedrooms."

"Sanders, you don't have to explain," I said, trying to stop her.

"It's okay. Nothing actually happened. I mean, one of the guys shoved me into his bed, but he forgot to lock the door. Apparently, Indi had seen me wander off and ended up using pepper spray to get me the hell out of there. If it wasn't for her, it would've been really, really bad."

"I'm so sorry. I don't understand how people can be so cruel." I didn't know what else to say.

"I'm past it now. So, what do you do for work?" she asked, quickly changing the subject.

"Hmm . . . guess."

"You work on your computer a lot at Dolce . . . never making calls, just typing," she said, thinking out loud. "How many guesses do I get?" Her eyes sparkled as she paused to take a sip of her coffee.

"How about three? That sounds like a good even number."

"That's literally the opposite of the number three," she laughed.

"Do you want to make it two?"

"Fine." She looked at me playfully. "You're a salesperson who deals with clients in different time zones. That's why you email rather than call."

"Go fish," I said, shaking my head.

"You're a writer? But not a journalist. A writer for instructions for contests or maybe for games."

"What kind of games?"

"For a casino. You write the rules."

"Guess again."

"Hmm." She took a deep breath, closed her eyes, and took another sip. I didn't understand how her tiny hands could hold a mug, let alone claw someone's face so forcefully.

She opened her eyes and locked in on mine. "I've got it," she said.

I slyly grinned, awaiting her third and final guess.

"You work for AnaScape."

"Holy shit. How did you . . ."

"You have the latest Scape laptop, your backpack has the logo embroidered on it, and you have a bumper sticker."

"Well done, but you still don't know what I do there."

"I can't take anymore detective work. Please fill me in."

"You were close. I'm a tech writer and developer. I come up with app ideas, and when ones that I don't come up with are developed, I usually write the rules and regulations."

"That's pretty cool. It sounds complicated. Did you go to law school? Rules and regulations sound pretty legal."

"I took a few courses in pre-law and got my degree in computer engineering. I can show you so many cool things on your phone that you didn't even know existed."

"Like what?"

I grabbed her phone. "Let me set it up."

"You don't know my passcode."

"Don't need it. This will blow your mind. Are you ready?"

She nodded.

"I need you to look directly at the phone. It has to memorize your face."

She rolled her eyes, then looked up, and that's when I took the picture without her knowing.

"Come on! Stare at the phone."

"Okay," she said and looked into the camera. I opened her Wi-Fi sharing app and sent myself the photo. Then I quickly flipped the camera lens to front-facing and said, "Okay. Now laugh."

"What?"

"It has to memorize all your facial features, including when you move your face. Just think of a *Friends* episode."

She started laughing, and in that moment, I snapped a picture of myself.

"Okay, cool. You're set. It takes eight hours to fully set it up since you have an older version."

"What?! That's such bullshit!" she laughed.

"Honest," I said, putting my hands up in defense.

She sighed and looked around. "Don't you love being surrounded by people? I always feel more inspired when I'm in a crowded place than when I'm sitting at home. It's everyone's energy."

"I know what you mean. I like that no one knows what I'm working on, and I have no idea what everyone else is working on, but we're all on our computers while sipping caffeine to keep us awake enough to do what we need to."

"Like knowing other people are human like us."

"Yeah."

"Excuse me. We're closing in ten minutes," one of the baristas informed us.

"What time is it?" I asked.

Sanders glanced at her phone. "Holy shit. It's almost midnight."

"What time do you have to be at work tomorrow?"

"I'm working at the café, and I open. So . . . 6:00 a.m. We should head out."

I opened the door for her. As she climbed into my truck, I felt like there was so much more I needed to know.

Sanders slept most of the way home. As I turned onto her street, I gently pushed on her arm. "Sanders, wake up. Hey, we're at your place."

She woke up seemingly in a daze. "Sorry, I fell asleep. I guess today was kind of a lot for me."

"You're good. I'm just glad you're okay."

"Me, too," she said sleepily. "I'll see you later."

And with that, she was out of my truck. I wished I had said something more, but she was already inside of her house. Would hangouts with her ever be normal? A part of me hoped they never would.

Nine

MOVING LIKE A cog in a well-oiled machine, or espresso machine in her case, Kelynn was pleasantly busy getting lost in each order she took; two pumps of vanilla, a sprinkle of cinnamon, a drop of honey, while pouring the steamed milk in the most intricate designs she could manage in ten seconds or less.

"Hey!" Blakely said across the counter, breaking her rhythm.

"Hey," she reluctantly replied, unable to match her bubbly energy. "What're you doing here?"

"Remember, we're thrifting today?" Blakely laughed at her friend's disheveled appearance.

"Oh, right. I get off at 2:00. Want to come back then?"

"Kel, it's 1:30. I figured I'd just get a drink and wait for you."

"How is it already 1:30?!"

"Where has your mind been today? You seem out of it. Are your 'haunting thoughts' back?" Blakely teased.

"No, thank God. Not since the party." She knocked on the wooden countertop for dramatic effect. "Half an hour sounds good. What can I get started for ya?"

Blakely dressed her best every day, always wearing clothes that would grab people's attention. Today she sported a long trench coat with a crop top turtleneck and high-waisted jeans. Her crop top barely covered her bra, mere centimeters above, teasingly swaying and inviting an array of looks.

"Mmm," Blakely hummed as she looked over Kel's shoulder at the menu. "How about a peppermint mocha, but make it nonfat. I'm trying to lose ten pounds."

Kel rolled her eyes as she grabbed a cup and started pumping the "healthier" version of the jolly drink.

Kelynn was oddly excited to hang out with Blakely. It had been a while. Although she was normally overdramatic, whenever the two of them spent longer periods of time together, they got along really well. It typically took Blakely about a half-hour to drop the snobby façade, and then everything was good, especially when they went thrifting. Thrift shopping was their thing. They had the best time laughing at all the old styles they found, breathing new life into them. Mom jeans, Dickies coveralls, fur jackets, graphic tees from the eighties, even men's robes which worked as long cardigans—nothing was off limits.

"Bon appétit," Kel said, placing the picture-perfect latte on the wooden countertop. Blakely grabbed the drink without looking up, glued to her phone.

"Hey, did you hear about Preston and Lliam?" Blakely asked while texting.

"No, what now?" Kel asked, annoyed already.

"Apparently, Pres tried to hook up with him at that party where you blacked out. He rejected her."

Kelynn rolled her eyes again, feeling like they were going to fall out at this rate. "I'm so over that nonexistent relationship."

"Ditto," Blakely said, raising her to-go coffee cup and nodding her head in gratitude.

After Blakely sat down, Kelynn started prepping for the next shift. While she did the dishes with her co-workers taking orders and making drinks, Kel got lost in the sensory details of La Vita Dolce. The sounds of the clinking mugs, milk steaming, and the grinding of beans filled her ears. The sight of sunlight peeking through the blinds, the frothy milk tulips, and people greeting each other with hugs and hand-shakes danced across her eyes. The smell of crisp fall air leaking in from patrons coming and going mixed with freshly brewed coffee, toasting paninis, and the ever-popular pumpkin spice aroma teased her nose.

"Seriously. What's with you today?" Blakely asked, disturbing Kel's tranquil state.

"Sorry. What's wrong? Is your drink not okay?"

"I downed that in the first two minutes. Delicious," Blakely said, touching her thumb and forefinger together, modeling the Italian gesture for exquisite. "Kel, it's time to go."

"Right. I knew that," Kel said, turning off the faucet. "I'll meet you out front," she said, feeling unsettled.

Kelynn hung up her apron and joined her friend with the breeze coaxing her out of her daze.

"So I figured we'd start at Rumors, and then go to Club Nova, and then a couple of Goodwills if there's time," Blakely said, pulling onto Market Street.

"Or should we start with Goodwills, then build up to Rumors and Club Nova?" Kelynn asked.

"Ooh, that sounds better! Let's start there."

The windows were rolled down to fully embrace the fall weather, and a mixture of folk music, including The Lumineers, Mumford & Sons, and Houndmouth spilled out of them.

Taking a deep breath, Kel said, "I don't know why we don't do this more often."

"We both work a lot and try to limit our spending, so . . ." Blakely trailed off.

"No, I mean just hanging out. It's days like this when I don't doubt our friendship," Kel said, gazing out the window at the changing leaves.

"Are there times when you do? Ouch, Kel," Blakely said, obviously hurt.

"I mean, sometimes you and Pres act like I'm a pain in the ass, or I'm not part of the group."

Blakely went quiet and looked out the window, refusing to make eye contact with Kelynn for the rest of the drive. Each of her fingers sported a ring, amplifying the awkwardness as she tapped her fingers on the steering wheel. With each tap came a clink that made Kel cringe. Finally, they were parked. The two got out, and Blakely purposefully walked ahead of Kelynn into the store.

"Perfect example of what I mean," Kelynn said under her breath.

Blakely loved finding unique cocktail glasses, so she went straight to the back of the store, while Kel began flipping through racks of clothes. She started with the women's and grabbed a few denim items, then went to the men's section.

Mmm, flannels and giant shirts. It's like I'm home, Kel thought, the oversized fit of retired men's clothes reminding her of her dad.

She'd always been closer to him, even before her mom left. At the age of eight, Kelynn watched her mom take everything she could fit in her biggest suitcase and walk out the door, deciding she liked the comfort of wealthier men over the actual loving souls of her family. She remembered when her mom used to save the leftover popcorn kernels that didn't pop in the bag until she had enough to make an entire bowl, even though her dad's job held them at an upper middle-class status. Something shifted, and she went from living a life irrationally restricting her spending, to wanting to spend radically. Whenever she thought about her mom, she felt like that small child once again, remembering the nights her mom would come back in the early hours of the morning, barely past midnight, begging her dad to find a higher paying job so she could stay with him. But Kelynn always heard the soft putter of the engine of whatever Benz class or BMW series sat in the driveway; a gift from her latest affluent man. She listened intently on those nights, waiting for it to grow quieter, trailing off like her mom. Even now, her memory wasn't fully clear, but the sinking feeling that accompanied it was enough for her to want to retreat back to the present as fast as she could.

She found Blakely searching through old record albums.

"Blake, can we talk?"

Blakely continued flipping through the old music legends, squatted on the floor like she hadn't heard a word.

"Yeah," Blakely said, still not acknowledging her presence, yet she spoke first. "I'm sorry. I didn't know you felt that way. I want us all to hang out and be cool with each other. I'm only playing when I give you a hard time," Blakely said, stopping to take a breath before continuing. "I can't look at you right now because I suck at apologies, but I said it and I'll say it again. I'm sorry."

"Blake, I love you. Can we please put this behind us and get back to our day of fun?"

"*Day of fun*?" Blakely finally turned to look at Kel with a smirk on her face.

"Quit making fun of me!" Kelynn laughed.

"This is the stuff I'm talking about!" Blakely said in between giggles. She stood up and hugged Kel. "Come on. Let's get you to a fitting room. You HAVE to try this on!" she said, touching a denim tube top Kel found. "This is hot!"

They went to the checkout with only a few items, not wanting to blow all their money at the first stop.

"Okay. Let's hit up Rumors!"

"SHHH," the girls said in unison, laughing as they placed their index fingers on their lips, mocking the cleverly named store.

They found a few solid pieces at Rumors before moving on to Club Nova.

The car ride to the third store made for a more pleasant time with the tapping of Blakely's fingers replaced with the nonstop flow of conversation.

"Hey, Al," Blakely said as she walked in, the bell above the door ringing behind her.

"Hey, ladies. It's been too long since I've seen ya," Al, the store owner, replied. Blakely leaned over the counter to talk with him as Kelynn made her way to the back of the store. She always started there and worked her way up to the front, mostly to avoid the ever-flirtatious ol' Al, but Blakely liked them older. It worked out for their friendship, as they never fought over guys since Kel liked men without receding hairlines and fingers that grew the hair their heads could not. After only a few minutes with no luck in the back of the store, Kelynn made her way to the front, where Blakely had finally moved on from Al to a hat rack.

"What do you think?" she asked Kel, sporting a beret.

"A little too French," Kelynn said.

"I like it!" Al said.

I'm sure you would like it French, Kel thought. *Ew.*

Something caught Kel's eye in the glass case where the "expensive" vintage finds were.

"Hey, Al. Can I see that necklace?"

"Of course. This is a very rare blue opal on an 18k gold chain."

"Blakely! Get a look at this," Kel said, touching her neck. "I think I lost mine. Maybe this is it?" she said, her eyes wide.

"I'm sure you just forgot to put it on today," Blakely said.

"I forgot to check the house after work yesterday," she said quietly to herself. "How much?"

"Today it's $100, but if you come back next week, we're having a sale. It'll be $85."

"That's too much. I might be back if I can't find mine, though. How long have you had this one here?"

"Someone brought it to me about a month ago."

What are the chances it's mine? I never take mine off. I don't even know how I could've lost it. It must be on my nightstand or something, Kel thought, trying to reassure herself.

"What about this one?" Blakely asked, this time wearing a floppy beach hat.

"Better," Kel said, glancing at her while still holding the necklace.

"Real talk. I'm getting it," Blakely said, approaching Al's dated checkout counter.

Kelynn handed the necklace back.

"Thanks, babe," Blakely said, wearing the hat out of the store, sending a wink his way.

"Now, that is what I call a hot piece of man," Blakely said once they were out the door, but all Kelynn could think about was the necklace.

SHIVERING FROM THE sunless fall evening, I wrapped the blanket tighter around her. She nestled close to me, leaning her head against my chest, like she truly trusted me. I pulled her closer, smelling the pine-like scent of her hair. The moon reflected on her cheek, making her face glow. The freezing cold steel of the bed of my truck didn't feel so cold while I was holding her.

"Can I give you some advice?"

Sanders and I both jumped, an intimidating man in a suit standing next to my truck, having appeared out of thin air.

"What?" I asked, the only thing I could think to say.

"You should quit now. Stop trying to get a better job."

"Huh?"

"You're not smart enough," said a girl who looked an awful lot like Preston standing on the other side of the truck.

Thud.

Just then, I jolted as someone landed on the roof of my truck. I arched my neck as I turned to see another woman who said, "You're so entitled. You think you deserve more money? What about everyone else who worked just as hard?"

That's when the crowds started coming. They were shouting over one another, yelling conflicting statements.

"You got this! Just work harder!" one shouted.

"You suck. No one thinks you're good enough!"

"You're so beautiful," another said in a calm voice.

"You're not destined for success."

"You don't belong here."

They grew louder and louder as they started to climb onto the truck while I held Sanders. Her body felt lifeless in my arms. I kept holding her tighter and tighter . . ."

Ding-ding, Ding-ding. Ding-ding.

Whoa, I thought, hitting snooze on my phone's alarm clock, noticing the opal necklace lying next to it. Had I taken it to bed with me?

With my alarm silenced, I started looking through my phone notifications, seeing a text from Hastings that read, *Heard you're halfway. There's no way she's going to agree to a second night out after what happened with that guy on the street. My girl, Kel, talks. Kiss that $100 goodbye. At least that's something you'll get to kiss.*

I rolled over trying to comprehend what I had just dreamt while also annoyed at Hastings. I began typing a spiteful message back when I noticed something terrible; something you *never* want to see on a workday. The sun was out, and not just a little bit. It had fully risen and was high in the sky. The alarm that went off was to remind me to pick up more food for Willie on my lunch, not the alarm I was supposed to wake up to.

"Shit," I said, turning to find Willie whining, sitting next to the bed with her chin resting beside my pillow. "I'm so sorry, bud. I guess I needed some extra sleep today. Let's go eat breakfast."

I walked into the kitchen and gave Willie her usual bowl of bits while I fixed myself a mean breakfast of over-easy eggs, sausage, bacon, and toast. If I'm late, I might as well eat a hefty brunch so I won't need a lunch break. Mr. Maté would understand. He was the most chill boss I'd ever had, always letting employees work from home or make up time. To ease my mind further, I played Bob Marley in the background as I showered and got dressed.

On the drive in, I kept going back to the dream, reliving the nightmare. What did it all mean? It made me want to see Sanders as soon as possible. I needed to know she was okay, but I had to put that aside as I opened the office doors and went straight to my cubicle. I had a lot to catch up on from the morning and wanted to get started right away. I hadn't fully settled in when I felt a heavy hand on my shoulder, an angry hand.

In a low tone that only I could hear, he uttered, "You better have a damn good excuse for this morning."

My stomach dropped as I realized Mr. Maté, in fact, did not understand. "Mr. Maté, I apologize. There's no excuse. I forgot to set my alarm . . ."

"Clayton," he said, cutting me off. "Do you remember what important meeting we had this morning?"

"Shit." I buried my head in my hands and exhaled a heavy sigh as I looked up at him. "Was it a disaster?"

"It went," he paused, "surprisingly well, even without your presence. I was able to present your apps with a customer's perspective since I didn't know them as well as you do."

I looked at him in suspense, noticing his softened expression.

"We sold all three."

I had barely begun to let out the breath I had been unintentionally holding when he said, "But they're coming back next week to hear from the creator himself on the marketing vision for each damn one."

"Yes, sir. I will not let you down."

"You better not," he said, "but I do have to say well done on the creation. If anyone asks, I didn't give you any slack, nor did I smile."

"Understood," I said as he walked briskly away from my desk.

I let my shoulders drop and took several deep breaths to slow my heart rate before returning to my task list for the day.

I looked up at the fluorescent-filled ceiling with gratitude.

Headphones in, I plugged away at what was left of the day. I didn't take any breaks, except to use the restroom and refill my (what felt like) "worst employee" insignia mug. When I got back to my desk after my third refill, my phone vibrated with a text from Sanders.

What is this? it read, followed by the picture I took of myself the other night.

Just seeing her name across my screen made me smile. *Thought you needed a contact picture of me,* I texted back.

Does this mean you didn't even do anything cool on my phone? I trusted you! she wrote back.

My thumbs moved quickly, sliding over each letter as I typed and deleted my response three times before replying with, *I mean . . .*

You used your nerd powers for evil, she wrote back. *Now you're gonna pay for that.*

She started to type again but stopped. I waited a little longer and then said,

How about I pay . . . for dinner. Say Friday?

I took a sip of my coffee and realized I'd let fifteen minutes go by without working.

Get yourself together, I thought, kicking myself.

I put the phone down and got back to reviewing the apps Mr. Maté was miraculously able to sell when her text came through.

Sure, was all it said, but that was enough. I was taking Sanders out on a real date.

As the last person left the office, I kept my light on and continued to work.

I jumped when I heard a knock on my desk partition. "Burning the midnight oil?"

"Mr. Maté, you know I owe it to you."

"Thank you," he said with a nod. "The custodian comes in a couple of hours. Just a heads-up."

"Great. Thanks," I said, turning back to my computer and onto a new project.

I started researching current market trends on millennials. Anytime I got stuck, I turned to the generation I understood the best—my own. Diving deep into how we tick was one of my favorite hobbies and, lucky for me, part of my job. I'd never stayed this late at work before. The now dimly lit office had a peaceful feel to it. Paired with my computer screen, my desk lamp provided just enough light. I felt hyper-focused with nowhere to be and zero deadlines to meet. I was in the zone. I drafted two solid development ideas to pitch to Mr. Maté and backed them with consumer-based data. I liked practicality in applications to make the day-to-day easier. Getting outside of that box and designing games or something to add to someone's life for the sheer purpose of wasting time was like forcing me to only eat kale, and not in a flavorful salad but alone. Unseasoned, bland kale. Torture.

I passed the cleaning crew on the way out, ending my day as they started theirs. It was strange how two lives could be so similar, yet so different, operating on two totally different timetables. It was then that I realized I needed to get home and see Willie. She was probably hungry, even though I fed her a hearty breakfast. As I dug for my keys, I felt my phone vibrate in my pocket.

So, are you going to tell me where we're going?

It was from Sanders.

Are you going to let me drive? was all I replied as I walked outside.

Ten

KELYNN FINALLY HAD a day off. With balancing two jobs, she had a hard time keeping track of what day it was. To "reward" herself, Kelynn took a mental health day each month to recenter.

"Good morning, sleepyhead," Indi said as Kelynn climbed down the carpeted stairs still in her pajamas—a giant T-shirt and fuzzy socks—trying to hide her giant yawn.

"Hey, Bradshaw," she said in reply, her eyes half open, threatening to shut all the way again.

"Did you just call me Bradshaw?" Indi asked, confused.

"Yeah, Clay calls me Sanders, and I kinda like it. Thought I'd try it out on someone else."

Indi let out a giggle. "It's not bad, but let's not push it," she said. "By the way, how's it going with him?"

Indi had been Kel's best friend since high school. They'd gone through the same Chapel Hill school system for elementary and most of middle school, except for eighth grade when Indi's family moved to Ocean Isle for a year and came back shortly after. But it wasn't until their freshman year when Kel was smacked on the ass by an upperclassman that Indi stepped in and their two worlds collided. Together, they didn't put up with anyone's crap, yet tried to be inclusive in their friend group, which is how they picked up Preston and Blakely later at UNC. Even still, an unspoken bond existed between them. Indi knew all of Kelynn's secrets, including why she was guarded when it came to men. She'd seen her go through hell in high school with several guys who treated her like she was a second-rate movie. They put on a big show in front of people but ended up finding a side of popcorn or a more "mature" piece of cinema they liked better by the end of it. Because of her past, Kelynn had never had an adult relationship, just immature dating experiences, which was part of the reason she took a hiatus from relationships while at UNC.

"I haven't seen him since we got coffee that one night, but we're supposed to go out Friday," Kel said. "I think he likes me."

"Well, do you like him back? Maybe a lot?" Indi pressed.

Kel could feel the heat on her cheeks. "Indi, I'm still trying to figure it all out. I barely know him. Plus, I'm not one to rush into things."

"Oh, please! In high school you gushed at the attention guys gave you," Indi laughed.

"That was high school. Relationships never amounted to anything back then," Kel rebutted, her thoughts traveling back to the days when getting a boyfriend felt like the most important thing on the planet. She hated all that drama and feeling like the world was ending if some-one didn't like you back.

"I'm happy you're taking things slow, but he seems pretty nice, Kel. Just don't risk ruining a good thing based on your past, okay?"

Kelynn nodded, grabbing a mug and pouring the freshly brewed Traveler's Blend Indi picked up at their local farmers' market. The smell of it drew her out of bed, with notes of blueberry, cocoa, and the rich dark roast beans.

"In other news, what are you doing today?" Indi asked, changing the subject. "Your usual gym run and trash TV?"

"I think I'm going to head to the Villas today after the gym," Kel said.

"Oh yeah? It's been awhile since you've seen her, hasn't it?"

"Yeah, it's harder now, but I need to."

"Well, I'm off to work, but enjoy your day, babe," Indi said, hugging her roommate and heading out the front door, making sure not to let Roscoe run out behind her.

Kelynn put on her no-slip running leggings and a cropped sweatshirt that peeked at her abs as she grabbed her gym bag and headed out to start her day. Kel loved to run. As soon as her feet hit the treadmill, it was like she was transported somewhere else. She pictured different scenery each time: The Blue Ridge Mountains, the beach, a hiking trail, a grassy field, her neighborhood. She was able to zone out for most of it, her breathing controlled. Once she hit mile three, she turned off the treadmill and headed for the weights. She hated the meathead guys always crowding that part of the gym, staring at themselves in the mirror. Regardless, she grabbed a barbell and did some leg work. Leg day was Kel's favorite, and probably her most intense workout each week. She grabbed a much needed peanut butter-flavored protein smoothie from the front counter and went to the locker room to change. Freshening up, she swapped her sweaty clothes out for some dry ones, put on some extra deodorant, and tried her best to fix her sweat-soaked hair.

Good enough, she thought as she looked herself up and down in the bathroom mirror. *Monette won't mind*. She grinned at that thought, leaving her reflection as she headed out to her next stop.

Clay.

IT WAS WEDNESDAY on my lunch hour, and I hadn't seen my grandmother in two months. Honestly, I didn't like to see her. Not like this. When I was younger, my Omi was my best friend. The name Omi is German, just like my grandfather. It was just like her to accept his heritage as her own. I remember adventures we would go on every time I visited her. I can still smell the pines from our hikes, the ocean air from the sandcastles we made, feel the wet kisses of her weiner dogs, and taste the cookies she'd insist on making every time I visited, even when I was no longer a little boy. When Opi, my grandfather, left this earth, things became unbearable for Omi. She wasn't herself anymore. His loss corrupted her entire life, leaving a shell of the woman I used to know and love.

On the drive there, I listened to her favorite music, Frank Sinatra, Dean Martin, and James Dean. I could still see her terrible dance moves in the back of my mind, her apron used as a prop to gently smack me as we spun around and around in a kitchen from years past.

I parked my car in front of the Villas and took a deep breath as I said a quick prayer and shut my door, reminding myself, "She's still your Omi. You can do this."

I knocked on the door, expecting a nurse to answer, but when it swung open, Sanders was standing there. She looked at me with the most confused look, her brows furrowed together, almost angry.

"Hey," I said hesitantly, just as confused as she was, "Can I come in?"

"What? Are you stalking me now?" Sanders replied back sharply.

"I gotta tell you. That's the nicest greeting I've ever gotten here."

"Seriously, Clay?"

"No, really. Those nurses can get pretty snippy," I said, squeezing through the small crack in the door frame Sanders left open.

She looked at me disbelieving as Nurse Regina said, "Clay, so good to see you. She's missed you."

"See? So snippy," I said so only Sanders could hear me.

I followed the nurse, looking back at Sanders with a wink before entering Omi's room. She was looking out the window, as usual.

"Hey, Omi," I said sheepishly so as not to startle her.

She turned to face me. "Clay, my sweet boy. I've missed you." She reached out and kissed my cheek.

She wrapped her frail arms around me and squeezed me tighter than usual. I couldn't keep it together for long. I could feel the tears already stinging the backs of my eyes as I pulled her in close. "I'm so sorry, Omi. I shouldn't have waited this long." She held my waist a little longer. "I'm so, so sorry."

"Ah, don't you cry now. It's okay. I'm doing fine," she said, sounding like her old self.

"You seem better," I said, looking at her sunken face.

"You know, I feel better. I recently started having some fun again."

"Oh yeah?"

"Yeah, I've been going outside more. Just taking in the Lord's beauty. It's good for the soul."

"Yeah, I know what you mean," I said, seeing a tiny spark in her eyes.

"Do you want to go out there with me now?" she asked, her head angling toward the window in her small room.

"Of course," I said, taking her arm in mine to help her balance as we slowly headed through the doorway.

I pushed the sliding doors open and cautiously escorted my grandma outside to the back patio. We sat in two large rocking chairs like you would find at Cracker Barrel while we talked about my job, my life, and what "exciting" things were happening.

"What gets you out of bed every morning, Clay?" Omi asked.

"Well, I enjoy my job. I like what I do, and I have a few friends there."

"Are there days when it's hard?"

I felt like she was looking for inspiration to get out of bed herself, so I said, "Not really. I know this is how the world works, and I'm just doing my part in it. I get out of bed to survive."

She faced me, stopped my rocking chair and said, "Well, that's pathetic. You need the excitement of a new day with its endless possibilities, all of God's great nature, and most importantly, passion, to get you out of bed."

"You're right," I said, a little stunned by Omi's bluntness. "I could use a little more excitement and challenge in my days." I elbowed her hoping to ease the conversation.

"You're comfortable, I can tell," Omi said, eyeing me with her classic grandmotherly *you better mind me* look.

"I know. Comfort can be nice from time to time, but I'll work on it."

"Damn right, you will," she said. "Life's too short. I wish I would've stopped all the nonsense in my life to enjoy more of it and put myself out there. Challenge is good, too, but you need fun and excitement, Clay."

"Omi, when I look back on all our memories, all I see is fun. You made everything we did fun, even cleaning."

"I'm glad you see it that way, but a lot of that was just when I was with you. I wish I had taken in more of what God put right in front of us. More of this," she said, fanning out her arms.

I nodded, lost in contemplating the details of my life.

She pulled me out of my thoughts when she said, "Now, how's your love life?"

"Omi . . ." I said, giving her the look.

"Clay. Don't give me any of that crap."

"Alright, alright," I said, looking to the end of the patio where I saw Sanders and who I assumed was her grandmother.

"There is someone, but it's too early to tell where it's going."

"Tell me about her."

"I can't figure her out, Omi."

"You never will. That's part of the fun."

"She keeps surprising me with how connected to herself and everyone around her she is, or at least seems to be. It's like she's living a raw human experience, without anything artificial. That probably sounds weird."

I looked back at Omi and saw tears in her eyes.

"Clay, she sounds like what you need. I don't care how close you are to her yet, don't lose her. Keep figuring her out. Fight for her."

"Omi, I barely know her."

"I can already tell by how you talk about her," she said, her voice sounding weak. "I miss your Opi," she said, letting the tears flow now.

"Aw, Omi. I know." I held her hand as she searched for a tissue. "I miss him, too."

"Will you tell me your memories of him? I want to hear about him from a different perspective, from someone who knew him in a different way than I did."

"Of course, Omi."

I spent the next hour recalling several little moments with Opi, both serious and comical. We laughed a lot, with Omi holding my hand the entire time. I occasionally glanced over at Sanders who seemed so serious, talking with *her* grandma. She kept turning to the side and looking off into the distance and then plastering on a smile before turning back to the elderly woman. It was as if Sanders was trying her best to put on a good face for her.

I walked Omi back inside and promised her I'd be back sooner next time around. She hugged me just as tight as before. I walked out of the Villas' heavy door, feeling like it now held the weight I had walked in carrying. Omi finally had a spark in her eyes again. Even though it was tiny and hard to see sometimes, it was there, and that was enough.

Eleven

KELYNN WALKED INTO Radical, her mind preoccupied with the evening's festivities with Clay. She prepped for their date that morning, since they'd be headed to dinner right after she got off. She didn't like putting on loads of makeup, so she just put on a slightly darker shade of eyeshadow and a hint of red-tinted lip gloss.

"You look so good today," Julie, her coworker, said as she passed Kelynn on her way to her workstation for the day.

"Oh, thanks," Kel said, eager to brush off the compliment.

"What's different with you?"

"Tried a little harder this morning."

"Well, I love it."

"Thanks," Kelynn said, now self-conscious that Clay would notice she was trying to look good for him. She wanted it to appear effortless, but the attention made her uneasy.

Her day was less than exciting, with her assignment consisting of grabbing screenshots of social media posts involving clients who'd attended an awards show put on by Radical.

Sitting at a desk all day was not her ideal work environment, but she reminded herself that she was working towards her future, no matter the task. As she scrolled through the Twitter-verse, Kel put her earbuds in and turned on Radiohead. She could feel the hours slipping by while taking screenshot after screenshot and compiling them into a presentation. Her phone vibrated, pulling her out of her concentrated state. It was a message from Clay.

Hey, we still good for tonight?

Yeah, Kelynn typed, trying not to sound eager.

Cool. You may want to dress up.

Dress up? Where was he taking her? Cocktail dresses weren't her thing, Kel thought before replying with, *So, my best tux with heels?*

Somewhere between hiker and album release party.

Very funny, she typed back.

Just a little nicer than going to a street fair.

Got it.

Clay must've remembered what she wore the night they ended up at Starbucks. She liked that.

Pick you up in t-minus 3 hours.

Three hours? she thought.

That meant she still had two hours of work left before she had to rush home and wade her way through traffic. She started to panic when her boss tapped her on the shoulder. "How are the recaps coming?"

"Almost done!" she replied.

"Let me see what you've got so far," he said, leaning in.

She opened the presentations as her boss hovered over her shoulder.

"They look great! Why don't you go ahead and head home for the day? You can finish this up next week. Don't worry about the extra hour. You've put in enough hard work that we'll count it."

"Are you sure? I don't mind staying and . . ."

"Yes, have a good weekend. You must have plans, looking so nice today."

"Well, yeah, actually, I do. Thank you, Joe," Kel said, again slightly bothered by the extra attention.

She grabbed her purse and jacket and headed out of the office, letting out a sigh of relief as soon as she shut her car door. As she headed home, she tried to redirect her thoughts to Roscoe. She couldn't wait to see him. He always gave her the BEST greeting as soon as she stepped foot in the house, never getting tired of her.

What a life, she thought, envious of the effortless joy Roscoe felt.

Clay.

FINALLY, THE WORKDAY had come to a close. I was more than ready not only for this hellish week to be over, what with me missing that huge meeting with my boss, but also I had only two hours before I had to pick up Sanders. Time was moving so slowly, barely creeping along. Every time I glanced at my watch or phone, only a couple of minutes had passed. I guess that's what I got for checking it incessantly. I hadn't let something mess with me this much since my college days. This was another level of pathetic.

On the way home, I made a mental list of the things I could do in the two-hour window I had before dinner. I could work out, take a shower, play with Willie, and trim my beard—all of which only added up to a little over an hour.

I went straight to my weight room and started knocking out rep after rep and set after set of flies, curls, and bench presses. After exhausting my upper body, I took a quick, piping hot shower and fed Willie before grooming my beard. I paid careful attention to keep from nicking my jawline. Slipping on my go-to tan corduroys, I tucked in my grey dress shirt, leaving the top two buttons undone. I did a once-over in the mirror, and Willie let out a whimper, knowing that once I got dressed, I was about to leave. I gave her a pat on the head as I sprayed the tiniest amount of cologne possible and grabbed my keys.

My Dodge made the most pleasing deep hum every time it started. I flipped through the radio as I made my way onto Sanders's street.

I hope she's ready, because I'm freaking starving, I thought, placing my feet on the pavement.

As I rang the doorbell, I could hear Indi yell, "Kel, he's here!"

"Coming!" she yelled back.

Sanders's front door had little slats of glass but was made so you couldn't clearly see inside the house, just blurry shapes and colors. I saw Sanders running down the stairs, and even though she was hazy, I already knew I was in trouble. I didn't need clear glass to tell what a babe she was.

She opened the door, seeming rushed and a little out of breath as she said, "Ready to go?" Her eyes glanced up at me for a brisk moment before returning to the ground.

"Yeah!" I said. "I hope you're hungry because I'm ordering the entire menu."

"Starved," she said, my eyes caught hers that time and she didn't force them away as her wavy hair blew in the chilly fall breeze. I couldn't help but stare at her as we walked towards the street. She looked different tonight—good different. Her hair was straight, she had on red lipstick, and her eyes looked more dramatic, more vibrant somehow. It was like she had opened up her soul a little more than usual, and it was shining through. "Hey," she said, breaking my fixation, "should we get going?"

I half smiled and shut her door, quickly trying to hide the warmth spreading to my cheeks as I headed to my side of the truck.

"How was your day?" she asked as I buckled my seatbelt. It felt like we'd been asking each other that very question for years.

Twelve

THE BRIGHT LETTERS above the awning caught Kelynn's eye, reading "Kipos" while Clay put the truck in park, choosing a space near the back of the parking lot.

Good thing I didn't wear heels, she thought.

She reached over to unbuckle her seatbelt, and as she looked up, she realized Clay had already gotten out of the car and was opening her door. Kelynn almost got whiplash as the door swung wide, startling her. She tried to play it off as she gracefully stepped onto the blacktop.

"Sorry I parked so far away. I enjoy the fresh air."

"I don't mind," Kel said, "At least not when I have the time."

"You can always make time."

"Not always," Kel said, thinking of how many times she rushed from place to place. She knew they were just talking, but it felt like they were almost arguing. Tangible tension existed between them. Kel couldn't tell if it was because of her long day, or if something wasn't right.

You can't force love, she thought as she held her blazer together against the breeze.

I can really feel that fresh air now, she thought. It was filled with the aroma of food, which made the silent walk feel even longer.

He leaned over as they slowly approached the restaurant and said, "You look cute."

"Thanks," Kel said, barely glancing at him as the tension drained from her rigid stature.

Before Clay could grab the door for her, a hostess let them in. The double doors opened up into a homey, yet modern room. Edison bulbs hung from the high ceiling, varying in height, looking almost as if they were competing to see which one could hang the lowest without touching the bar. The rest of the light was coming from fixtures that took the form of glass balloons, giving off a radiant glow. For such a small restaurant, its presence felt big, like the two of them had walked into a family reunion, where every busy staff member made it a point to smile at them.

They followed the hostess to a small table in the back by a window. Kelynn sat down, unable to stop fidgeting with her hands. The last date she'd been on was with Hastings, and that was about a month ago. Still, she'd never felt this uneasy and aware of her every movement. Meanwhile, Clay sat across the table from her looking cool as a cucumber. He knew exactly where to place his hands. Every maneuver seemed natural. He wasn't overly conscious of the perspiring glass of water sitting on the table like Kel was. Instead, he would occasionally sip from his, totally comfortable. He held eye contact like it was his job, making Kelynn uneasy and aware of the tiniest normalcies, like blinking.

Blink. Look up at him. Blink. Get a drink of water. Blink. He's looking at me again. Blink. Look out the window. Kel thought like this for what felt like twenty minutes, when in reality only five had passed.

"How was your work week?" Clay asked, finally breaking the silence.

"It was decent. I took a day off this week, and that always helps."

"Oh, right. To visit your . . . grandmother?" Clay asked, squinting his eyes at his guess.

"I forgot you were there, too. She's not my grandmother," Kel said, glancing down at the floor this time.

"So, an aunt? Family friend?" Clay pressed, running his hand over his mouth and letting it rest on his beard.

"No, actually. I, uh, started volunteering at the Villas earlier this year. I felt like I wanted to do something more meaningful with my free time," she said, still looking away.

"Wow. I barely visit my own grandmother, and you go there for fun?" Clay asked dumbfounded.

"I mean, I'm not some hero. I have my fair share of demons. I used to know someone who lived at the Villas. I visited once and didn't go back. I'll regret that for a long time. Hanging with Monette helps me forget that, like I'm making it up with her." Kel smiled at the thought of their long conversations that never had any sense of continuity to them. "She had a stroke two weeks ago, and now she doesn't remember my name or anything about me. Just my face."

Clay sat across from her, silent. Suddenly, the table felt like it was a mile long separating them.

"Kelynn, I'm sorry. I know this may not mean much coming from me, but I'm telling you, I'm sure she still enjoys your presence. No matter what she remembers, the feeling she has when you're there matters so much more."

Kelynn looked up and smiled, like Clay had just told her a joke.

"You called me Kelynn," she said.

"Well, I guess you're right. Damn," he said with a soft laugh.

"Can I get you something to drink other than water?" the waiter broke in.

"Heineken," Kel said, still looking into Clay's grey-blue eyes.

"Blue Moon," Clay said, staring right back at her.

"Okay, guys. I'll have those out in a few minutes for you," the waiter said hesitantly.

"Great," the two said in unison.

Once the beers were delivered, the conversation turned to lighter topics.

"Hold on, hold on, hold on," Clay said, still laughing. "Let me get this straight. You went on a first date with a guy you had already dated before? And you didn't know it?!"

"Listen. We had only gone on one date previously like two years before, and I didn't want to be rude, so I sat through the evening. He didn't recognize me either!"

"What gave it away?"

"I didn't know for sure it was him until the end when he started talking about his Lego hobby. That's why we didn't go on a second date the first go around."

Clay shook his head, smiling, his cheeks red from laughing so hard.

"Okay, your turn. Tell me your worst first date," Kelynn said, cocking her head sideways in expectation.

"Alright, fine. But nothing can top that story."

Kel smiled as she dipped a French fry in ketchup.

"So, I met this girl at . . ."

"Opa! Opa! Opa!"

Before Clay could get another word out, the entire restaurant staff began shouting "Opa" and motioning for everyone to get out of their seats. They went table by table, pulling out guests' chairs as jubilant music blasted, each person joining a line of dancers who were showing them how to move to the rhythm, called tsifteteli—the Grecian version of belly dancing.

What the hell did Clay get us into? Kel thought, sending a playful glare Clay's way, just as the waiter reached out his open hand to take hers while pulling her chair out from behind her.

Clay.

NEXT THING I knew, Sanders was taking off her jacket. I hadn't realized she'd kept it on all evening. The waiter helped her slip it off, revealing an open-back shirt. Seeing her entire back, her lightly tanned, luminescent skin, felt like all of the oxygen in the room had been removed. She looked at me over her shoulder and mouthed the words, "Come on!" I hadn't realized the waiter was now trying to pull my chair out and get me to join.

"I'm not doing this alone!" Sanders shouted over the music as we were rushed into a circle of belly dancers.

I impulsively grabbed her hand while spinning her. She giggled, and I couldn't look away from her red-lipped smile. The belly dancers filled the yolk of the circle, moving their bodies like a wave from head to toe. I began to panic when they turned to face us, grabbing several customers' hands, bringing them into the middle. I avoided all eye contact as the music grew louder.

"Ahh," Sanders squealed, shaking her head no as a belly dancer extended a hand in her direction. "I can't dance," she insisted.

But the dancer wouldn't take no for an answer and coaxed Sanders towards the center. She taught her some basic steps, and boy, was I surprised when she caught on, almost instantly. She moved her body back then forward, right then left, all the while moving her hips just like the professionals. Each time she spun around provided glimpses of her tanned back. Then, the lights went out, and laser beams bounced off of walls. That's when Sanders really got into it. She was at the very center now, the belly dancers all dancing around her, taking turns spinning her. She looked up at me, still swaying to the beat of the Greek bop. Her eyes spoke, "I dare you," in my direction. With one look I was making my way to the center to grab my date and spin her for myself. Everyone cheered as my feet took me towards her like a magnet. Then it was just us. The rest of the patrons disappeared from view. All I could see was Sanders and her red lips, straight hair, and vibrant eyes. As the song came to an end, I dipped her backwards, watching her neck arch, waiting patiently for those red lips to come back into view. She lifted her head, and I drew closer to her. Our faces were almost touching when the forgotten crowd began to clap and cheer for us, jolting us back to reality. Sanders looked startled as she blinked and broke eye contact to smile at the crowd. She was standing next to me with one hand around my back and one hand on my chest, like a real couple. The waiters started pulling out swords, a type of dance I didn't care to stick around and see, or be forced to take part in, for that matter.

I pushed my lips into Sanders's hair next to her ear and whispered, "You ready to go?"

I felt the deep breath she took before looking up at me and nodding, a definite sparkle in her eye. I took care of the check, grabbed our jackets, and took Sanders's hand, heading for the door. Her fingers intertwined with mine made me feel strong, like I could protect her against anything.

"Clay, what in the actual hell was that?" Sanders asked, swinging our hands and laughing as we made it outside.

"I swear, I had no idea they did that. The place had great reviews. I just didn't take time to read any of them," I said, playfully presenting my case. "Did you like it?"

"Until the swords were brought out, yes," she said, still laughing.

"Yeah, I'm not a big weapon person either," I said, thinking back to my father's hunting. I never fully understood it.

As I opened Sanders's door, I pinched her side, tickling her. She let out another giggle as she jumped into the passenger seat. Sanders filled the empty air with laughter, reliving the evening the entire ride home.

"I mean, that was like a movie. That shit doesn't happen in real life!" she said, hugging her knees, her body language portraying a much more comfortable ride home than to the restaurant.

"I didn't know you could, uh, dance," I said, glancing sideways at her with a smirk.

"Are you making fun of me?" she asked, shoving my arm.

"Hey! I'm driving here! But I'm serious. You're good," I said, raising my eyebrows at her.

"I danced competitively when I was little, but now it's just for me, and there's no technique anymore. That's for sure," she said.

"You should do it more often."

"I dance all the time at home. You just haven't been around when it happens."

"Solid point," I said, hesitating before adding, "We should change that."

"Are you asking to come inside?" she asked as I pulled into her driveway.

"Not necessarily," I said. "I only meant we should hang out more, so I *will* be there when you're dancing."

She looked at me from the passenger side. I didn't want her to leave yet. Those eyes. I could feel that electricity again.

"Don't get out yet," I said, hopping out to grab her door.

"Thanks," she said, avoiding eye contact like she did at the start of the night as I let her out.

I walked her to the front door, wondering if she was as nervous as I was.

"Sanders?"

"Yeah?"

"I had a really great time with you. That was probably the weirdest but best date I've had."

"My weirdest one is still the one where I unknowingly went on a date with a guy I'd already dated, but I definitely liked this weird one better," she said. "Thanks for dinner."

"No problem," I said, turning back towards the truck, when she grabbed my hand.

"Clay?"

I looked at her expectantly.

"I'd like to hang out more, too," she said, swinging my hand back and forth.

"Goodnight," I said and smiled, releasing her hand and heading down the driveway.

I couldn't help thinking I'd just made it through my second date with Sanders, the memory of the bet with Hastings resurfacing. I tried my best to ignore that fact, hating that I even thought it, as I watched to make sure she made it inside, wishing the night had never ended.

Thirteen

KELYNN WOKE UP, unable to remember where she was. She sat upright and looked around her room, the sunlight flooding in, overwhelming her senses. This is how she usually felt after blacking out, but that hadn't happened since Clay's party. The night came storming back. She gazed out the window, twirling her hair, thinking about it all—the awkward beginning that turned into something so beautiful; something that brought out a feeling Kel hadn't experienced in a while.

What was that feeling? Kel thought.

Then it struck her—it was freedom. She felt fully alive with Clay last night. It had been a long time since she'd really let go and laughed like that.

"Geez. Is there a hot air balloon out there or something?" Indi asked, Kelynn's eyes still glued to the window.

"Oh, hey," she said, her mind still on replay.

"Breakfast is ready. I made our favorite," Indi said, her head leaning through the door.

"Eggs and potatoes?" Kel asked, turning around in excitement.

"Ah, so you are alive," Indi said. "I'll be downstairs whenever you want to eat, but don't wait too long. I'm starving. By the way, you have a friend out here."

"What?" Kelynn asked as Indi headed downstairs to finish setting up breakfast.

She cracked her bedroom door open a little farther to find Roscoe laying outside her room, looking up at her.

"Roscoe, buddy! I missed you," she said. He came bounding into her room, covering her with kisses. "Okay, Ro, that's enough," she said laughing, petting his head to calm him as she walked into her bathroom to brush her teeth. As she looked in the mirror, sleepily moving the brush around the inside of her mouth, she noticed the vein in the center of her forehead. It was a little swollen, a common result of her blackouts, comparable to the pulsating headache of a hangover.

How could I have blacked out? Last night was so fun, I never once felt stressed, she thought.

She rubbed her forehead where the vein was and realized it was enlarged, yet smaller than usual. Her eyebrows creased in confusion as she headed downstairs to indulge in Indi's cooking. She took bite after bite of egg, then potato dipped in ketchup, then toast, then egg again.

"Are you gonna come up for air, or . . ." Indi asked, taking a casual bite of toast.

"Sorry. I'm starved," Kel said, suddenly realizing how quickly she was shoving food into her mouth. "Roscoe was so cute this morning."

"Uh-uh. Nope. You are not avoiding telling me about last night. Spill," Indi said, shooting her a glare.

Kel smiled. "It was amazing, except for the end of the night, which I can't really remember. He was so brooding, hanging onto every word I said."

"What do you mean you don't remember the end of the night? Did he kiss you?"

"Well, no. He walked me to the door, and everything ended fine, but I woke up and all signs pointed to a blackout. I don't remember ever feeling it consume me though."

"Your vein is a little swollen, isn't it?" Indi said, examining her.

"Yeah, normally I remember feeling everything go black before I'm unconscious, but I only felt the aftereffects this time."

"Do you remember what you were thinking about?"

Kel blinked hard a couple of times. "I was picturing hanging out with Clay again, and then I started thinking about the future with him . . . Wait, that's it." She rubbed her head, pinching her eyes shut again. "My thoughts were going in a million directions, but my blackouts have always been super intense. I didn't even wake up with a headache."

Maybe it's because I was with Clay. Last time, my recovery wasn't as bad either, and it was after I'd been to his party, Kel thought to herself. *Maybe being around him subliminally calms me.*

"That's good, at least. As long as you're okay."

"Really, I am, Indi. I'm not that concerned with my blackouts right now. Especially if they're this mild," Kelynn reassured her.

"Okay, then neither am I. Now, you have to tell me everything about the date!"

"Indi, you're not going to believe what happened."

Kel dished all the details of the night, from each look Clay sent her way, to every butterfly that threatened her from saving face, to the belly dancers bringing out her inner extrovert.

After her debrief with Indi, Kel needed a run to clear her head. She had a surge of energy this Saturday morning, and she wasn't going to waste it. She threw on a pair of muted green running tights, her favorite white cropped tank, and a baseball hat.

She started the engine of her Jeep and took off towards the ocean. Carolina Beach was about two hours away, but Kel knew the run would be worth the drive, not to mention she could use the extra solo time. It was a perfect day, the clouds rolling across the sky, giving in to the breeze while the sun shone through them, radiating heat to all the living things below. Kelynn rolled down her windows to let the fresh air in, blowing her ponytail left and right. She stopped at a red light, closed her eyes and inhaled deeply, letting the full scent of fall enter her lungs. The evergreens put off a comforting smell, Kel's favorite smell, like Christmas mixed with a musty fire. She approached the intersection right before the beach and her heart started pumping. She was excited. She was ready and long overdue for an outdoor run. She pulled into the lot that basically touched the sand and hopped out, shoving headphones in to block out all other sounds but her music. Looking out over the ocean, she felt a sense of peace. Kids were playing nearby making sandcastles, while several housewives browned their already tanned bodies, and a few boys jumped waves. She felt the sun hit her face, warming her, as if it were pushing her to run.

Kel took a deep breath as she stepped forward with her right foot and began to run. Step after step, breath in after breath out, she felt more and more at home. Her rhythm evened out, and before she knew it, she was gliding. Each song pounded in the background, controlling the beat of her steps. Knowing the ocean inhaled and exhaled the waves next to her motivated her to keep going, like it was connected to her lungs. As her chest rose and fell, the waves built and crashed. She felt fully alive, her adrenaline pumping as she ran as fast as she could. Her feet pushed off the wet sand, leaving imprints with every step. Kel always wondered how many footprints of hers could be found after one of her runs. The mystery and enormity of it all enticed her. She reached her peak, her body operating at optimal capacity. She ran with urgency, like she would lose someone or something if she didn't run faster, run harder.

It was only in moments like these she caught a glimpse of clarity and felt powerful enough to accomplish whatever she wanted. Kel thought about the possible manifestations of her future, compartmentalizing as usual. It was easier for her to picture each part of her life separately: career, friends, philanthropy, bucket list–infused crazy dreams, and love. Thinking about one area at a time made her feel like her goals weren't impossible, but trying to put the puzzle together caused chaos.

She could see the flag ahead. Today it was yellow, meaning mildly stronger waves than average, but still safe. As her right foot crossed the imaginary finish line, she came to a light jog and then stopped. She bent over, breathing heavily with her hands on her knees, and then looked up at the ocean and smiled. She did it. Four miles behind her, and she could now feel great about whatever the rest of the day brought. She untied her running shoes as the sweat dripped out of every pore. Kel shoved her socks inside and tied the shoe strings together. She held them by her side as she ventured towards the water. It, too, had been warmed by the sun but sufficed as it tempted Kel's toes with relief. She rolled up her tights and went in up to her knees. She took five deep breaths, still recovering from her cardio session. With each breath, she felt grateful for something in her life; her ability to run, Roscoe, the sun, the ocean, and . . . Clay.

Ah, Clay. Why didn't he kiss her last night? Maybe he was just being a gentleman, being polite. Too polite, Kel's mind wondered.

Kel was used to guys making moves before she was ready, and the one time she was more than ready for it, he didn't.

Ironic, she thought as she turned towards her parked Jeep.

Clay.

AT FIRST, ALL I could see was the pavement below my feet, my unusually small feet. They were moving in a way that my entire body felt steady, yet I knew I was hauling ass. My breathing had a rhythm, too. I'd never experienced running like this. It didn't feel like I was running but rather coasting, like I was on a moving sidewalk. It felt exhilarating and almost cleansing; both feelings I didn't get when running. I was in Chapel Hill; I knew that much. The streets looked familiar, but I noticed random faces that stuck out in the crowds lining the street. They were cheering me on. Every few looked right at me, like I knew them. Then something changed, and I was no longer in Chapel Hill but a totally different state. I looked around, trying to read my environment, when I noticed a banner above that read "Boston Marathon." Shit! Was I running the Boston Marathon? This was not possible. My experience with running ended with gym class in high school. Sprints were one thing, but long distance had never been my gig. How was I doing this? I looked down again to see if my feet had somehow grown to their actual size and realized I was wearing very tight pants. My legs looked feminine—very muscular but still feminine. I could feel my body growing tired. I tried to ignore the fact that I wasn't actually in my normal body and pushed through. I crossed the finish line with the best feeling of accomplishment I'd ever had. I let out a yell of victory as the people surrounding me started to disappear. Suddenly, I was standing at the front of an auditorium. Every seat was filled, and the people in them were clapping. I looked beside me and there was a table with books—a lot of books. Make that a lot of the same book. They all had the title, *Out of the Black*. I walked over and opened one. The title page was signed. I blinked twice to make sure I read it right. The autograph was none other than Kelynn Sanders's. I turned to look at a woman beside me on the stage, holding a microphone in my direction.

"Kelynn, tell us the inspiration behind your captivating novel?" she demanded in an excited voice.

Why was she calling me Kelynn?

I stepped up to the microphone and felt a little uneasy. Thousands of pairs of eyes were looking at me, and I kept trying to open my mouth to speak, but it was as though it was sewn shut. I couldn't pry my jaw apart. I closed my eyes, hoping they would all disappear, and when I opened them, it was pitch-black. I thought I had fallen into a black hole, until my eyes adjusted a little and I saw a glow from tape adhered to the ground beneath my feet. I was now wearing all black, as well.

I heard someone say, "Sanders, Cyrus is ready to enter from stage left." I turned to see who was there, but no one was.

"Hello?" I whisper-yelled.

"Sanders, do you copy?"

Where was the voice coming from? I reached up to rub my forehead in confusion and felt a headset resting behind my ears.

"Copy that," I said into the tiny microphone resting against my cheek, my voice reflecting more assurance than I was actually feeling. I walked a few feet in front of me towards a curtain where light was fighting its way through. I pulled it back slightly only to see a room full of the most popular musical artists. Beyoncé and JayZ, Coldplay, Katy Perry, and Lady Gaga all sat stage left. I scanned the room to stage right where Taylor Swift, The Jonas Brothers, Selena Gomez, and Drake were all seated. My eyes moved slowly over the crowd to the stage in front of me, which had a giant Moonman statue proudly displayed. That's when it hit me. Holy shit! I'm at the MTV Video Music Awards. Wait. I'm not just *here* at the awards; I'm *working* them.

I blinked several times in disbelief when I heard, "Hey, I'm ready. Just tell me when." It came from a deep, well-saturated voice standing beside me. I turned to see her face, her bleached blonde hair framing it, tattoos scattered across her arms.

"Miley?" I asked, starstruck that she was standing so close and speaking to *me*.

"Yeah, aren't you the placement coordinator?"

"Yep, that's me. They're ready for you," I said, pointing to the stage, having no idea what I was saying, only that I was saying it to Miley.

"Great, thanks," she said, winking at me as she sashayed onto the stage.

I'd never thought much about Miley until now. I never cared much about her. Her music was decent, but I'd never imagined feeling overwhelmed by her presence. Maybe these weren't *my* feelings.

I could hear a muffled voice surrounding me, but no one was in sight. It sounded almost like it wasn't coming from backstage, but rather from the back of my brain.

"Dude, helloooo? Are you in there? Clay!"

I closed my eyes trying to concentrate on whose familiar voice was booming in the depths of my thoughts.

"Hey, man. Thought I was going to have to take you to the hospital."

I opened my eyes to find Gunner standing in front of me holding the opal necklace.

"What're you doing here?" I asked, forgetting I had even picked it up again.

"We're going hiking today, remember? What drugs are you on?"

"Sorry. I guess I'm a little out of it," I said, eager to put the necklace in a safe place.

"Why were you holding this?" Gunner asked, extending his arm to me, the necklace seeming so tiny in his hands, yet so powerful.

"I found it after my party."

"Your party? Wasn't that like a month ago? What are you doing with it now?" he asked as he set it on the kitchen table.

"Just wanted to move it so I remember to ask around. I think I know who it might belong to," I said in shock, realizing for the first time that maybe somehow this piece of jewelry was connected to the vivid daydreams I was experiencing.

"Are you sure you're okay? When I got here you were just standing with your eyes open, but you acted like you were asleep, like you couldn't even hear me."

"Yeah, I'm fine, man. Let me grab my gear."

I turned to gather myself before heading out on a hike. I could probably use some fresh air after that out-of-body, time-warp-like experience.

"Hey, Willie! Are you coming with us today?" I heard Gunner ask.

Everything started to come back to me. It felt like I was getting used to my brain again, like someone else's thoughts clouded all of mine—most likely Sanders's. How was this possible? If I told her what I'd seen, she'd think I was crazy. For now, I was going to keep the necklace in a safe place, hidden where only I could access it. I checked my phone for the time before locking the door behind me. It had only been thirty minutes since I grabbed the necklace to move it in the first place, yet it felt like days had passed—maybe even weeks.

This isn't real. You're imagining this, I thought to myself, not even believing my own voice of reason. Gunner seemed unaffected when he held it, which made me doubt what I saw even more.

Fourteen

KELYNN STARTED HER Monday morning with some yoga stretches. She didn't have to be in to work until 9:30 a.m., and she was soaking up every minute she had to herself. Those 6:00 a.m. shifts had been killing her, draining her of energy to do the things she loved when she got home. As much as she loved to refresh, Kelynn couldn't just be. She had to be doing something that felt active in some sense, even when she rested.

Deep breath in through the nose and out through the mouth, she thought, opening her mouth and exhaling all her demons: stress from lack of sleep, the actual lack of sleep, pushing herself and feeling like she was getting nowhere, and her necklace, which was still MIA.

She pushed her legs back and rocked her hips side to side until she maneuvered into downward dog. As she took another deep breath, she recalled when her dad first gave her that necklace. He was more like her than her mom ever was, which made Kel feel like they were connected in a special way. He seemed to understand her overwhelming thoughts, and although he had never experienced blackouts like she did, he constantly showed deep empathy. When Kel turned eighteen, her family threw her a one-of-a-kind party. She remembered waking up to her dad telling her one thing—to wear her favorite nineties outfit, which was difficult since Kel had quite the collection from thrift shops. With *Friends* being her favorite show, they surprised her by setting up their living room using vintage furniture they found at Goodwill to mimic Central Perk. They had one of her best guy friends dress up as Gunther, bleach blonde hair and all, and serve coffee to the guests. As she came down the stairs, she noticed little props based off the show scattered throughout the house. There was a picture frame on their front door, a small white dog statue in the office, and the French poster Monica loved so much hanging in the bathroom. When she entered the living room, everyone yelled, "Surprise!" It was the best birthday she could've asked for. The rest of the afternoon they played a *Friends*-themed trivia game, ordered coffee from "Gunther" and danced around to the theme song "I'll Be There for You" played by her brother and his band. Near the end of the party, after most of her guests had left, her dad pulled her aside.

"Hey, I know today was a great one for you, but I wanted to give you something for the days that aren't always this way," he said, handing her a delicate box wrapped in brown paper and tied with a simple canvas ribbon.

She smiled at her dad, confused as to what could fit in a small box yet could handle such big problems. She ripped the paper and carefully opened the lid to find the most stunning necklace she'd ever seen. A minimal gold chain held an impeccable spherical sea-blue opal that showed a prism of colors when the light hit it just right.

He pulled her chin up as he looked at her with the most sincere look she'd ever seen, like his heart was breaking in the most beautiful way for her. "Whenever you have your haunting, overwhelming thoughts, I want you to hold this opal in your hand and visualize them all escaping into this. Good or bad thoughts—any thoughts that cloud your vision—okay?"

"Thanks, Dad. I love it."

"I want you to know something. No one else knows about this necklace except for your great-grandmother." He paused. "It's been *blessed*. According to tradition, your thoughts will actually live inside of it. It will hold them like a time capsule."

Kelynn remembered looking at him in disbelief. Magic was the kind of stuff you told little kids, not someone on their eighteenth birthday.

"Your great-grandmother knew more about it because she had it consecrated by a Romani traveler, a gifted nomad. The Roma told her all about the possibilities of its powers, but she was so old by the time she gave it to me that she couldn't remember all of them. I don't even know if it works, but just always keep it close. You don't want those thoughts to get lost." His words echoed through her mind as Kelynn lay on her stomach, pushing her chest up with her arms in cobra pose as she smiled reliving the memory.

Sorry, Dad, she thought as she tried her best to relax her muscles, letting the stretch reverberate throughout her body. Endorphins swam through her brain, calming her.

She took one last deep breath as she finished her yoga practice for the day and checked her phone. It was only 7:00 a.m. She lay on the floor next to Roscoe for a little longer. He shifted his head to her stomach as she pet him. Kel loved it when he cuddled her. She tried to force it so often that he would only cuddle with her when she least expected it. Finally, she pushed herself up from the soft, carpeted floor and reached for her jean jacket.

"I'm heading out! I'll be back before ya know it, bud," she said, looking at Roscoe who was now sitting up and whining at the fact that she was leaving without him.

"Indi?" she yelled up the stairs.

"Yeah?" Indi said, sounding half asleep from her late shift the night before.

"I'm off to the farmer's market. You want anything?"

"Can you give me five minutes, and I'll come with you?" Indi asked, now peering down the stairs while rubbing her tired eyes and running her hands through her half-washed hair.

"Sure!" Kel said.

"I love that they started this farmer's market up again in the fall. I know summer is prime-time for produce, but a girl needs her whole foods."

Kel smiled over at Indi, wondering how she could be in such high spirits after an exhausting night.

"How was your shift last night?" Kel asked as Indi drove towards the market.

"It went well. I actually doubled my tips."

"Really? What was different?"

"An orchestra concert let out, so the place was full of high-class people, and I put on my best fake smile for each and every one of their pretentious asses." Indi winked. "In all seriousness, they weren't that bad, and I met someone."

"Tell me everything," Kel said.

"He was there with his mom. He took her as his date to the orchestra. Isn't that the cutest?"

"Yeah," Kel agreed, cringing a little. "But also kind of sad. Like he can't get a date."

"No, it was his mom's birthday. She *loves* the orchestra. He doesn't even like it, but he went for her."

"Oh, okay. That changes things. What's his name? Did he give you his number?"

"It's Gunner. I think I've seen his face before, but I can't place him. He seemed familiar; comfortable. Maybe it was because we were vibing."

"Wait," Kelynn started. "Did you say Gunner? What's his last name?"

"I think he signed the check *Gunner Chapman*," Indi said, her face suggesting she was searching back through her memory.

"INDI!"

"What?!" she asked, almost wrecking the car.

"That's Clay's best friend!" Kel said, still yelling.

"Is this going to be a problem?" Indi asked, her voice a little softer.

"Is something actually going to come of this?"

"I don't know. To answer your question, he did give me his number when he left. I was thinking of texting him tomorrow."

"This isn't good," Kel said, getting out of the car and making a beeline for the fresh okra.

"Kel, wait up. I'm sorry. I had no idea you wouldn't be okay with this. I didn't even remember he was friends with Clay. Can you please just stop for one minute!"

"This just reminds me of Preston. Remember Matt?" Kelynn asked, checking each nearby Roma tomato for its firmness.

"Shit, Kelynn. I completely forgot about that," Indi said, referring to the time Kelynn was interested in Matt but was unsure if she should break her "no dating in college" rule for him. Preston suggested they go out on an innocent double date, since she was interested in Matt's best friend. After the date ended, they all went their separate ways. At least that's what Kelynn thought until she went back to the restaurant to get her sunglasses she left on the table to find Matt and Preston making out in his car.

"But I'm not Preston. I wouldn't do that to you. Not ever."

"You're right. I just feel a little possessive, which is weird for me. I'm still trying to figure out Clay, and I don't want something complicating it or someone invading that unknown territory. I'm sorry. I know it doesn't make sense. I'll try to shake it off," she said, paying the farmer for a bushel of okra and shrugging her shoulders.

"Okay, so are we cool?" Indi asked.

"Yeah, I guess. I'm still not one hundred percent on board with it, but I can't try to control your life. That's not fair either. Come on. Let's find the squash," Kelynn said, eager to move past the current topic, clearly uncomfortable with her irrational yet still present feelings.

"Okay. By the way, how was Monette?" Indi asked, clearly feeling similar.

Kelynn sighed. "She's worse now, after the stroke. She doesn't really remember me. There are times I see a spark of recognition in her eyes, but she's fading, or at least her mind is. It makes it hard to visit her, ya know? We used to laugh so hard together, and now it's sad to see her so confused."

"That's rough, Kel. It seems funny now, but remember when you used to debate on even going? Look at you now. You've made a great friend. I'm sure she still loves having you around. Maybe those little sparks of recognition make her day. You never know. Promise me something, okay?"

"What?" Kel said, busying herself with another stand, this one selling asparagus.

"Don't stop going. She may need you more now than ever. I bet her memory is fading the less she sees people she knows."

"I promise. I'll make a point of seeing her every other week." Kel sported a forced smile. "Did I tell you I saw Clay there?"

"At the nursing home?" Indi asked.

"Yeah, funny story . . ." Kel started.

Clay.

I WANTED TO see more—to go back into that dreamland where I could somehow see Sanders's thoughts and prove to myself that her necklace was the gateway to them. I didn't want to lose track of time, though, or not be able to stop it. I was whooped after the hike with Gunner. All I wanted to do was watch a movie, so why not watch one Sanders was in? I went into the mud room and untied my hiking boots. Willie went straight to her bed in the living room. She always crashed there after a long day in the sun on the Blue Ridge Mountains. I sat there trying to come up with a way to wake myself up. If it was actually the necklace that allowed me to dream, then Willie stopped the vision the first time around, and Gunner interrupted the second. I needed a plan this time, some way to "wake" myself up. I couldn't pinch myself or force myself to drop the necklace. Or could I?

I grabbed a protein bar to recover and headed for my fishing gear. I unzipped the front pouch of the tackle bag. Score—fishing wire. I searched in the kitchen, digging through all the drawers. Bingo. Pushed to the very back of my junk drawer was Omi's old-fashioned kitchen timer, shaped like an apple, the top moving in a circle each time it ticked. I pulled out my pocketknife and took the supplies to my bedroom. I tied the knife to the kitchen timer with the fishing wire, so every time it ticked, the knife moved with it. I grabbed a light piece of wood from my firewood pile out back and tied fishing wire around that, as well. This was getting good. I tied the fishing wire attached to the board to the top corner of the bookshelf next to my bed. All I had to do was set the timer, grab the necklace, and then, if my invention worked as it should, the pocket knife would cut the fishing wire holding the board, which would drop, making contact with my arm, ultimately forcing me to drop the necklace.

"I just MacGyvered the shit out of that, Willie," I said, but she was already passed out on her dog bed.

I set the timer for twenty minutes and sat down on the bed. *Here goes nothing*, I thought, reaching for the blue opal.

My fingers traced the tiny gold chain as my room began to disappear before my eyes, suddenly replaced with a field. I felt the cool breeze rush past me, blowing the hair off my face. I closed my eyes, letting the sun warm my skin as I leaned back, my elbows resting behind me on a picnic blanket. I could hear a small, high-pitched voice in the distance. It was yelling something, but I couldn't make out what it was. I heard tiny footsteps getting faster and faster, and with them came the word, "Mommy!" Over and over, the little boy yelled as he giggled up the hill towards me.

He fell into my lap and said, "Mommy, I picked you a flower." He extended his little arm towards me, holding a dandelion, flashing a mismatched smile that showed gaps where his teeth hadn't grown in yet.

His hair was brown, his eyes a deep green like Sanders's. I felt an overwhelming sense of love for him as I held him in my lap, where he seemed perfectly content. Then, a man began walking towards us, up the same hill where the little boy came running from. He was tall and strong, but when he got closer, he didn't have a face.

Well, this is trippy, I thought.

He sat next to me and told me of the adventures he and the boy had at the bottom of the hill. The words I spoke weren't mine, nor was my mind thinking them before they came out. I was merely in the body that was saying them.

"I love you so much. I don't want Kale to get any bigger. Did I tell you, the other day he came up to me and told me I was his best friend?"

"What? No fair. I thought *I* was his best friend," the man said.

"I'm being serious. How long is he going to think I'm cool enough for that?"

"Like, two weeks," the man said, now sitting next to me, chuckling.

"Exactly."

"Well, then we'll just have to have another one," he said, his tone more serious now.

"I don't know. Pregnancy was really hard."

"Yeah, but you did it, and you look amazing," he said, grabbing my hand. He began to lean in for a kiss.

Plunk! I opened my eyes to see my bedroom wall before me again.

"That was a close one," I said out loud, as if to reestablish that I was back in the real world.

I looked beside my bed to see the plank of wood and opal both resting on the ground with a small pink spot spreading on my wrist from the impact. My invention worked! I sat there on my bed for a minute trying to rewind the "dream" I had just seen, while still terrified that this was somehow possible. One thing I was sure of, the necklace was definitely connected to what I was seeing. I just didn't know how, and if this was indeed Sanders's necklace, she had so many different dreams and goals for her life. Parts of her dreams seemed so independent, and yet that one was the exact opposite. I also didn't understand how I was able to see the face of her future child but not the face of her future husband. Didn't the two go hand in hand? I was beyond confused. These futuristic visions made me feel closer to Sanders, yet also a little guilty—like she was telling me what she wanted out of life without actually telling me, making me feel like I was eavesdropping. It was as if someone was letting me in on her secrets, and I liked knowing them. This was beginning to feel heavy. I didn't know what my future held, and I preferred it that way, but seeing each one of these opal scenes made me feel like I would have to adjust my lifestyle if I wanted to be with Sanders. Although, I still couldn't wrap my head around how any of this was real at all. Maybe it wasn't.

Sanders! It hit me. I hadn't talked to her since our date. I searched the bed for my phone and checked my messages from her. The last one was her agreeing to the date. Shit. She probably felt like I was avoiding her. I guess the opal made me feel like I was spending time with her. Maybe being around her more would reveal which one of these futures she wanted the most.

I pulled up her contact info, seeing the picture I took of her on our first night out and hit *Call.*

"Hey," she answered. I could hear the smile in her voice.

I echoed her greeting and added, "Are you busy tonight?"

Fifteen

"WELL, GOOD MORNING, Miss Monette. You have a visitor here to see you bright and early," the nurse said, moving to reveal Kelynn standing behind her as she walked closer to Monette's bed.

Monette had been woken up before Kelynn arrived and was sitting up. Her hair had clearly been brushed, her nails freshly done. She blinked a few times before a small smile crept across her lips, but it didn't match her eyes. They looked distant, perplexed.

"Hey, Monette. I thought I'd stop by before my shift at work. Are you feeling better?" Kelynn asked, taking a seat on the bed next to her, knowing that she'd felt weak ever since the stroke.

Monette reached out her hand like she always did for Kel to massage as they talked, only this time Kelynn did the talking with little nods from her elderly friend. She was glad she decided to get up early today. Something told her that Monette needed to see her, or maybe she needed to see Monette. Either way, Kelynn could see the decline in her health. She wanted her to go back to the way she was—spunky, always telling Kelynn about life and how to not take it so seriously. Normally, she loved talking about her daughters and grandchildren. Some of them had gone into modeling, something she did herself in her youth. She was always pointing at photos of them in her small bedroom, marveling at each one, and repeating their names to Kelynn each time she visited. For the first time since she's started coming to the Villas, Kelynn realized that Monette, while much older than her mom, felt like the female parent she never had; one that wasn't always searching for something better. Tears filled her eyes as she recognized the missing piece, listening ear, and cheerleader Monette had become. She was someone who not only had pride in her family but in Kelynn, as well. She imagined her mom talking about her the way her elderly friend talked about her granddaughter while thumbing the edges of photographs. Through the lens of this new perspective, Kelynn talked with her for about an hour before she had to say goodbye and head to the café.

"Love you always, Monette," she said as Monette squeezed her hands like every other visit prior, making it harder to leave.

Kelynn was working a midmorning shift at La Vita Dolce. For the most part, it was slow. Kel liked it this way, when the music playing over the café's speakers was actually audible. It made her feel peaceful as she organized the coffee mugs and took her time putting everything in its place. It also gave her time to talk with her coworkers. When they were slammed, they worked on autopilot, each part moving as fast as possible to keep the vehicle of the café going. Today she worked with Carter, who was a little younger than her, still in college studying pretty much anything and everything. Kel glanced over her shoulder after positioning the scones inside the glass case to see Carter staring at yet another new textbook.

"What are you studying now?" Kelynn asked.

"I wanted to branch out this semester, but it's heavier than I thought. I'm taking a class on family dynamics in sociology."

"I always liked the classes that make you rethink how our world and systems work. Isn't it crazy how society affects how we act without fully being aware of it?"

"Yes! It's very interesting, but a lot to digest. I can only read a little at a time before I start overanalyzing everyone and every interaction in my life."

"I get that," Kel said. "How are you doing outside of school?"

"School and work are my life, so I guess I'm doing okay. I don't have time for much else."

"When do you graduate?"

"Kel, I literally have no idea what I want to be. I have a jumble of credits that go toward different degrees, but I'm still technically an undecided major as a junior," she said, looking downcast.

"Hey, it's okay. I have a degree, but I'm also still undecided about what I want to do in life. You're not alone."

"Thanks," Carter said, unconvinced.

"What's something you wish you had time to do?"

"Write," Carter said without thinking twice.

"You should look into studying journalism! You could write about anything and everything, including those sociological interactions."

Carter cocked her head as though she were considering it.

"I feel like we just had a breakthrough!" Kel said.

She wanted to know more about Carter, what her passions were, and why she felt the need to dance around them. She was about halfway through her shift when her phone buzzed in her back pocket. She looked down to see the picture of Clay he'd taken the very first time they hung out.

"Carter, are you cool if I take a call out back?"

"Kel, we've had two customers in the past two hours. It's chill," she said, adding a wink.

Kel nodded and answered the phone, turning the handle of the heavy back door to the coffee shop.

"Hey, are you busy tonight?" Clay asked.

"I haven't heard from you in awhile. Are you sure you know who you're talking to?" Kel said, teasing him yet slightly hurt that he hadn't reached out to her since their first official date. It had almost been a week, which she didn't understand since that night was pretty perfect in *her* memory.

"I think I remember your voice. Plus, *I'm* the one who called *you*. And if that wasn't enough, I have your picture to help me out, remember?"

"Yeah, I have one of you, too. Clay, is it?"

He laughed. "So, Sanders. You busy tonight?"

"Well, I was planning on reading, but I might be able to get out of that."

"I wouldn't want to impose on your lively evening, but I need to see you," Clay said.

"That sounds serious. Is everything okay?"

"No, can I pick you up at eight?"

"Sure. . . . What's going on?" Kel hesitantly agreed.

"I just need to see you. I'll explain tonight."

Kel hung up the phone and began to head back inside when she heard, "You're in love, aren't ya?"

Roger was back, propped up against the brick wall of the alley in his dirty coat with his shopping cart full of souvenirs from the street.

"Roger, you scared me!" she said, taking a seat next to him.

"So who's the guy?"

"I met him about a month ago. I still can't quite figure him out."

"Does he have a heart as good as yours?" Roger asked.

"I think his is softer than mine. I like that about him."

"I was in love once," Roger said. "But now my main love is sand-wiches, whenever I can get one."

"I hear ya, Roger. I'll be back. Egg with ham and cheese on a croissant?"

"How about a bagel today?"

"Roger that," Kelynn said, winking.

She shut the door behind her and weaved her way through the obstacle-ridden back room. She could maneuver through it in her sleep. Bypass the rack of T-shirts to the left, swerve by the boxes of hand-thrown mugs, step next to the burlap bags of coffee beans, two more turns, and 'voila,' back behind the counter. She grabbed the ingredients for Roger's sandwich and turned on the toaster oven.

"Hungry, Kel?" Carter asked, moving her thumbs back and forth, not looking up from her phone.

"It's for Roger."

"Sure, 'Roger,'" Carter said, putting his name in air quotes.

Kelynn rolled her eyes and headed out back again, her shift ending with Roger being her last customer. She sat with him while he ate, listening to his stories about friends he'd made on the streets. He reminded her how friendships can be fragile, making her rethink her response to Indi's news about Gunner. She checked her phone. It was 6:30 p.m. She gave Roger a hug and headed home to wash off her coffee-scented sweat. Her phone buzzed on the bathroom counter right as she was getting out of the shower. It was a text from Clay.

How's the book? he texted.

Better when I'm not being distracted by you, she jokingly replied.

He didn't respond, and she liked that. Maybe he was respecting her time. She threw on mascara and the lip tint that enhanced her natural rose color. She grabbed her favorite denim jacket and, like clockwork, the doorbell rang.

Sixteen

KELYNN ANSWERED THE door to find a very confused Clay on the other side. She took him in, starting from bottom to top. He was sporting all black Chuck Taylors, worn black jeans, a grey striped henley, and to finish it all off, a denim jacket, the wash almost identical to hers. In fact, their outfits practically coordinated. Instead of a grey top, Kel had on a white shirt, also paired with black jeans. She wore black lace-up boots, not Chucks, but still, the two definitely modeled the same aesthetic.

"Did you plant a hidden camera in my place?" Clay inquired, his gaze darting back and forth between him and Kelynn.

"I should ask you the same thing," Kel said, a little embarrassed. "I'll go change." Truthfully, Kelynn hadn't noticed their coordination as much as she noticed *him*.

I would kill to touch those eyebrows. Actually, I'd kill to touch any part of that face right now, Kel thought, her eyes moving to his lips and then back to his eyebrows.

They looked soft to the touch. Just above them were two shallow lines, probably caused by deep thought—lines that weren't too rigid yet, but deep enough that they added to his alluring stature. Then there was his hair. His dirty-blonde hair coiffed to one side. He kept it neat, just long enough to tempt Kel to run her fingers through it.

Clay grabbed her hand as she started to turn away. "Don't. I like that we match."

"You sure? We might get some weird looks."

"It's fine. Let's go," Clay said, still holding her hand and pulling her out the door.

She looked into his blue-grey eyes and smiled sheepishly. Her heart raced with their faces so close together. For a minute, Clay didn't say anything. He held her chin in his hand and took a deep breath. He started to move closer, almost closing the gap between them.

"Roscoe! What are you doing out here?!" Kel said as Roscoe jumped on Clay, nearly knocking him over. "I thought I put you inside. Come on, bud," she said while searching her pockets for her house key.

"Looks like someone needs some attention," Clay said under his breath while laughing. After a few minutes of trying to distract Roscoe with treats, they were out the door.

Clay turned on some slow alternative music on the way to wherever he was taking her.

"What's this playlist?" Kelynn asked. Some of the songs sounded familiar, but she hadn't heard them in this order before.

"Don't judge me."

"Never," she said.

"It's the Walter Mitty soundtrack. I found it on Spotify after you told me you met Ben Stiller. It's one of my favorite movies of his."

"Shut up! Why have I never looked for that before?"

"It's pretty good, right?"

"Yes! That movie is just . . ." Kel sighed, "I can't even describe it, it's so good. Perfection, no doubt."

Clay smirked at her. He laid his hand on her thigh and said, "I like the way you talk when you're passionate about something. It's cute."

A bunch of butterflies shot up from Kelynn's leg all the way to her stomach. She took a deep breath, in shock he was blatantly flirting with her. She hoped he didn't notice her chest move sharply as her breath filled her lungs. The two didn't speak for the rest of the ride as Clay's hand rested lightly on Kel's very alert left thigh. She tried to shift her attention to the setting sun, indicating it was officially time for the night-life crowd to inhabit the streets of downtown.

"Have you ever been here?" Clay asked, opening the door to what looked like an average bar.

"I don't think so, but ya never know."

Clay cocked his head. "What do you mean by that?"

"I'm sure you've done this, too. You go out with your friends and start at one bar, have a few drinks, and then go to another, and another, and by the end of the night you can't remember where you started or finished, let alone all the stops in between," Kel said, taking a seat at a bar stool.

"Well, actually . . ."

"Oh, don't tell me you never binge drank in college," she said, shoving him. Her hand drifted down, and he grabbed it, interlacing their fingers.

"Yeah, of course," Clay said. "But what I was going to say was, we're not actually sitting up here."

"I'm confused," Kel said, still very aware that Clay was playing with each of her fingers. His hand felt so big holding hers; like he could pick her up using only that hand.

"I take it you *haven't* been here before, then," he said, pausing. Kel looked confused as ever as he said, "We're going downstairs."

Clay guided her through the rush of people who had magically arrived at the same time they had and knocked on what looked like a storage room door. It was painted like a bank vault.

A bartender opened the door. "Just the two of you tonight?"

"Uh, yes," Clay said.

"We've still got room. Go on down."

Why did Clay know all the wildest spots in town? Kel wondered. She'd lived here almost as long as him and had no idea any of these places existed.

The two walked down a long wooden staircase that creaked with every step, yet they could barely hear the noise from their feet above the music. Compared to the upstairs bar scene, the stairs opened up to a fairly large room, with six mismatched couches, a pool table, several booths, and a bar. Kelynn took in the scene, the colorful lights strung across the top of the bar where it met the ceiling, reflecting blue, red, green, and orange glows in her eyes.

Kelynn looked up at Clay, who was clearly anticipating her reaction. Her eyes got big as she said, "Clay, I love it! This is freaking legit!"

He squeezed her hand and went up to the bar. "Why don't you go get us a couch? Anything you want in particular?"

"Surprise me," she said.

Kelynn walked towards the couches, all of which reminded her of *Friends*. In fact, this entire bar felt a little like the set of Central Perk. Except here, there were four couches, two on one side of the wall with the other two facing them with tables in between. It felt so homey. After a quick scan of each couch, she chose the one that most closely resembled the orange one the group of six used to all pile on day in and day out on the sitcom. She sat down and bounced a little. It was perfect. She crossed her legs and right when she was about to look to see if Clay was almost finished ordering, a beer bottle was directly in front of her face as Clay had handed it to her from behind the couch.

"Cheers," he said, tilting his bottle towards hers as he made his way to the couch across from her. "Well, cheers to *Friends*. Drinking with you is like hanging out with my best friend, Chandler," he said as he tapped his bottle against hers. Kelynn looked at him and cocked her head, confused.

"That would make me Joey," he said, taking another drink.

"How did you know I liked *Friends*? I was just thinking about how this whole place reminds me of Central Perk," she said.

"We joked about *Friends* when we got coffee instead of going to the street fair, remember?"

"I guess I was a little shaken up that night. My memory is a bit jumbled," Kelynn said, reliving the traumatic evening.

Clay got up to sit next to her on the couch she had chosen. He moved in close so she could hear him over the music, but not so that everyone else could.

"I'm glad you kicked his ass, Sanders. You're a real badass," he said, clinking his bottle against hers again.

"Clay?" she asked, feeling bold.

"Yeah?"

"What's your family like?" The question hung in the air for a moment. It was a topic she wouldn't normally press into this early in a dating relationship.

"Funny you should ask. I was going to invite you to a beach brunch with them. My mom puts it on every year right before it gets too cold to go to the beach anymore, like the last hurrah of the season."

"When?" Kel asked, a little taken aback.

"Uh, Saturday. Is that too soon?" Clay replied, scratching the back of his head, his bicep clearly visible under the sleeve of his shirt.

"No, Saturday's good," Kel said, not wanting him to look any deeper into her eyes.

"But, since you asked, my mom and dad are still together. I have two sisters, one younger and one older, making me the middleman."

"My parents haven't been together since I was young." She shifted in her seat, the following words coming out slower. "My mom, if you want to call her that, left when I was eight. My dad raised me and Alex, my brother. He's younger, still in college. He's busy being on his own for the first time, and we don't keep in touch really."

"You don't talk about this much, do you?" Clay asked.

"No, not really." She sat up straighter.

"Did you get to say goodbye to her?"

"She came back a few times but in the middle of the night. I tried to pretend it was all a dream. I came out of my room once when I heard her, and she wasn't exactly excited to see me. I stayed up the rest of the night wondering if she'd stay. After that, if I heard her, I didn't leave my room. My brother sees her occasionally. He's a bit more susceptible to her . . . games."

Kelynn breathed deeply before telling Clay everything. It came out in broken sentences and fragmented stories, but eventually he understood.

Her mom cared more for the comfort she found in status and rarities money could buy than she did for her family.

"Thank you for letting me in." He traced her fingers with his as he watched her face regain its small smile. "You're sure you're cool with Saturday?" Clay asked, which seemed irrelevant after going down the traumatic path of Kelynn's past.

"Yeah, I just didn't know I would be meeting your family this soon," she said, her eyes repeatedly darting back and forth from his drink to hers.

"What do you mean?"

"Nothing. I just feel like I barely know you . . . without adding in family dynamics."

"Sanders, you know me pretty well."

"Before five minutes ago, I had no idea you even had siblings or parents that were still living, let alone still married."

"Okay. Fair enough. What do you want to know?" The smirk she'd seen when he teased her at the assisted living center returned.

Kelynn took another swig of beer, then replaced the bottle with her thumb. She nibbled at her nail bed, suddenly uncomfortable, feeling like she was sitting next to a stranger. She tried to think of things to ask him, but the list was so long she didn't know where to begin. She started with something simple, yet clever enough for him to carry the conversation and let her listen for a bit. She hated answering personal questions, especially when she felt exposed every time Clay looked into her eyes.

"Who's your favorite band?" she asked after what felt like an eternity of silence.

"Hmm. That's a tough one. I like most genres of music. When I don't like something, I know it immediately, but I'm open, usually. I'll listen to a song three or four times before making a decision on how I feel about it, unless it's just flat-out trash first listen."

Kelynn was laughing now.

"If I had to choose, then I'd say Coldplay. You probably think that's a cliché answer, but their songs take me to another dimension. I can sit and listen and be in a whole other world until the song ends."

"I totally get it. I love them, too. It's like their music has magical powers or something."

"I don't know if I really believe in magic, but yeah, I get what you mean," Clay said. "My turn. Do you like the MTV VMAs?"

"CLAY! I'm obsessed. That is my go-to awards show."

His smile made her feel like he was expecting that to be her answer. "Do you remember that one year when Miley Cyrus came out of that teddy bear?"

"Okay, you're starting to freak me out. That's one of my all-time favorite performances. Miley Cyrus is *my* celebrity. I would kill to meet her!"

"What about *work* with her?" His expression seemed as though everything Kel was saying was funny.

"That's definitely the dream, but I doubt I'd be able to form complete thoughts around her, let alone actually do a job for her."

Kel was nervous by how much they connected. It was like he already knew her, like he knew everything she was about to say before she said it.

"Have you ever been in love before?" Clay asked nonchalantly, like he'd just asked her the most basic question.

Holy shit, Kel thought, in shock that the superficial conversation she'd started took a sharp turn to the deep end.

"What?" Kel asked, hoping he would retract his question.

"You heard me. It was bound to come up at some point," he said, waiting for her answer.

She looked down at her boots resting comfortably on the table in front of her.

"Sanders, come on," he said in a sing-song voice.

"More drinks?" she asked, getting up from the table and taking the empty bottle from his hand.

"Sure," he said, the smile disappearing from his face. "I'll be back," he said, making his way to the restroom.

Holy shit. I totally blew it. He's not going to want to hang out again.

He's probably regretting that he even invited me to that beach thing with his family. Damn it. Kel panicked while standing at the bar waiting for their drinks. She headed back to the now empty couch when she heard a familiar voice.

"Kelynn? Is that you?"

"Max?!" she said before she even saw his face. She could pick out his laugh in any crowd. She hadn't run into Max since they worked together in college.

"Oh my gosh! It *is* you!" he yelled, giving her the biggest hug before they both took a seat on the couch. "How have you been?" he asked, his voice dripping with excitement.

"I've been good. I'm still trying to figure out the job sitch, but who isn't? What about you? How's the social media gig?"

"Kel, I love it there. The office is so modern. It's going to change how the world works. You just wait. One day you're going to have a nap pod room and it's going to be the best thing you ever experienced."

"That sounds amazing and, honestly, a little weird."

"Right! Totally strange, but it works! They don't conform to corporate America ways of looking like you're working hard all the time. They give us so much time for play and rest and it works. It's like everything you have been told not to do at work, they encourage."

"That's so cool," Kel laughed, falling right back into her and Max's easy friendship groove.

Kelynn could see Clay out of the corner of her eye as he walked over behind the couch and put his hand firmly on Max's shoulder. "Hey, I'm Clay," he said, practically shoving his hand in Max's face for him to shake.

"Hey, man! Sorry. I didn't mean to overstep. Kel and I are friends from college. We also worked at a pet store together for a while."

"Oh my gosh, Max!" Kel said, slapping his leg. "Do you remember when that family came to buy that pug, and he had explosive diarrhea all over Andrea's shoes right before they left?"

Max burst out laughing, "Oh my gosh! I totally forgot about that!"

"Andrea was our boss," she started to explain, looking up at Clay, who was clearly uninterested.

"Max, why don't we catch up another time. It was so good running into you."

"Sure thing, Kel. You can text me. I'm still at the same number," Max said.

"See ya!" Kel said, while watching Clay watch Max walk away.

Clay sat back down, this time across from Kel. "Thanks for the drink," he said without a smile.

"No problem. Is everything okay? Did something happen in the bathroom?"

"What? No, I'm fine."

"Clay, talk to me."

"Let's go outside," he said, extending his arm for her hand. She reluctantly gave it to him, definitely feeling different this time walking up the stairs than when they first went down them. She felt like she was moving in slow motion. The air felt thicker than before, like she was wading through water. Clay led her through a crowd of people, crammed into the street level section of the bar. She could barely see two feet in front of her when the cool air hit her face. Ah, they were outside. Clay still didn't let go of her hand as he led them to the side of the building. An alley with lights strung above it connected two rooftops on either side of them. He faced her and took a deep breath, the heat from his breath clouding the air.

"I'm sorry. I just didn't expect you to fill my seat so quickly . . ." he said, stumbling over his words, "especially after avoiding my question."

"I ran into an old friend," Kel said, feeling as small as a child.

"I shouldn't have reacted that way. I'm sorry. I guess I feel kind of protective of you," he said, swinging her hand back and forth.

"Because of what happened with that guy on the street who attacked me?"

"No, not that."

"Then what?" She released her hand from his. "Clay, I'm not some kid you have to protect. I'm a grown woman," she said, now angry.

"I know that. I just . . ."

"You just what? I was talking to a friend. We were never anything more than that."

"Sanders. I'm sorry. I can just feel something strong between us, and I didn't want anything or anyone to threaten that."

"Maybe your feelings aren't real. Maybe you're confused," Kel said, arms crossed.

"Come on, Sanders. I know you feel the electricity between us. I can feel it right now, connecting us."

Kelynn shook her head, refusing to look at him.

"Sanders, look at me," Clay pleaded, sounding like his life depended on it.

She slowly turned her head back in his direction and locked eyes with him. She could feel the wave of electricity he talked of. It made her feel like she could stand on top of the world, do anything she set her mind to, like his eye contact made her fearless.

"Clay, I'm not deny . . ."

Before she could say anything else, Clay's hands reached for her face. The air grew thick and it became hard to breathe. Then his lips met hers. She felt the tension drain from her as their lips moved together. She'd never felt heat like this before. Every inch of his lips sent a new wave of fire rolling through her. It was as though they were meant to kiss and their lips were made to fit together this way. She could feel the fire growing as Clay's lips seemed hungrier. He moved them harder, pressing her against the brick wall of the bar. Kelynn stopped to take a breath, and as she did, she met Clay's gaze. She felt fully alive, watching him look back at her like no one had ever looked at her before. She stayed still only for a second before pressing her lips firmly back against his once more. The way he held her felt like he needed her to survive. He gently pulled away and kissed her forehead, lingering there for a moment with his hands resting on her shoulders.

"Sanders," he said, speaking into her forehead. "I'm sorry. I'm sorry for talking to your friend that way. Now you know why."

She put her arms around him and pulled him close, hugging him. "Is that beach brunch invite still on the table?" she asked, looking up at him.

"It was never off," Clay said, holding her tight.

Clay.

I WOKE UP to my alarm signaling me to get up for work. I hit snooze. I just needed ten more minutes. I was so exhausted. Even Willie didn't get up for breakfast, a sure sign we both needed more sleep. My thoughts rolled back to last night, my mind swimming in the half-asleep stage when the memory flooded my brain. I kissed Sanders. She was about to try and break things off. I bit my lip, remembering how it felt against hers. The way she moved when we kissed, her hips dancing back and forth, how it made me feel like her body was doing the talking for her. She could've told me she hated me, but I would never believe her after a kiss like that. After last night, I knew I needed her— that somehow, being that close to her gave me clarity. I walked away feeling almost refreshed, like I'd just taken a dip in a pool. How in the hell was I supposed to go to work for the rest of the week after a night like that? All I wanted was to be near her, like gravity was pushing me towards her, completely out of my control. My ten-minute snooze was up. I dragged myself out of bed and got in a quick workout before showering and heading out the door.

"Willie, I might be home a little late. I think I'll be working outside the office most of the day," I said, but she was already mostly asleep again, peering at me through one eye as I shut the front door, locking it behind me.

Work had settled back into its normal groove after my oversleeping incident with Mr. Maté. I found myself back in the daily grind, which was kind of nice. My nerves were at ease, and I could go about my workday with minimal effort. Except for today, when all I could think about was Sanders. I wanted to text her but didn't want to scare her like I had last night. I couldn't stand the silence. Restless, I made a quick decision. I grabbed my laptop and headed out the office doors. I sent Lliam a text to meet me. I needed an excuse to grab coffee other than to see her.

"Working outside the office the rest of the day, Mr. Fogerty?" Mr. Maté asked, leaning back in his chair so he could see me from his office.

"Yes, sir, I'm in need of some inspiration outside these walls."

"Understood!" Mr. Maté said, nodding his head in approval.

I turned to go and didn't look back. I needed to see her.

I parked in a spot directly in front of La Vita Dolce. As I made my way inside, the lunch rush was heading out. Perfect timing or so I thought. I snagged a table by the window, dropping my stuff on the cushion, reserving it. I looked out the window for a second to gather my thoughts before heading up to the counter.

"Hi. What can I get started for you?" a worker I hadn't seen before asked.

"Is Sanders . . . Kelynn working today?" I asked.

"No, she called in today."

"Did she say why?"

"Sir, I'm not allowed to give you that info. Besides, she talked to our manager, not me," she said. "Do you want me to start a drink for you?"

"Yeah, I'll take a cold brew." I paused as she wrote on the cup. "Actually, make it a latte."

She eyed me as she crossed out what she originally wrote. "Any flavoring?"

"Nope. Just plain, and before you ask, here is my rewards card."

"Great, thanks," she said in a sarcastically enthusiastic tone. "Name?"

"Clay. What's your name, by the way?" I asked, wanting to be able to reference her if I ever saw Sanders today.

"Who wants to know?" she asked.

I could sense a shift in her tone. *Did she think I was flirting with her?*

"Nevermind," I said, taking my seat by the window.

Great. Now she's gonna tell Sanders I came in looking for her, and then flirted with her instead, I thought, frustrated.

"Flavorless latte for Clay," the barista teasingly yelled, looking directly at me with a "come here" smile.

"Thanks," I said, grabbing the cup from her, trying to show the least amount of emotion possible, in hopes of not leading her on any further. As I walked back to my seat, Lliam walked in and with a nod, headed to the counter to order.

Good luck, I thought.

At least I was out of the office. I liked looking out the window, thinking about the world, thinking about things bigger than me. This always calmed me. Even so, I couldn't shake the thought that Sanders was avoiding me. Wait, that's crazy. She didn't know I was planning to come here. But what if she was shaken up about last night? Clay, focus. I tried my best to work for a solid thirty minutes before I finally gave in.

Hey, last night was fun.

I hit send and tried my best to distract myself with work.

"Hey, is that her? She's cute," Lliam said, pointing over his shoulder at the barista.

"No, apparently she isn't working today. How have you been, man?" I asked, picking up my coffee.

After several sips, I understood why Sanders liked lattes. They were simple, yet more decadent than a cold brew. Although, I must say, during working hours, I prefer a cold drink. The temperature alone jolted me awake. Lattes feel more like relaxation and nostalgia than a lifeline. I spent the next few hours working and talking with Lliam mostly about what was going on with him, which I was happily distracted with until I went home, annoyed with the silence on Sanders's end of the phone. I couldn't stand it, so I went to the one place I knew I could find her, or at least her thoughts. I knew I should give the necklace back, but I couldn't—not until I knew more about her, about the things she wasn't telling me.

I carefully picked up the timer and wood block from the drawer beside my bed and set up the contraption with new fishing wire. I pet Willie, put the opal in my right hand, and closed my eyes.

I blinked a few times and saw nothing but blackness. Complete darkness surrounded me, but I could hear the intro of a song playing. The beat sped up, as did my heart. I looked around, waiting for my eyes to adjust. In the distance, I could see a small glint of something, make that two somethings—a pair of eyes staring at me. I blinked a few more times, scanning the room and realized thousands of pairs of eyes were on me. *Bam!* A spotlight hit me from above. I was suddenly holding a microphone. I opened my mouth and began to sing. I could feel my body moving in ways it had never moved before. I heard back-up singers and turned to see The Lonely Island behind me. Their energy made me feel even more alive. My hips swayed, and I dropped it to the ground as the crowd cheered. It felt like I was watching the performance inside my body. I had no idea how I was singing or moving, or rather, how Sanders was singing and moving. It was such a rush. Everyone loved me and seemed to approve of me. When the song ended, I struck a pose, my back to the crowd but my eyes facing them. They all stood and cheered as Jimmy Fallon made his way out onto the stage, clapping for me.

"Wow, just, wow. Give it up for Kelynn Sanders, everybody! That was her new song, 'Not Changing for You' featuring the Lonely Island."

He turned to me then, looked me in the eyes, and held my hand between both of his. "Seriously, that was amazing. You're so gifted," he said, so only I could hear him. I waved to the cameras with him, and we talked a little longer. I turned to go backstage to talk with The Lonely Island, but as I went to pull the curtain back, I was transported to another country. The people around me were all speaking what sounded like Spanish. I scanned my surroundings and saw a small make-shift shelter with several people piled inside it. As I walked towards it, a little boy came running up to me, speaking in Spanish. All I could make out was a name.

He was shouting, "Kelynn! Kelynn!" with Spanish words intermixed. I stopped in my tracks and turned towards him.

"Hola," I said to him, using one of the only Spanish words in my vocabulary. Then, just like when I was singing on that stage, I began speaking in Spanish—fluently.

Where are we? I wondered, pushing the thought towards the front of my brain. Apparently, the part of my brain that was speaking the native tongue heard it, because the boy began laughing and responded with "Cooba," meaning Cuba.

"Tu eres mi mejor amigo. Te amo. ¿Quieres ir a comer?" the little boy asked.

I was smiling, and I felt my eyes burn with tears, but I didn't know why. I repeated what he said several times in my head so I could remember later. I responded with similar words, and he hugged me and held my hand while we walked towards the shelter together. I could smell the food cooking inside. I actually felt my stomach growl. I started to open the door for the little boy and *smack!* The wood plank hit my arm, knocking the opal onto the ground once more.

Damn it! Every time a dream ended, I kept trying to think of some explanation of how it started in the first place. It felt like whiplash. That feeling quickly subsided when I thought about that Cuban food. I looked over at Willie, who was whimpering, and then it dawned on me. Neither of us ate dinner when I got home.

"Aw, bud, I'm the worst. Let's go get some grub."

Willie shot up off the bed and ran to her food bowl. I gave her a scoop and cooked an egg sandwich. After shuffling through my bags of chips, I settled on classic Lay's. Willie happily scarfed down the bits of egg I put in her bowl. I turned on Netflix and grabbed my phone. Still no sign that Sanders was alive. Great. That was it. I was going to call her. The phone rang and rang. *Voicemail.* I didn't leave a message. I didn't even know what to say without coming on too strong. My memory hit me like a lightbulb as I opened Google Translate to see what the little boy said to me. "You are my best friend. I love you. You want to go to eat?" were the words the app generated. I smiled at that, feeling satisfied as I put my phone facedown on the table and went back to watching my show.

About five minutes into it, my phone buzzed. I turned it over to find a text from Sanders.

Finally, I thought.

It read, *Hey, now's not really a good time for me. I'll see you on Saturday. Just send me the time and place.*

I sat staring at my phone as Netflix played in the background. How was I supposed to respond to that? I guess it was a good sign she didn't try to cancel again for Saturday, but still. I replied back with the address.

359 West Crisp Dr. in Sunset Beach.

I looked at my phone a little longer before setting it face down again. I heard from her; that was all that mattered.

Clay.

TWO DAYS HAD passed since I'd seen Sanders in person, and I felt like I'd been punched in the chest. All I could think about was her perfectly cute face with her forest green eyes and naturally wavy hair. I sat on the porch of my parents' beach house watching the sunrise as I thought about her. I matched my inhales and exhales with the rolls of the waves and hoped to God Sanders would actually show up today.

"I've never seen someone sleep like that."

My eyes startled open at the sound of her voice.

She smiled. "What're you doing out here, Clay?"

"If you must know, I was breathing in the ocean air; just closed my eyes for a minute." I stood up to greet her as I tried to play off my unplanned nap and, to my surprise, she hugged me.

"Where have you been?" I asked her, still taken aback she was one of the first guests to arrive.

"I thought I was early," she said, side-eyeing me as I led her inside.

"No, I mean for the past two days. You haven't talked to me. Did I upset you that night we . . ."

She cut me off. "No, it wasn't that." She paused, looking down. I could tell she was struggling to talk. Her chin quivered.

"Sanders, what's going on?" I asked, concerned.

"It's Monette."

"The woman from the assisted living place?" I asked, searching her face for clues.

She pulled me into a side room off of the kitchen.

"She's gone," she uttered, holding back tears. "They took her to the hospital the night we went out. She had another stroke, and this time she didn't recover. She's gone, and I just couldn't handle it."

"Sanders, I'm so sorry," I said, pulling her close to me. "You didn't have to come today."

"I wanted to, to get myself settled before the funeral. It's later today."

"I'll go with you."

"No, you should stay here with your family. I know they'll need your help after brunch."

"Sanders, let me be there for you."

She nodded and laid her head on my chest, her arms folded against me. She seemed like she was trying her hardest to hold back the tears that were already flowing.

"I may have gotten your shirt wet." She laughed a little, which was a relief.

"That's the least of my worries," I said. "Is this why you called into work?"

"Yeah, how'd you know that?"

"I may have gone there that day, and your new barista now thinks I'm hitting on her, even though I asked for you."

"Glad I got to hear your side," she said, smirking. "Carter told me a fine piece of ass came looking for me on Thursday, and he seemed like a player."

"Sanders, I swear I did not flirt with her."

"I know. Carter thinks every guy who talks to her is flirting," she said. "Just don't talk so much next time, and you'll be fine," she said, lightly punching my arm.

"Are you sure you want to do this?" I asked, turning the conversation back to today.

"Yeah, I'm sure," she said. "Hey, Clay?"

"Yes?"

"I don't normally say this, but I think I need you."

I lifted the side of her face to look into her eyes and there it was. That electric wave.

"Sanders, I need you, too," I said as I closed the gap between us and pressed my lips against hers. A rush went through me as I kissed her gently, holding back every ounce of instinct. I felt her tongue dance against mine, shooting another flame down to my toes.

"You must be Kelynn," my mom said, immediately breaking up the moment.

I looked at Sanders, whose cheeks had turned pink. "Yes, hi, nice to meet you," Sanders said, putting distance between us.

Seventeen

KELYNN SAT AT the Fogertys' kitchen bar, a few feet away from the raw wood table that so eclectically enhanced the room. What appeared to be a family friend was behind the bar making drinks. Bloody Marys, frozen Irish coffee, and mimosas were all on the menu. He turned to her with his eyebrows raised. "What'll it be, Miss Kelynn, is it?"

"Yes, and I'll take a mimosa. Hold the orange juice."

He looked at her quizzically before giving a nod of approval. "My kind of girl."

Clay turned to face her and laughed. "So, champagne? At 10 a.m.?"

"What's the difference? I don't like orange juice, and champagne is so light and airy. It's like having sparkling water in the morning."

She gracefully stretched out her tanned arm to take the glass flute from the bartender.

"Thanks, Dad," Clay said, putting his hand on Kel's back, guiding her outside.

She waited until they were out of the kitchen before asking, "That was your dad? I figured he'd be mingling."

"Oh, he will be, but he was a bartender in a past life and misses it. He always starts parties behind the bar, getting everyone loosened up and ready to talk before he joins them."

"I get it. Making drinks is oddly satisfying," Kel said, sipping her bubbly. "Can I try your frozen coffee?" she asked, leaning close to Clay's glass.

"Whoa, whoa. Paws off. This is the best brunch drink ever. If you wanted one, you should've ordered one, Miss Fancy Champagne," he said, holding out his pinky as he tauntingly took a sip of his frozen treat.

"Come on. Just a taste," she giggled. "Clayyy," she taunted, as he thwarted her moves towards his glass.

They walked towards the tiki hut outback when Clay slipped on a damp tile. He opened his hand to grab the bar just under the cabana and the drink went flying and crashed to the ground. The two burst into laughter as the drink hit the sand. Kelynn looked over her shoulder to see Clay's mother watching them. She shook her head as she walked in their direction.

"Clay, why don't you and your guest go inside and clean up," his mother said, looking disapprovingly at the two.

"Sorry, Mom. Didn't see you there," Clay said.

"Make sure and change your clothes," she insisted, eyeing his pants where the drink had splattered.

Kelynn turned quickly to avoid exploding into laughter again. As they walked towards the house, she glanced up at the giant kitchen windows. She could see Clay's father smiling at them. He'd been watching the entire time. Kelynn definitely knew who the disciplinarian of the family was within the first twenty minutes of meeting Clay's family. Clay opened the front door for her, and she made her way back to the indoor bar.

"I'll just be a sec," Clay said, taking the stairs two at a time, already unbuttoning his shirt.

"Hurry back," Kel said, unsure about being alone with Clay's family.

"So, another orange-juiceless mimosa?" Clay's dad offered, grabbing the bottle of Moët & Chandon.

"Actually, I'm going to need two frozen Irish coffees. One for me and one for Clay. I tried to sneak a sip of his, and that's why he's upstairs right now changing."

"I saw that. He could use a girl like you who doesn't back down," he said.

"I'm sorry. I didn't catch your name," Kel said, watching him toss several shots of Irish creme into the blender.

"That's my bad. No need to apologize. I'm Ken."

"Well, Ken, it's nice to meet you."

"So, tell me about yourself. What makes you tick?" Ken asked, his eyes sparkling with genuine interest.

"I *love* the music and film industries. Basically, I gravitate towards anything media or entertainment-related."

"That's refreshing. It seems like you're truly following a passion."

"I have many, but that's my biggest one. I hope to work in marketing or event planning one day, maybe at awards shows."

"Now, that would be cool. You'd have to score us some seats. Tell me, what's another one of your passions?" he asked while passing her a frozen coffee.

"I'm a bartender of sorts like you, except I work with coffee. I enjoy it. It has a sort of rhythm to it like nothing else."

"That's the truth," Ken said, looking deep into her eyes like Clay did, like he was reading her thoughts.

"Did you think I'd lie to you?" Kel asked, almost sarcastically.

"Maybe embellish. Most people embellish, but when you talk about the things you love, your eyes . . . they seem to no longer see what's directly in front of them. I can tell they're looking at another view, one in your head."

"Yeah, you're right. I never thought of that, but it happens."

Clay was secretly seated at the top of the staircase listening to them talk. He walked into the kitchen in a fresh shirt and shorts. He put his arm around Kel and took a sip of her coffee.

"Hey! Yours is right there!" she playfully yelled, pointing to the opposite side of the bar.

"Oh, come on. It's only fair," he said, refusing to give it back.

"Clay! I didn't even get a sip of yours!" she said, moving fast, snagging the one made fresh for him from across the counter.

"Now we're even," she said, turning her back to him and heading out of the house.

"They're about to serve brunch finally," Clay yelled as she jogged ahead of him towards the ocean.

"Okay," Kel yelled back, coming to a slow stop.

Clay walked up beside her and grabbed her hand. "I know this is a lot today, but I'm glad you came."

Kel looked over her shoulder at him. He leaned in and kissed her. She kissed him back with the fire she could feel billowing deep inside her stomach and gaining oxygen as it hit her lips that met his. Clay broke away and made an odd face.

Was he not feeling what I was? Kel thought, suddenly self-conscious.

"I have to tell you something," Clay said, biting his lip like he was holding in a laugh.

"What . . .? You're weirding me out," Kel said, studying the grains of sand instead of Clay's face.

"You dance when you kiss."

He had her full attention now.

"What?"

"You dance when you kiss—like, you sway."

"I sway?" she asked, her eyebrows squeezed so close together a needle wouldn't fit between them.

"You sort of move your hips. Don't be offended," Clay said, smiling at her defensiveness. "I like it . . . a lot."

"Well, glad you enjoyed it because that's the last time I'm kissing you," she said, shifting so her back was to him.

"Sanders. Come on. You're cute."

She refused to acknowledge him.

"Come on, Sanders," he said playfully as he took a giant step and tickled her sides.

"Clay, stop it!" She could barely get the words out between laughs.

"Come on, Clay," mimicked a voice behind her. "You must be Kaitlin," the voice said as Clay stepped to the side to reveal a perfectly tanned blonde a few inches shorter than Kelynn.

"It's Kelynn," she corrected.

"Or is it Sanders?" Another girl approached them from the house, this one brunette. She resembled more of Clay's features and seemed kinder than her striking comrade.

"Hey, only I'm allowed to call her that," Clay said, standing beside the two girls.

"Well, hi, Kelynn. I'm Candace. I promise we don't bite," Candace, the brunette, said with a genuine, but close-mouthed smile.

"And I'm Chloe," the blonder sister said abruptly.

"So, Clayton, Candace, and Chloe," Kel said, trying to hide a smile. "Your parents must love alliteration."

"I like the way you say Clay's name," Candace said. "It just kind of rolls off your tongue."

"It's nice to meet you," Kel said.

"Shall we eat?" Clay asked, guiding all three girls with his outstretched arms back towards the beach house.

"Yes, I'm starving," Kel said, feeling her energy slowly drain away. Between Monette and Clay's family, her emotional gas tank was hovering on *E*.

Things got easier as food was passed around and conversation started flowing. Kelynn's guard began to come down as she talked, even with Candace asking her a million questions about her style and what it was like to live on her own. For an hour, Kelynn was happily distracted. Her joy deescalated when her phone buzzed with a text from Indi.

Hey, Kel. It's time. I love you.

Indi always knew when Kel needed the least amount of words possible. She knew when to push and when to step back. When Kelynn left her apartment this morning, she asked Indi to send her a reminder for Monette's funeral. She had a feeling that Clay would work his magic and distract her from the pain, but it was something she couldn't miss. She had to say goodbye.

"Will you walk me out?" she whispered to Clay. "Goodbye everyone! It was nice to meet you all," she said as she got up from the table.

"Of course," Clay said, trying to keep up with her as she made record time exiting the house.

"Wait up!" he shouted, hoping to stop her. "Let me take you."

"No, that's okay."

"Let me try that again," Clay said, his lips forming a straight line. "Let me go with you."

"Really, I'm fine," Kelynn protested.

"I know, but I want to."

"Clay, it would be different if you knew her. I need to say goodbye on my own. Okay?"

"Yeah, I get it," he said, wrapping his long arms around her.

"Thanks for forcing me to have fun," she said, a small smile creeping across her face and into her eyes.

"Anytime. I'll call you later."

She nodded, opening her car door.

Clay.

I WOKE UP in a state of confusion. I wasn't in my bed but on a couch almost as comfortable as my bed. I blinked a few times and realized I was still at my parents' house.

"Well, good afternoon, sleepyhead," my mom said, sitting at the end of the couch where my feet rested.

"When did I fall asleep?" I asked, mid-yawn.

"Once your friend, Kelynn, left, you went straight to the couch instead of rejoining us at brunch. Are you alright, sweetheart?" she asked me.

"Yeah, guess I didn't sleep great last night, and I feel for Sanders. A friend of hers passed away. By the way, Mom, she's not my 'friend.'" I was irritated.

"So you two are official?" she asked.

"Since when do you use the term *official*?"

"Isn't that what you guys say now?"

"We're more than friends, but I haven't called her my girlfriend yet, if that's what you mean."

"I see. Sounds complicated. Just don't let this complication affect your life too much."

"Mom, she's more than a complication. Geez. I'm gonna head out."

"Clay, I just think you should be more focused on your career right now," she said.

"Bye, Mom. Love you," I said, done with the conversation and ready to be back in my own place.

It was already five o'clock. The funeral should have ended hours ago. How could I be so exhausted and careless? Sanders probably thinks I've been ignoring her. I checked my back pocket to see if my theory was true. I had two missed calls and three texts from her.

Monette's family was kind to me, just how she described them.

The funeral is over.

I'm home.

None of them seemed to shove any negativity in my direction, but I could tell she was down. Instead of heading home, I drove straight to Sanders's place.

The doorbell rang as my finger held the button down. Indi answered the door.

"Hey, Clay," she questioned, her face downcast. "She's upstairs."

"Thanks," I said, entering the house and turning right at the top of the carpeted stairs.

I looked down the hallway, realizing I'd never been in Sanders's room before. After looking both directions, I saw a shut door with a sign hanging on it that said "I like naps a latte." That had to be her room. I knocked gently and barely heard a "come in" from the other side of the door.

"Clay?" she said, cocking her head sideways, craning her neck backwards to see me from her bed. "What are you doing here?"

"I'm sorry I didn't come sooner. I had a feeling you'd need a friend."

She looked at me, her swollen eyes blinking, still processing I was standing in her room.

She lifted her blanket as an invitation. Slipping off my shoes, I climbed into the bed. I could tell her eyes were puffy from crying. As

I wrapped my arms around her and held her, she cried more. Her body felt so small and fragile against mine. She laid her head against me, her hair draped across the left side of her face. Her roots started out dark and melded into a white-blonde near the ends. The sun had lightened it in a way that it resembled a sunset.

"Clay," she said, through her sniffling.

"Yeah?"

"Can I talk to you about it?"

"Of course," I said. Her head moved back and forth as she told me about the funeral. Monette's family gathered around the casket. Not a soul knew Sanders. She talked of the bond between them and how she felt like Monette sensed her presence there. The stories people told of her only reinforced her love for Monette and her hilarious feistiness.

She talked until I could tell she'd gotten everything out. Her mind was exhausted. We both lay there, the weight of her head still resting on my chest. I noticed her breathing change. She was asleep. I closed my eyes, in disbelief at how honest she was with me. I thought she would've told me to go home, but her tough exterior had broken today. Monette made a difference in Sanders's life, and that was enough for me to respect the woman I never had the privilege of knowing. She didn't bring her up, but I pondered how Sanders's mom leaving had seared her heart, so much so that Monette, whose relationship to her wasn't nearly comparable to mother and child, meant the world to Sanders. I knew this malformed maternal relationship would most likely affect her life indefinitely, but it allowed me to better understand her, and I wanted to help her start to see how it was already manifesting. I lay there listening to Sanders inhale and exhale. She was so peaceful and calm. I looked down at her and noticed, for the first time, she wasn't wearing makeup. I liked it. It felt like she could completely trust me. I shut my eyes again and matched my breathing with hers as I drifted off into another round of sleep.

"Clay. Clay. Wake up." Sanders sounded so far away.

"Clay," she said again. I felt pressure on my chest. I slowly opened my eyes to find her pushing against me, trying to wake me.

The room had grown dark. "What time is it?" I asked, still in a stupor.

"It's seven o'clock. I'm so hungry."

"Let's go get something to eat," I suggested.

"I don't feel like going out," she said.

"Sanders, I think you need to get out of here for a bit. It'll be refreshing."

She gave me a look of protest, half slumped over in the bed.

"Come on. You don't have to get dressed up. You just need fresh air and food."

"Okay," she said in a sleep-laced, whiny voice.

"I'll get us a couple of bottles of water to help us wake up."

"Sounds good. I'll be down in ten," she said, grabbing my hand and dragging it with her, pulling me up from the bed.

I started to go down the stairs when I heard her say, "Hey, Clay."

"Yes?" I asked, looking back up the stairs at her in the doorway of the bathroom.

"Thank you."

I smiled at her perfectly imperfect self—her barefooted, bed headed, flawless self.

Eighteen

KELYNN MADE HER way into her and Indi's shared bathroom. She did a once-over in the mirror and laughed out loud.

I cannot believe I let Clay see me like this, she thought, her puffy eyes staring back at her.

Her hair was a mess of kinks and tangles. The remnants of her eye makeup stained her under-eyes, making her look like a drug addict. She pumped a blob of face wash into her hands and rubbed in a circular motion, starting with her cheeks and being extra careful around her eyes. She turned the faucet to cold and let the refreshing water glide down her face, taking the soap suds with it. She ran a brush through her nest of a hairdo and looked back in the mirror.

Maybe just a little mascara and lip gloss, she thought.

She didn't want to hold Clay up too long and make him think she was high maintenance, so Kel slapped on the slightest amount of makeup and went to change. She overheard the conversation coming from the kitchen.

"Long day?" Clay asked.

"Yeah, you could say that," Indi said. "I think it was a longer day for Kel, but . . ." She trailed off.

"I feel bad for her. I'm going to take her out and try to cheer her up."

"She agreed to this?" Indi asked.

"Yeah, why?"

"Well, Kel's not usually one for surprises, especially not after a day like today."

"I think I've got a good plan to take her mind off it all." He paused. "By the way, Kel tells me you're seeing Gunner?"

"Mhmm. Make that, *saw* him."

"My bad. We went hiking the other day, but we usually talk about career stuff, so I didn't ask him. Maybe I should have."

"No worries. We're better as friends. When I talk to him, it's like talking to the brother I never had."

"Is it going to be weird with all of us hanging?"

"When are we all hanging?" Indi asked.

"No plans yet, but it's bound to happen at some point," Clay said. "He's my best friend; you're hers.

"We should be fine. Nothing to worry about. Like I said, he's like a brother," Indi said.

"You ready?" Kel asked, her voice trailing down the stairs.

Her hair flowed on either side of her face. It had a natural, unkempt look that worked. Clay glanced over, his head nodding and speaking for him as he did a once-over. Kel shut the door behind them, making sure she'd turned the lock. "Okay," she said, taking a refreshing breath of cool, fall air. "Where are we going?"

"Well, according to Indi, you don't like surprises, so I'll tell you. I was planning on taking you to Nightlight."

"Hmm," Kel said, fidgeting with her keys. "That place is super pretentious. Blakely and Preston go there all the time. They're probably there right now," Kel said, visualizing the bar instead of noticing his blue-grey eyes staring at her.

In her mind, she could see her friends sitting there, all sipping their vodka tonics, like she used to do in college. They would wear their best outfits, spend a minimum of two hours getting ready, and usually end up overdressed. She could see them waiting for a cute guy to pass by or look at them from across the room, remembering how they would fake laugh in hopes of attracting them, waiting to be noticed.

I used to be so dumb, Kel thought.

"Hello? Earth to Sanders!"

"Sorry," she said, blinking several times. "We're not going there. I know a place," she said, reaching for Clay's keys.

"You want to drive?"

"Please, Clay. I love the truck!"

"Say no more!" Clay said, mimicking her raised voice, and threw the keys her way.

"So, have you gone on any more runs lately?" Clay asked as Kel took off down the road.

"Yeah, I actually did four miles the other day." Kel merged onto the highway. "How did you know I like to run?"

"I think you told me," Clay said, searching for the memory.

"I would've remembered that," Kel said, speeding faster, swerving in and out of the lanes.

"Sanders, are you sure you should be driving tonight?" Clay asked, gripping the side of the door for stability.

"Yes! I've felt numb for way too long!"

"Sanders, look. I get that you're in an intense emotional state, but can we not drive with a vengeance?" Clay asked, pulling on his seatbelt that had tightened one click too far.

"Sorry. I felt like I was running. You made my mind go there," she said, tapping the brakes, the odometer slowly climbing back down from 90 mph.

Clay reached over and laid his hand on her thigh. "Sanders, we're going to have a simple night of distraction and fun. After everything you had going on today, I just wanted to put you at ease."

"You're right," she said, grabbing his hand and interlacing her fingers with his. "It is going to be fun. Let's talk about something else."

"Deal," Clay said, relieved.

"Tell me about your sisters. What do they think of me?"

Clay grabbed the side of the truck for support again, hearing Kel's tone inch up a few notches again.

"Shit, Sanders. I'm serious. We can talk about that stuff another time. I'm here for you, but you have to let me in. What happened between the time when we were in your bed an hour ago and now?"

"I'm not used to being so open with people," she said, her voice cracking. "I don't want you to think I'm a weak person who can't handle the shit that goes on in her world, or the type of person who needs to rely on someone else to make it through."

"Sanders."

"Because I'm not that person, Clay," she said, her voice sounding rushed, like she was running out of air.

"Sanders."

"I can do this on my own. I don't need you."

"Sanders, stop," Clay said, referring to more than just her mouth.

"No, Clay."

"Sanders, stop the car now!"

Kelynn pulled over onto the shoulder, barely dodging a car that was merging onto the highway.

"Sanders, look at me."

"No."

"Sanders. You've had a long day."

"Clay, that's not what this is about."

"Look at me," Clay said in a tone that let her know he meant it.

She turned her head towards him and slowly met his ever-passionate gaze.

"You are independent. You are strong. You are beautiful. You are also human. I don't care if it's me. I don't care if it's a man, or Indi, or whomever. But people care about you, and I need you to let them in."

To her own surprise, she didn't look away. Tears fell from the corners of her eyes as he talked, but she never moved to wipe them, her eyes locked on his. She felt her nostrils flare with every word he added. Clay touched the ends of her hair. He wrapped a strand around two of his fingers. Then, his hand glided up to wipe her tears away. Kel rested against his hand. He moved in closer, wiping one last tear before kissing her. He moved slowly with intention. He kissed her again and again. She couldn't tell if her heart was beating faster because of each lingering kiss or because of the cars passing by at 65 mph, the wind from each one rocking the truck.

She placed her hand on his chest and gently pushed him away.

"Clay, there's something you don't know about me."

"Tell me," he said, breathing her in.

"I black out . . . a lot. I actually blacked out at your party. I didn't want you to know. I didn't want to have to explain, but I want to now." She paused waiting for Clay to say something, but he didn't. "When my fears become too much, I lose my ability to see, and I pass out. Everything goes dark. I don't know why, but for some reason, when I hang out with you, those thoughts grow smaller and smaller. The longer I'm around you, the less consistent my blackouts are."

"So that's what happened that night. I wondered why your friends were being so protective about it. But what does this mean? Maybe you should see a doctor?"

"I have. They can't figure it out—not completely. But I think this means, somehow, my thoughts need you. I'm not used to needing any-one. It's taking everything inside me not to fight it."

Clay kissed her again, his bottom lip resting on hers.

"Sanders, it's okay. Why don't we switch places? No more thinking tonight, okay? You just tell me when to turn right or left and we'll go to the place you planned on going."

She nodded. "Deal," she said, climbing over him as he climbed under her.

"Take it away," he said as he pulled back onto the highway.

"Right," Kel said, referring to the next exit, feeling more like Clay was right; right for her, which scared her more than words could explain.

$$C\!.lay.$$

"LEFT!" SANDERS SAID, excited we were almost to our destination.

"Okay, right!" Each direction was louder than the last.

Today had been a turning point for both of us. She had finally let me in. I didn't know exactly what this meant for us, but I was happy to know I could calm her. I didn't understand how our connection helped her mysterious medical condition. It sounded like something from a sci-fi movie. I tried to shove it to the back of my mind for now because she was finally feeling better. I didn't want to do anything to jeopardize that and have her fall back into a pit of sadness, or as she called it, darkness. The title of the book in that opal dream came rushing back to me—*Out of the Black*.

"Okay! It's on the left!" Sanders yelled, her feet up on the seat, hugging her knees.

"I think I've been here before," I said, looking at the exterior of the bar as I read the sign.

"The Crunkleton," I said, rubbing my chin trying to locate the memory. "I swear I've been here before, but something's off about it."

"Clay, let's go inside," Sanders said, opening her car door and hopping out.

I followed her as she rushed through the door.

"Hey, it's Kel!" a booming voice said from behind the bar, not more than a couple seconds after Sanders entered.

"Ferdinand!" she shouted. "How are you?"

"I'm good. It's been quite some time since you've stepped foot here. I should be asking how you are!"

"Today wasn't my best day, but I knew you guys could cheer me up."

"Glad you came to us," he said, with rosey cheeks like Santa. He wore a button-down shirt with a tie that was connected to his left shirt pocket by a small gold chain, and his mustache curled on either end.

What a hipster, I thought to myself, feeling a little skeptical.

"So, what'll it be?" Ferdinand asked. "Your usual? The Champ drink? Chambord and champagne?"

Sanders smiled, mulling it over. "I'll just do a Jack and Diet Coke," she said. Ferdinand raised his eyebrows.

"Clay, you want something?" she asked, turning to find me.

"Yeah, I'll just do your hoppiest beer."

"Wise choice," said Ferdinand. "We've got some insanely hoppy beers, all brewed locally."

"Perfect," I said.

I scanned the room as Ferdinand made our drinks. It felt familiar but like everything had been rearranged. There was a pool table in the left-hand corner and a deer head surrounded by plates that hung flat against the wall on the right. Frameless photos of established-looking men smoking cigars covered the back wall, and ladders stood behind the bar, leaning against the shelves of bottles. They looked like ladders you'd find in an old library or mansion with dusty books scaling to the ceiling.

"Here you go!" Ferdinand said, the ends of his mustache moving as he talked.

"Thanks," I said, grabbing both drinks. "Hey, by the way, do you guys have another location?"

"Yes, sir, we have another spot in Charlotte."

"That's why this place is familiar! I thought you'd rearranged all the furniture since I last came in," I said as the memories of past spring breaks rushed back. I used to visit the twin bar with Lliam. We had many, many girl talks over that pool table.

Ferdinand's laugh echoed through his stomach. It sounded almost like an evil villain's laugh, making me feel even more uncomfortable.

"Just so you know, well, Kel knows this," Ferdinand paused to wink at her, "but there is a secret passageway over there by the books. Just pull the right one and it will lead you into another section of our bar."

"Yes, I love that room!" Sanders said.

"We've got karaoke in there tonight," Ferdinand said, rubbing a towel over freshly cleaned glasses, furthering their shine.

I handed Sanders her glass. "Want to go? Maybe make fun of the singers?" I asked, hoping to move somewhere away from Ferdinand.

"I'm game." Sanders sipped out of the tiny-mouthed stirring straw.

She led the way to a bookcase that had a giant red book in the center. She pulled on it, unlocking the thick door. She leaned all her weight forward until it finally opened into a speakeasy. It smelled like cigars and instantly sparked my craving for one. The bar had a cabin-type feel, but this secret room exuded an entirely different ambiance. I could see why Ferdinand worked here. He appealed to both the cabin hipsters and the speakeasy snobs. Thankfully, tonight the room was full of twenty-to-thirty-year-old adults who put off a relaxed vibe—the perfect environment for Sanders to let go and forget about the day.

She walked me to two living-room-style chairs, one green-and-white striped, the other orange with little white polka dots. Each was showing wear from what must have been decades of use. Her hand felt strong as she walked us to our seats. We sat down without Sanders letting go of my hand. She was playing with my fingers, looping hers around mine, tracing their length. She sat comfortably in the chair, partially slouched.

"How're the hops?" she asked.

"Pretty good," I shouted over the karaoke. "What's the story with Ferdinand?" I asked, moving my thumb and forefinger in a gesture of a curly mustache above my lip. To my surprise, Sanders laughed.

"I used to come here a lot in college, usually after a hard test or rough day. It felt homey; worn-in. No one comes here to impress anyone else. They come here to have a good time and relax, like a home away from home. Ferdinand got to know me. He's really nice. He's like forty. Can you believe that?"

"Actually, no. He looked like he was thirty," I said.

"Right?! I think the facial hair helps hide his true age."

"So, Sanders."

"So, Fogerty," she said, leaning over and grabbing my hand dramatically with both of hers.

"I have to know. Did you take a nap earlier, or was that considered a blackout?"

"Oh," she said, taking both hands back and filling them with her glass. She toyed with the small black straw for a bit. "It *was* a blackout, but they haven't been the same lately."

"What do you mean?"

"Normally, all my dreams and fears, or as I sometimes call them, my haunting thoughts, cloud my brain and it shuts down in a way. I usually wake up with a pounding headache and the vein in my forehead bulges. But lately, they don't last as long, maybe an hour or so, and my head feels almost normal when I come out of it."

"And you think that's because of me?"

"I'm not saying the two are related, but it is weird that the more I hang out with you, the more bearable they become. Like today, for instance. I came home from the funeral and laid in my bed to take a nap. All of a sudden, my thoughts multiplied, as they tend to do."

"What were you thinking about?" I was intrigued.

"Monette—that I should've visited her more. What our friendship could have become. What it actually was. All these 'what ifs' popped into my head, and then I started contemplating if I could even go back to the assisted living center and visit someone new. I wondered how the workers handle it so well, which turned into the thought that maybe I should get into the business, but that has nothing to do with my dreams. After that, I started thinking about my career, and all these voices started swarming—telling me lies and truths about myself."

"Did you tell me about the voices before?" I asked, feeling like I'd known about them somehow. I could recall how each one sounded. I had heard them.

"I don't think so. Tonight was the first time I told you about my blackouts in general."

"You're right. I'm not sure why that sounded familiar."

"Anyway, today was different because normally when my thoughts get congested like that, all I see is black, and then I pass out. But today I didn't see black. I saw memories of Monette. It was like I was reliving it all, like a movie. I probably sound insane now, or at least more so than I already did."

"Did your head hurt when you woke up?"

"Not really. My eyes hurt from crying more than anything."

"You don't sound crazy. It just sounds like you have some sort of medical condition. Intense anxiety, maybe?"

"It feels almost supernatural, though. I don't know. It doesn't follow any of the typical medical cases like mine. I've seen several different specialists—neurologists, psychiatrists, even sleep doctors. They can't give me an exact answer or cure, but part of me thinks it's you, like being around you somehow causes my thoughts to decrease, or maybe your presence is somehow an antidote."

I leaned in close, reaching over my Victorian armrest. Our lips met briefly before I said, "I like that you're not normal."

She blushed and turned back to her drink.

"So, what song are you singing?"

She looked up at me with a "no way in hell" look as she threw back the last of her drink.

"Aw, come on, Sanders," I said, shoving her leg that was now draped over her armrest. Clearly, the Jack and Coke had begun to take effect.

"Clay, I don't sing."

"Well, we'll never know that unless you prove it."

"I'll prove it to you when we're alone."

"I'm going to grab us more drinks," I said, extending my hand for her empty glass.

"I'll take the Drink of Champs for the next round," she said, pointing and winking at the same time. Oh, I was so going to get her to sing. It was one of the dreams I had seen when holding the opal. There's at least some part of her that wants that future, to perform and to be in the spotlight. I was going to make it happen for her. Tonight. She just needed a nudge, and maybe a couple rounds of the Drink of Champs. I headed back to the bar out front since the one in the speakeasy was packed.

"Say, Ferdinand, who do I have to ask to announce Kelynn as the next karaoke contender?"

"Oh, man. Are you sure you want to do that?" he asked, his voice loaded with hesitation. "Kel's the type of person who enjoys being in the background."

"Maybe she did when you knew her, but I know her better," I said, taking the drinks from him.

"Just tell Julio. He's running the system in the back."

"Thanks," I said over my shoulder as I walked towards the secret entryway once again.

Sanders seemed totally focused on the current singer, who was stumbling over the words to "Escape" by Rupert Holmes. *Yikes*. I made my way through the misaligned chairs and handed Sanders her drink.

"Hey, I think I know that guy back there," I said, referring to Julio sitting behind the karaoke station, which consisted of his laptop and two microphones.

"Who?" Sanders asked, stretching her head around the side of her chair.

"I'm gonna go say hi," I said, setting my drink down on the table next to her.

"Okay," Sanders replied, more interested in her drink than what I was saying.

The crowd booed the guy off the stage as I made my way to the back of the smoke-filled room.

"This place goes all out for karaoke night, doesn't it, with the smoke machines and all?" I said, trying to make small talk.

"Yeah, you could say that," the man said behind his laptop, eyes glued to the screen.

"You see my friend over there on the striped chair?"

He looked up, trying to find who I was describing.

"She's right over there. Her legs are hanging off the side of that chair, moving to the beat."

"Ah, yeah, what about her?" he asked, only pausing for a minute before getting back to his computer.

"She loves to sing. It's actually a dream of hers to sing in front of crowds, but she needs a little push. If you get the crowd excited first, she will most likely get on stage and belt it out. And man, can she belt it!" I said, trying to persuade him. I was taking a chance, since I'd never actually heard Sanders sing, except when her voice came out of my mouth in that opal dream, and even that seemed a little cloudy now.

"Look, man. I'm not a DJ. I don't announce things," he said, like I was a fly he couldn't seem to swat away.

"Okay, I hear ya. Can I announce it?"

"You want to introduce your friend on stage?" he asked, turning to face me.

"Yeah, look, I'll buy you a drink."

"Deal," he said, extending his hand which held a microphone. "Just give me the name of the song."

"Right. Um. Let me think. She loves Miley Cyrus."

"I have the song 'Party in the USA,'" he suggested.

"Perfect," I said, walking much more confidently towards the stage than I actually felt.

Nineteen

KELYNN SIPPED HER Drink of Champs and looked around at the crowd surrounding her. Most of the people here looked to be in their thirties—their lives seemingly figured out. She envied people she had never met as they conversed with others about their "line of work."

Am I ever going to have a "line of work"? She thought about her two part-time jobs. Her mind wandered off, playing the "what if" game, yet again.

What if I had studied a major with a focus in a specific area? What if I had taken different classes that scared me and pushed me? What if I wasn't afraid? What if I was in a different town where more opportunities existed?

Out of reflex, she touched her bare neck where the opal necklace once hung. She desperately needed to shove her thoughts into the gem to prevent a blackout. This time, her overloaded mind was slowly dragging her down rather than the normally rapid pace, which was odd. She could feel the decline, as though her thoughts were tempting her, not forcing her this time. Her mind started to follow them when she heard, "And now, we're going to hear from someone who has been wanting to do this for some time now. She hasn't had the courage to get up on stage in front of people in a while, if ever."

She knew that voice. That voice was pulling her out of her clouded thoughts.

"Please give a warm Clunkerton's welcome to Kelynn Sanders!"

It was Clay, and he was extending an arm in her direction from the stage. Kelynn blinked a few times, the cloud vanishing from her mind. Everything was crystal clear—even more than that every*one* was crystal clear. Their eyes were all staring at her, waiting for her to get up and make her way to the stage. She was so mad her cheeks were turning red. She could feel their warmth as she stood up and walked towards Clay. The crowd began to clap for her, encouraging each terrifying step she took. She shook her head at Clay as she took the mic from him, refusing to make eye contact. She started to turn back, when Clay grabbed her hand.

"You got this," he whispered into her hair. He kissed her on the forehead and then left her alone on the stage.

"Hi, everyone," she said rather shyly.

The intro of "Party in the USA" began to play, and Kelynn was transported to another realm. She closed her eyes, hoping that would end the reality that a crowd was staring at her. She opened her mouth to sing, and a confidence took over she'd never experienced before. She sang the first verse with her eyes still shut. The song continued, and as she kept going, she slowly opened her eyes. The packed seats began clapping along to the beat. She took a deep breath before belting out the first half of the chorus.

"YEAH!" the crowd shouted in response.

She sang the second half.

"YEAH!" they shouted again.

Kel moved back and forth across the stage like she was born to perform, swaying her hips from side to side, owning the beat. The song ended and Kelynn felt a rush of satisfaction as the crowd clapped, the loudest response anyone had received all night. She took a bow, and Clay walked up with an outstretched hand. She gladly took it, hopping down off the stage. Clay walked her back to her seat. "Let's go home," she said, smiling so big that the corners of her mouth almost touched her ears.

"You sure?" Clay asked, surprise lining his voice.

"Yeah, I want to stop while I'm ahead," she said, feeling powerful, a mixture of her champion drink and her champion-level performance reverberating through her.

Clay followed her out as she slowed to say goodbye to Ferdinand with a long parade wave and then continued to the front entrance.

Clay opened the passenger door, and Kel hopped in without hesitation, a smile still plastered across her face. He walked around the front of the truck and climbed in. He didn't start the car at first, but turned to face Kelynn.

"Sanders, I need a freaking high five."

She laughed as she smacked his hand with added force.

"You can actually sing!" he said, still in shock that taking a chance on a mystical opal worked to his advantage.

"It's always been a dream of mine to sing in front of people—to really perform."

"I had a feeling," Clay said.

"How could you possibly know that about me?" she asked, confused.

Clay leaned in close to her face, so even the crickets couldn't hear him.

"I had a feeling you're a woman of many hidden talents," he said under his breath, pressing his lips hard against hers.

Kelynn pushed back harder. She kissed him like she'd been waiting for hours. She shoved him back farther and climbed over into the same seat.

"Sanders," Clay said, stopping the kiss, his hands on her hips as she sat on top of him.

She kissed him again.

"Sanders, not like this," he said.

"What's wrong?" she asked, her hands on either side of his face, her fingers dancing on his beard.

"I don't want you to do something you'll regret. I haven't ever seen you like this sober, so . . ."

"That's fine," she said, falling backwards into her seat.

"Sanders, don't be mad."

She crossed her arms, looking out the window, refusing to respond to him.

He pinched her sides, and she erupted in laughter.

"Okay, fine. I'm not mad at you. Sometimes, I just wish you were a jerk and wouldn't care if I was drunk."

"Sanders, you need water."

"No, *you* do!" she said, still laughing. "Can I at least hold your hand?" she asked, giving him overdramatized puppy eyes.

"You can always hold my hand," he said, reaching over and resting his on her thigh.

"I like you, Clay," she said, looking out the window, her face softer now.

"I like you, too, Sanders. Maybe even more now that I know you can really sing."

Her drink-influenced laughter was gone. She was left feeling calmer, still looking out the window, replaying the night.

Clay had helped her achieve something she never would have on her own, and she didn't know if she liked that he had that power over her—a power she couldn't tap into herself.

SANDERS WAS COMING over. It was official. My mind raced as I hurried to clean up my place. Normally, I was pretty good at keeping the place looking nice, but I recently had the guys over for a euchre night—a storm that left cards and snacks littered in the living room. Not to mention, I had been preoccupied with the thought of Sanders. The way she kissed me and how I saw her future change over and over again still trying to decipher what it all meant. One future seemed to include a relationship, but several others did not, at least from the limited opal "visions" I'd experienced.

What if I wasn't a part of her future? I thought as I gathered several empty chip bags.

Willie watched me from her comfortable bed. She didn't even lift her head as I moved frantically. She only moved her eyes to and fro, lazily watching my every move. The place was clean enough. I threw on my favorite concert tee and opened a bottle of sweet strawberry wine. Cheese and crackers paired well with it in the past, so I put some out on a plate in the center of the kitchen. I needed Sanders to want to come back and hang out at my place more often. Willie slowly walked into the kitchen and dropped her ball at my feet.

"Good idea, girl," I said, picking up the ball, along with the rest of her scattered toys, and putting them in a basket. She laid back down and thumped her head to the ground, sighing at me. I grabbed a can of air freshener and held my finger down, refusing to let up until I'd hit every room of the house.

Ding dong.

Perfect timing, I thought, putting the air freshener back, running my fingers through my hair and across my beard once more.

"Hey, welcome," I said, opening the door.

"Thanks," Sanders said as the once-sleepy Willie came bounding towards her. "Hi, cutie," she said, extending her hands and squatting down to her level. "That's such a good girl," she said in a baby voice as Willie licked her.

"Alright. Come on, Willie," I said, attempting to pull my dog off of a dog lover.

"It's okay, really," she said, laughing.

"I know you don't mind, but I really wanted to be your first kiss through the door," I said, putting my arms around her waist and pulling her in towards me as I pressed my lips against hers while simultaneously pushing the door shut with my foot.

She stopped kissing me and smiled. I kissed her once more. "Is that wine?" she asked, looking over my shoulder.

"Yes, I made wine for you."

"You make wine? Why didn't you ever tell me that?"

"I mean, I poured you a glass," I said, still trying to recover from the kiss. It was like I was transported each time we touched like that, and I had to return to Earth before my brain would function again.

"Looks great. What kind is it?"

"Strawberry," I said matter-of-factly.

"No way. That's one of my favorites. The taste is just so sweet and crisp. I'm not the biggest fan of the song, but I get why someone would sing about it," she said.

"Wait," I said. "A toast."

"To what?" she asked, her lips playing on the edge of her glass, tempting the wine to dance across her tongue.

"A toast to you being here again. This time I know you so much better."

"When have I been here?" she asked, her eyes looking away from the glass, trying to trace back the memory.

"Remember? My party?" I said.

"Oh right!" she said. "When I blacked out—it still seems a little fuzzy," she said, her eyes seeming like they were somewhere distant.

"Sanders?"

"Yeah?"

"Aren't you going to take a drink?"

"Right," she said, raising her glass with her eyes now looking into mine, back in the present. "So are you going to take me on a tour?" she asked, looking at me over her glass.

"Sure," I said, my mind racing back to each room I cleaned and ones I skipped.

"You're currently in the kitchen, and to your right is my living room."

She nodded, looking around. "What's that from?" she asked, pointing to a picture on the wall above the TV.

"It's a picture from the time I went mountain climbing in California."

"Whoa, that looks like a professional picture."

"I took it on my phone. I wish I could brag more about it, but . . ."

"It's gorgeous," she said. "Show me more."

I led her down the hallway to my office and then upstairs, past the guest bedroom.

"And this is my room," I said.

She walked slowly down the hallway as I looked over my shoulder to see the opal necklace sitting on my nightstand.

Oh no. How can I touch it without phasing out? I thought frantically.

I darted for the bed as she studied the pictures in the hall and quickly swept my hand across the nightstand, causing the necklace to fall to the floor behind it.

"This is nice," she said as she entered my room.

She walked around looking at each photo, examining every knick-knack before taking a seat on the bed.

I stood in front of her.

"What?" I asked, leaning towards her, placing my hands on her thighs.

"I like it. It feels like you."

"How so?"

"You somehow captured your essence within each piece of decor, and I really like this comforter," she said as she sat on a faded green bedspread.

"I really like that you're on my comforter," I said, pressing my lips against hers. I didn't open my eyes but took her wine glass and placed it on the nightstand. Her hands were around my neck as she kissed me over and over, her lips intertwining with mine. Her tongue was hot, and I wanted more of that heat.

"Clay." She pushed back against me, but I filled the gap again, kissing her harder.

"Mhmm?" I said under my breath as we stayed connected.

"Clay," she said, this time more sternly.

"What's up?" I asked, still standing, leaning over her as she sat between my arms.

She hesitated. "How many girls have been in this bed before?"

"What?"

"Remember when you asked me if I'd been in love before? Well, it's my turn to ask you."

"Sanders, no one has been in this bed." I could tell she was relieved by my answer. "And for the record, you never answered that question when I asked it."

"Shit. I didn't think that part through," she said, a small smile forming at the corner of her mouth.

I sat down next to her.

"What is that?" she asked, looking at my knife/kitchen timer/fishing wire contraption.

"No way. No more distractions," I said, panicking, hoping she would drop it and actually answer the question.

"Fine," she started. "I have loved one person." She took a breath. "But I wasn't in love with them."

"When?" I asked.

"It was my senior year of high school. He was a med student, and he seemed so sophisticated. He would take me to the nicest places and I think I was more smitten by the idea of him and who I was with him, than who he actually was. I liked being taken out and how he made me feel, but the chemistry was off. When I found out he'd been cheating on me, it felt like my heart physically broke, but in time I realized it wasn't really about him. I experienced that same feeling when my mom left."

"I'm sorry. No one should have to go through either of those things, especially not you," I said, taking a seat next to her, tracing her fingers with mine, her fists starting to release.

"Your turn," she said, turning to face me, shifting her legs into a cross-legged sitting position.

"Alright," I said, mimicking her seated position.

"I've dated several people, but there was only one that I thought I loved at the time. We were so young that now I know that's not what it was."

Sanders started to look away from me, so I grabbed her hands.

"I realized she was exactly who my mom would pick out for me, and that felt boring. I wanted someone that would throw them for a loop, someone who wasn't just like my family. So, I broke it off after two years of dating."

I played with her fingers as I talked, and she began to play back, her guard slowly lowering.

"Clay."

"Yeah?"

"Did I see cheese and crackers downstairs?"

I laughed, caught off guard. "Yes, would you like to go back down there? Willie probably misses you already," I said, starting to stand up from the bed.

"Yes, but first . . ." she said, grabbing me from behind my neck and pulling me onto the bed. She kissed me like I had been kissing her earlier. She stopped for a moment. "Clay, I'm scared of you," she whispered.

The sun had gone down, and only the moonlight shone in through the blinds.

"I'm scared of you, too, Sanders. I'm scared of how you make me feel," I said, kissing her again. She pushed against me, our bodies colliding for only a few minutes before she pushed me off the bed and sat back up.

"What's wrong?"

"I still want those cheese and crackers," she laughed and made her way down the stairs.

"Damn it," I said after she had left the room. I couldn't handle her, and that wasn't something I was used to.

Twenty

SHE WAS COMPLETELY caught off guard. When Kelynn walked into Radical Entertainment's grand front doors, she could tell the air felt different, lighter—like someone had taken all her negative thoughts and hand-picked them out of the foggy clouds of her brain. She felt confident in herself as she walked in, not knowing what the day would bring her.

"Morning, Kel!" the receptionist, Andy, kindly greeted her.

"Morning," she responded with a warm, genuine smile.

"Did you hear?"

"Hear what?" Kelynn asked, turning to face her.

"I got a new job. I'm leaving next week."

"What?! No! I mean, that's great! What is it?" Kelynn asked, excited and sad at the same time.

"I'll be assisting a production crew in New York."

"Oh my gosh, Andy, that's amazing! I'm so jealous!"

"Well, this could mean something big for you, too."

"How?" Kelynn asked, now leaning over the reception desk. She could smell Andy's perfume she was so close.

"I put in a good word for you. My job is the only one that doesn't require a master's degree. And the receptionist only gets hired from within, or if they have insanely stellar references."

"Seriously? I didn't think anyone could work here full-time without a master's."

"It's kind of a hush-hush thing around here because of that rule. I told Joe about you, and he already likes your work ethic, so fingers crossed!"

"Holy shit. Thank you, Andy! I owe you one. The next time I'm in New York, I'm buying you the most expensive coffee you've ever had. The kind made from beans crapped out by wild cats."

Andy burst out laughing. "Kel, that's the most grotesque thing I've ever heard you say. But, anyway, you should sit with me for a bit if you don't have a lot to do. I can at least show you a few things before I leave."

"Deal," Kelynn said, turning to go find her boss, Joe.

The air surrounding each step felt even lighter than when she'd walked into work. She felt like she was flying, partially from seeing Clay last night. The way he kissed her scared her, but in a good way. He was forceful—no, that wasn't the right word. He was passionate. She knew he would never hurt her or push her too far, but he moved with heat, like gravity didn't hold him to the ground but rather pulled him towards her, like an outside source moved them together.

"Kelynn? Kelynn?" Joe said towering over her, peering through his squinted eyes.

Kelynn shook her head before fully coming back to reality. "Sorry. Yes, Joe?"

"Are you doing okay?" he asked, concern distinctly coating his voice.

"Yes, sorry. Andy was talking to me earlier, and I guess my thoughts are going a hundred miles a minute."

"That's actually what I wanted to talk to you about. Come on into my office."

Kelynn followed behind him, hoping he still thought of her as a valid candidate after her daydream distracted her, transporting her back into Clay's world, her surroundings disappearing altogether. Joe motioned to the chair in front of his desk. Kelynn sat down, a little uncomfortable with having such a serious meeting. She worked in the entertainment business with an M.O. of fun. The mood was normally relaxed, but now she was conscious of her work attire and how straight her back aligned with the cloth-covered office chair.

"Since you talked to Andy, I'm sure she told you that she's leaving."

"Yes," Kelynn said.

"And that the position is now open," he said, continuing his train of thought.

"Yes," Kelynn said, waiting for the right words to come out of his mouth.

"Kelynn, she recommended you." She held her breath in anticipation. "And I like her recommendation. You've worked here diligently for two years now, filling in any hole or gap we needed you to. You worked with clients, film production teams, and record labels, and if you want it, I'm willing to offer the position to you."

He paused as Kelynn let out a sigh of relief.

"Before you give me an answer, I really want you to take some time and think it over. It would be Monday to Friday from 9 a.m. to 5 p.m. You would be greeting guests when they arrive and directing them to the floors where they'll be working that day. Your job would be to manage workflow, but also to perform administrative tasks. Knowing what you're capable of, we may throw random projects at you from time to time, but you will be at the desk all day. You won't be working on set for films. I know your heart is in those areas, and I want you to get there. That's not to say you won't be exposed to those areas, but your main duty is to sit at that desk and help those who walk into our office.

"Okay," Kelynn said, trying to process the job description.

"This job really helped Andy get to where she wanted to be. She started out like you, but as an intern, so you have even more to offer. I want this for you. I just want to make sure you know what you'll be giving up."

"I'd have to quit La Vita Dolce," Kelynn said, still processing the changes she'd have to make.

"Not necessarily. If you're still wanting to work there, it could be before or after your daily shift here, or on the weekends. It's completely up to you how you want to shift things, or if this is even something you're willing to shift for."

"This job has been my main priority over the years. I just hadn't thought about what it would look like to work full-time," she said, looking at her hands, playing with her rings. "I never thought it could be possible."

"Well, congratulations. I think this would be a great step for you, but please think it over," he said as she nodded in response. "I'll email you the official offer with numbers and benefits later this afternoon. That should help you decide."

"Okay, that sounds good," she said, still moving her tiny baby ring around the middle of her forefinger, and then her hand instinctively reached for where her necklace used to sit on her chest.

"Think you can let me know by the end of the week?" he asked, tilting his head like a father would to his child.

"That seems fair," she said, resuming eye contact and forcing a smile.

"Okay, great. Kelynn, I think you'd be a perfect fit. Just make sure it is for you, too."

"Thanks, Joe," she said, returning to her work area.

She opened her first email. She was going to be working on set today on the twenty-first floor for an indie film, maybe for the last time for a while if she took that job. She sighed, excited about the day's work ahead of her, but also confused about the decision she had to make. The air was no longer Cheeto Puff-light but had a heaviness to it; the kind of heaviness caused by the possibility of change. Kelynn had never been good with change. Once she got into a groove, it was like she was on cruise control, and her life felt okay. She had balance. When something shifted, it was as if her entire epicenter had been rocked and she had to find a new base, a new sun to revolve around. Yet, she always hoped for change, constantly talking about the future and the possibilities it could hold. She started to feel a cloud of thoughts sweep over her. It wasn't powerful enough to knock her out, but it was there. She envisioned herself keeping it at arm's length, and that seemed to work for her today. She kept the thought that it was Clay that made that possible even farther away.

Her job that day was to fill in for the boom operator. After almost six hours of holding up a microphone, she left, her shoulders a little sore, and headed to Clay's place again. He had texted her right before her shift ended.

You down to come over after work?

Hell yes was how she wanted to answer, but she held back, replying with, *Yeah, sounds good.* An answer without much emotion that wouldn't tell him how she was really feeling about him; a safe answer.

Kel headed out the entrance of the twenty-four-story office building. She plopped down in her driver's seat and leaned all the way back, needing a few minutes before heading to Clay's. She called Preston. She needed someone to get her mind off of the offer for a minute. For once in a long time, she wanted to be distracted with Preston's love life.

Kelynn parked on the street in front of Clay's place. She noticed the garage door was open as she hopped out. She knew he was expecting her, but she knocked twice before opening the unlocked door.

"Clay?" she yelled, her voice echoing throughout the house.

"Willie?" she called out, knowing she'd at least get a response from the dog if she was home.

Nothing. She made her way through the kitchen, searching for clues that Clay was there somewhere.

"Clay?" she yelled again, making her way slowly up the stairs.

Thump. She heard something hit the ground. Her steps grew faster as she skipped several stairs and dashed into the room where she heard it. Clay was sitting on his bed rubbing his eyes like he'd just woken up.

"Are you okay?" Kelynn asked, her words running together.

He shook his head, trying to remove himself from his stupor.

"Yeah, I'm good," he said, staring at her. He was looking at her like he just found out a giant secret of hers, like he was in disbelief over something.

"What?" she asked, uncomfortable with his expression. Her eyes searched his face for clues, but he just kept staring at her, almost like he was upset with her presence. Her eyes moved from his down to his half gaping mouth, to his unbuttoned shirt, to Willie sitting next to him on the bed, to the floor. Kelynn gasped. She couldn't believe what she was seeing.

"Is that my necklace?!" Kelynn practically shrieked seeing the luminescent glow of the gem her father gave her lying next to a piece of rough-cut wood attached to fishing wire.

"What?" Clay asked, following her glance towards the ground. "No, I don't know whose it is," he said, grabbing it and immediately falling back into his stupor, his body no longer moving. He was acting as if he was paralyzed.

"Clay?!" Kelynn yelled, furious now. "Clay, knock it off. Talk to me!"

He didn't budge. She walked over to the bed, and forcefully grabbed the necklace from his hand. He took a giant breath and blinked a few times before looking at her.

"What the hell?" she yelled again, her voice remaining at a heightened volume as she set the necklace down, afraid she'd hurt it; her anger extending to every limb.

"Sanders, you don't understand."

"Then please fill me in. What is going on?" she said, screaming at him, her body shaking.

"I . . . I . . . I found it after the party at my house."

"You what?!" she cried in disbelief, turning around and storming out of his room. She was headed for the stairs, but not before he grabbed her hand.

"Sanders, wait! Wait a damn minute!"

She thrust her hand out from his and ran down the stairs. Kelynn didn't stop. She made it just out of Clay's reach and was headed for the garage door. She threw it open and slammed it shut in the same motion. As she ran out to the driveway, it hit her. Her keys were in Clay's room somewhere. She couldn't escape. She started to run around the block when she heard a second pair of footsteps behind her.

Clay.

"SANDERS!" I SHOUTED as I picked up speed to catch up with her.

She was running hard, like she didn't want to be caught. Her form was perfect. She could definitely run the Boston Marathon.

Clay, you idiot. The fact that you know she even runs is the reason she's running away from you right now, I thought to myself, frustrated for keeping it a secret from her.

I was so close, her breathing was audible. I wasn't going to let her just run away. I needed to explain. As I picked up my pace, the gap closed between us. I reached out and grabbed her right arm. She fought me, trying her best to get loose of my grip.

"Sanders, please. Let me explain."

"There's nothing to explain. You had my necklace, and you knew it was mine," she said with her back to me.

"I didn't know it was yours at first," I started to say as she tried to catch her breath, tears starting to trail down her cheeks, "but you're right. I should've returned it to you the minute I knew."

I wrapped my arms around her, and she leaned her back against me. She cried harder, her body flinching. "Sanders, I'm so sorry."

"When did you know it was mine?" she uttered between broken breaths.

"When I saw one of your dreams about writing a book. It had your name as the author."

"When you what?" she asked, spinning around to face me.

"Yeah, I watched it play out. You were on a stage presenting your book called *Out of the Black*."

"Clay, how do you know that title?"

"I'm confused," I said, trying to read her face, her eyes tracing mine at a million miles a minute. "I told you already."

"No, what do you mean you *saw* one of my dreams?" Sanders asked, her tears drying as she spoke.

"I held your opal necklace, and it showed me the dream," I said, now sharing in her panic.

"You could *see* it?" she hissed.

"Yes, I don't know how it works, but anytime I hold it, I'm transported into one of your dreams, or thoughts, or goals, I guess."

"Clay, you're not making any sense," she said, sitting on the sidewalk.

"Remember how you found me today?"

"Yeah, you seemed off, like you didn't know I was there," she said, her eyes darting back and forth as if she couldn't process it all.

"Okay. Stay with me. That's because I got off early and wanted to watch one of your dreams before you came over. I thought I could start a conversation from it. I know that's terrible, but I didn't know you were there because I didn't see you or hear you. I could only see and hear what the opal was showing me."

"And what was that?" she asked, rubbing her forehead. Thunder boomed.

I looked up at the darkened sky. "I saw you in a pale-colored office. You were talking with someone who could help you adopt a child. You were explaining how you were qualified to be a single mother, and you kept trying to convince her of how much love you would give to a baby in need. The sunlight hit you through the small window, and all your freckles were popping. You looked so beautiful, yet so sad at the same time."

Sanders looked at me, tears filling the bottoms of her eyes, threatening to spill over, making the surface of her pupils look hazy. "How is this possible, Clay?"

"I don't know, but what I do know is a storm is about to come crashing down. Can we please go back inside, and I can try to explain this more?"

She didn't say a word but nodded as I held her hand, and we walked back around the block towards my place. Her hand felt so small and fragile, like I'd just told a kid that the Santa Claus they saw every year at the mall wasn't the real thing.

Rain started pelting the ground just as we made our way through my garage. I opened the door for her, and she went inside, walked a few more steps to the couch, and slumped down.

"Glass of wine?" I offered.

"Only if it's white," she said, staring at the wall. "And sweet."

I poured her a glass, thinking of how I was going to explain everything, how I was going to make it all better. The last thing I wanted to do was sound crazy and scare her off, especially now that I knew so much about her from the opal. This was going to be sticky.

I handed her the glass and she flicked her wrist, swirling the wine around in the glass, allowing it to breathe.

"Thanks," she said, her eyes still glued to the wall. She leaned over so her elbows rested on her thighs and took a small sip. The rain started to batter against the windows, adding to the heaviness in the house.

"Clay," she said before taking another sip of wine. "I'm scared of what you saw, of how far you got into my head, I guess."

"I . . ."

"Let me finish," she said, cutting me off. "I want you to know that what you did was wrong. I *need* that necklace to survive. Not to mention, it was an invasion of privacy and, more than that, manipulative. You used my thoughts to start conversations with me?" she questioned, shaking her head unbelievingly and taking a big gulp of wine. Before Clay could answer, she simply said, "I'm very angry with you, but for right now, I just need to know what you know and how you know it."

"Okay," I said, waiting for her to turn towards me. "I can start from the beginning, but can you promise me something?"

Finally, she looked in my direction.

"Just don't leave until I've said it all. If when I'm done you want to go, I understand. But, please, just . . . just stay until I've gotten it all out."

"Fine," she said, her face unwavering, her lips in a solid line. Her anger had subsided to give way to what seemed like a plateau of expressionless hurt.

"It all started the night of the party. That night, I felt the electric pull between us when I saw you with your friends. Even then, I knew we had a connection. Then, you left before I could track you down again, which now I know was because you blacked out. The next day, I found a necklace in my yard. I didn't put two and two together that it was yours at the time. I picked it up to put it somewhere safe, and it was like I was watching a movie, or rather living in one. It showed me New York. I was working in a big building with even bigger windows. It felt so huge, full of opportunities for my career. I, or I guess *you*, were a journalist. Then, I saw several flashes of images. To be honest, they're all a blur now, but I remember being transported to a film set, where I, or again, you, were the director. I looked down for a split second while on set, and suddenly I was on a mountain, trying to climb higher and higher, the cool air filling my lungs and igniting something inside me."

Sanders's face was locked on mine, like she could see the things I was talking about. Her posture had changed. She was fully listening to me, leaning in as if every word I said was pure magic.

"That was the first time I held the opal."

She sat there, her face a disposition of shock. "Those are my thoughts. Those are my actual thoughts. How is this possible?"

"I wish I knew," I said, in just as much amazement as her.

"No, you don't understand. My father gave me this necklace as a birthday gift. He told me that on days when my thoughts are too much to visualize putting them into the opal—that it would carry the weight of it all. How the hell did I know that it actually worked and the spiritual nomad was real?" she contemplated, rubbing her forehead again before drinking her wine.

"Nomad?" I asked.

"Yeah, he mentioned some Romani traveler from Europe blessing it for my great-grandmother and that it had magical powers, but he didn't know exactly what they were, other than it could supposedly hold my thoughts. Clay, we have to keep this a secret."

"I wasn't going to tell anyone, but why? What are you afraid of?"

"What if people think we're crazy or try to take my necklace away for good? What if they take away the one thing that actually helped me with my blackouts?"

"Wait. Are we talking about me or the necklace?" I asked, grinning and rubbing my finger on her leg hoping to ease the tension.

"The necklace," she said with a roll of her eyes, clearly not finding any humor in the situation. "Which, by the way, I'm going to go grab, so you can't do this anymore."

Twenty-One

SHE RAN UPSTAIRS and found it resting on the bed, exactly where she left it before running out of the house. She wrapped it around her neck and fastened its tiny clasp, then closed her eyes and took a deep breath. It felt like home, like a missing piece of her had been restored. She thumbed the tiny gem and stood up a little taller as she made her way back downstairs to face Clay again, unsure of where this conversation would take them. She promised him she wouldn't go until he was done explaining it all, and she had a feeling he had only scratched the surface. From the top of the stairs, she could see Clay still sitting on the couch, leaning over with his head resting in his hands, like it was too heavy for him to hold up on his own. He looked up at the sound of her bare feet walking down the wooden stairs, each foot making a sticky sound as it released and the other one planted on the next step.

Kelynn walked towards him, stopping directly in front of him as if to tower over him. She opened her mouth to talk, but he stopped her. She suddenly tasted the bitter rejection of her mother coupled with the cheating boys from high school. Trauma vomit was teasing her taste buds, threatening to turn into the real thing as she sat there looking at Clay.

Reaching for her hands, he said, "I don't want you to say anything. I know I messed up, but I want to keep talking."

She intertwined her fingers with his as he played with her rings. He thumbed them for a little while longer, and she sat down on top of him.

"I'm still mad at you, but I think if I sit here, like this," she motioned to her legs that were folded on either side of his lap, "I'll be more likely to listen and still like you while you talk." The dark cloud her memories had over her understanding of the current circumstance started to evaporate.

"That works for me," Clay said, putting both hands on the outer parts of her legs. "So," he continued, "I've seen several of your futuristic dreams, some of which make me think you don't want me in your life for the long haul," he started again, clearing his throat out of apparent nervousness. "Some of them feel very independent, like you want to do so much on your own, accomplish so many things that don't include someone else in your life along the way. I've seen you traveling, working as a performer, working on awards shows, writing, going to foreign countries . . ."

"What do you mean by performer?" she asked.

"You were, or rather I was in your body, singing on a stage for a large crowd."

"How long ago did you see this?"

"I don't know, maybe three weeks ago or so," Clay said, his eyes rolling back like he was searching the back of his brain.

"That was before you took me to sing karaoke. Did you know Clunkerton's had karaoke that night?" she asked, her face turning red. "Is that why you got me drunk and threw me on stage?"

"Sanders, I was just trying to help you. You were the one who directed us to Clunkerton's. I just took advantage of the karaoke night once we were there."

"'Took advantage' sounds about right! You used my personal thoughts against me!"

"Not against you. I just wanted to help you achieve your dreams, even if it was on a much smaller scale."

"I don't need your help!" Kelynn said, her emotions conflicting with Clay's hands rubbing her low back. Her body wanted his touch, needed his touch, but her mind wanted to be as far away from him as possible. His hands felt like fire, each finger sending a surge of heat rushing through her.

"Listen. You're one hundred percent right. I shouldn't have done that knowing what I saw. I should've told you. I just knew that if I did, you wouldn't have the guts to get on stage," Clay said in a much calmer voice than hers as he rubbed his beard with his thumb and forefinger.

"While that's probably true, you still deceived me."

"I know. Sanders, I didn't have bad intentions. I promise. I just care about you so much that I want to see you follow your dreams, even if they turn into something bigger that doesn't include me. I want you to try every possibility floating around in that complicated, clouded brain of yours until you've exhausted every dream and found the one that fits you best," Clay said. "I wish you would tell me more of the ones that are somehow locked inside of here."

Clay touched her opal as the words left his lips and was immediately transported into another vision. Kel quickly snatched it back from him.

"Did you just do that on purpose?" Kelynn asked after he'd clearly come back to reality, but there wasn't anger in her eyes.

"I wasn't trying to. I'm sorry. I wasn't thinking," Clay said, blinking away the dream.

"Tell me what you saw," she said.

"All right." Clay paused, closing his eyes. "I could feel the open air dangling beneath my feet. It felt so free. I started kicking them back and forth while looking up at the sky. I glanced down to get a sense of my surroundings when I realized my legs were dangling out of a plane. Then everything else became apparent; the loud engine of the plane reverberated in my ears, and the tight grip of the goggles around my eyes suddenly felt like super glue. A passenger behind me yelled, 'Alright, let's go!' as he gave me a light push out into the open air. I felt my hand slip off the doorframe and as I opened my eyes that were forced shut out of fear to see the scenery beneath my falling body, but all I saw was you sitting directly in front of me."

"I can't believe you saw that much in just a short moment." She hesitated. "To be honest, I kind of liked it when you were holding it, even though I'm still not able to fully believe it."

"Really?"

"Yeah, it gave me a brief feeling of release, like you just took some of my built-up anxiety away."

"Does that make you a little less mad at me?"

"Maybe for the moment," she said, astonished.

Kelynn felt like a deer about to be hit by a car. She could see the headlights, the seriousness of what could happen, but felt frozen. She didn't know what to make of Clay's words. She couldn't decide whether to be angry or to entertain the idea that she was falling for him. She didn't know which one would save her from the car that was coming at her head-on, so she impulsively put her hands around his neck and kissed him. His neck arched backwards, giving her a better grip as she pulled him closer to her.

The heat radiated from his hands as they moved up and down her back, as if mapping out every inch of her skin. She was suddenly very aware that she was sitting on top of him. He pulled the back of her shirt down, shoving her closer to him, leaving no room between the two of them. She ran her hands along his arms, feeling his veins that traced his skin. Those same arms shifted her weight, picking her up and maneuvering her to the length of the couch. One of his hands moved to her hip, while the other held his weight next to her head. His lips were radiating fire; fire she'd only had in doses from him, but never in full. Kelynn liked the fire, the spark that was making her feel so alive, so in tune with him. She could see clearly, and all she could see was him. She wanted him. She could feel his passion growing with each kiss, each touch. She took off his shirt as his hands moved up into her hair with his lips tickling her neck, bringing her back to reality.

Kelynn shifted, gently moving one hand into his and pushing against his chest with the other.

"What's wrong?" he asked, breathing heavy.

"Nothing, I just need a minute."

"Sanders. We don't have to do anything. I guess I just thought that's what you wanted."

"I did. I do. I just . . . Not yet," she said, fumbling over her words, her mind jumbled from everything Clay had told her, mixed with how it felt when she kissed him.

"Hey," he said, lifting her chin, forcing her to look into his eyes. "I'm not upset with you. If anything, you should still be upset with me."

"I am," Kelynn said without hesitation, "but I can't control this connection between us, Clay. I don't know what my future is, and I know you know that, but I don't want to force a future with you in it without trying everything you saw. But I also need you to know that some of those dreams you saw are probably just thoughts. If the opal works the way my dad says it does, then I've been putting thoughts into it that aren't necessarily something I'm serious about. They're just thoughts that clouded my mind at the time."

"Meaning?" Clay asked, his face sporting pure confusion.

"Meaning, I want to test the waters like you made me do with karaoke. I want to try out all my dreams and see what they feel like, see which one feels the most right. But that doesn't mean everything you saw is what I truly want. Some of them may not even exist as a true representation of my future, and this still feels insane even saying this. Part of me is in complete disbelief about all of this."

"I feel crazy, too, but I want everything you just said. Sanders, are you breaking up with me?" Clay asked, shifting, his back leaning against the couch.

"No, I don't know. I don't want to."

"Then don't," Clay said, kissing her again.

She kissed him back, feeling the spark ignite again, before forcing herself to turn away and break the bond.

"Clay, I need some time."

Clay.

I COULDN'T BELIEVE the words Sanders was saying. She was so confused, she didn't know what she wanted. How was this happening? Things were going so well. I got myself into this mess all because of that stupid necklace. As my eyes traced her face, I saw a glint of light dance in the opal necklace around her neck. Before I could form my next choice words, I got distracted by my own mess of thoughts. I sat there, trying to collect myself, and then I heard her voice, only it was in my head and not out loud. It was as though her eyes were saying, *"Hey, you've got this. You can show me the real you,"* removing any fear or hesitation I once had. I forgot I'd heard her voice before like this, but not as strong, so I didn't think anything of it at the time. It happened when I first saw her when she was with Hastings. When her eyes locked on mine that night, I swear I felt her telling me to find her. I could feel it in my gut that, for some reason, I needed to see her again. I genuinely felt a pull towards her, as though somehow she cleared my head, like the opal cleared hers. While being near her gave me confidence to move forward, her opal had a million crossed paths and no guide to know which one was right. Suddenly, I realized I'd been silent for an uncomfortable amount of time.

"Sanders, let's just take a step back for a second. Let's talk this through more," I said.

"Clay, I need to think on my own, without you, shirtless, staring at me," she said, leaning in towards me and running her hand down my chest before gently punching my abdomen.

I grabbed my shirt from the back of the couch and put it on, trying to focus on her and not her hands.

"Better?" I asked, fully clothed again.

"No, I liked it better before," she said.

"Sanders, I don't get it. You're sending me a million mixed signals right now. You know that, right?" I pushed back, trying to read her face.

"Was there ever a future with you in it?" she asked.

"Huh?"

"Did one of the visions or dreams show you a future with you?"

I took a deep breath, taking her hands in mine. "No."

I could see the hope drain from her.

"But you haven't had your necklace since we started hanging out, really. I did see a future of you with a man and a little boy."

"Who was the man?"

"He didn't have a face," I said, remembering how trippy that specific opal dream was. "The little boy had a face. He looked like you, but the man you were with didn't have any sort of face. He was blurry, but he was your husband. You both had rings on, and he kissed you."

She sat there, seeming like she was taking in the picture I was trying to paint. She reached up and thumbed her necklace, probably thinking back through all the times she'd mentally shoved her multitude of thoughts into it. Sanders shifted towards me again, kissing me.

I opened my eyes and blinked rapidly. "Did you just see that?" I asked, her eyes widening and blinking just like mine.

"What was that?" she asked, her hand no longer holding the necklace, her eyes in a daze.

"That's what I've been seeing! You just showed us both a future. How did you do that?" I asked, still unsure of what had taken place.

"I don't know. I had my hand on my necklace, and when I kissed you, I saw a beach, and I was sitting in a chair with my toes in the sand next to yours. I guess it freaked me out, and I let go of the opal."

"Do you want to try it again? I mean, that seemed like a nice-ass vacation," I said, running my hand through her hair. How could something that felt like contraband mere minutes before suddenly feel like a key that opened a door?

"Clay, stop playing around! I think I've had enough unexplainable weirdness for one day." She blinked a few more times, like she was still trying to comprehend the validity of her current reality.

Hell, I felt the same way, but I'd been feeling this way for weeks, whereas this was her *first* opal dream immersive experience.

"Let me take you home. You need to rest," I said, not liking the taste of those words.

"Yes, please," she said, unmoving from the couch cushion, as if gravity was the only thing she thought to be true and solid in her life.

"Come on," I said, helping her up off the couch.

"I drove here."

"Oh, yeah. I'd still like to drive you home," I said, feeling desperate for more time with her.

She paused. "I'll be okay, but thanks." She didn't sound completely sure of her choice as she kissed me on the cheek before heading out the door.

Twenty-Two

KELYNN WOKE UP feeling numb. She didn't know where to start in sorting out her thoughts. Her night with Clay had so many layers to it that didn't make sense or come remotely close to fitting together like a precut puzzle. She knew it would take time to try and form new puzzle pieces, maybe from an entirely new picture, and she wasn't ready to take a deep dive into that. She also had only two more days until she had to tell Joe if she was going to take the job. She didn't move. Her eyes still heavy with sleep, she extended her arm without shifting the rest of her body to find her phone. She had two texts from Clay. One was clearly sent last night.

Sanders. Everything is going to be okay. You don't have to have it all figured out. I just need to know if you want me beside you, figuring it out along the way with you.

Kelynn let out a much-needed sigh before reading his most recent text, sent at six o'clock that morning.

Morning, beautiful. I'm going to give you space today. Just know I'm here if you want to talk . . .

Kelynn felt a sense of peace. He had agreed to let her breathe, to try to see the clear water through the mud that clouded her senses.

"Thank God," she said out loud, waking Roscoe, who was resting on her stomach.

"Sorry, Ro. Didn't mean to startle you," she said, petting the top of his soft head.

He plopped back down and closed his eyes again.

I wish I could just sleep all day and not have to answer to anyone, Kelynn thought.

She checked the time. La Vita Dolce wouldn't be expecting her for another three hours. She closed her eyes, her hands still resting on Roscoe's fur-coated head, bringing her increased heart rate down. Kelynn tried her best to drift back off to sleep, but her mind refused. She got out of bed, frustrated, and put on her running clothes.

It was a chilly morning, but Kelynn didn't let that stop her. She threw on her half-zip long-sleeved shirt, one she knew would keep her just warm enough. She wasn't feeling the beach today. Although tempting, it made her soul ache when the water was this cold, and she didn't have time to drive there, so she headed for the track that circled her gym. Only one other runner was out on this weekday morning, as most everyone else was at work. Kelynn did one final stretch, took a deep breath, and started into a jog. The cold air hit her lungs like knives, each breath a duller pain than the former. The wind whipped her hair, smacking against her ears. Then her breathing fell into its usual pattern. Kel could feel her feet going faster, awakening her senses.

The other runner was only a few paces ahead. Kelynn picked up her pace even more as she passed him, feeling like she'd beat him at his own race even though he'd probably been out here for quite some time, his body moving slower now. She was running at full speed now, her breaths quicker. Now that she'd released some endorphins, it was time for her to start sorting out her thoughts. For some reason, it wasn't Clay that reached the surface but thoughts of Monette. She imagined Monette younger, running next to her, saying things like, "Is that all ya got?" Kelynn laughed at that. Her sassy nature and banter were Kelynn's favorite part of her. Monette didn't care if she was polite. She was a straight shooter but a lovable one. Kel's mind traveled back in time to their visits and then to the last time she saw her. Suddenly, she tripped, a raised piece of track catching the toe of her right shoe.

"Damn it!" she muttered as she stumbled to regain her footing. She kept running, but instead of feeling lighter, she felt anger, so strong it made its way to her face. Her cheeks were growing warm as she chugged along, the intense wind only aggravating her further. She was unarguably furious; furious that Monette was gone, furious that she never really said goodbye, and furious that Clay was involved in parts of her life she never asked him to be. Then a sinking feeling set in. The reason Clay asked her if she went running before was probably because he'd seen one of her dreams where she was running a race. Her lungs felt like they were going to burst and her legs felt waterlogged. Kelynn came to a stop, her face wet with tears of anger she didn't even realize had formed. She stood there, expecting a blackout to consume her, but it didn't. For once, she wanted it to. She wanted to fade into nothingness, if only for a few hours.

C. lay.

I TOOK A deep breath before walking into a building full of unfamiliarity; the smell of an office that reminded me of fresh paint blended with sunscreen, the sounds of announcements relayed over a loudspeaker by a voice that could soothe the angriest person, and the sight of an open, airy space with tall ceilings and inexplicably clean floors.

"How can I help you?" the receptionist asked, glued to her computer screen and keyboard, on which she seemed to type incessantly.

"I'm here for an interview with Mr. Bickel."

It was like I had said the magic words. She immediately stopped typing and smiled a genuine smile. "I'll let him know you're here. He's very excited to meet you."

"Thank you," I said, taking a seat on a ghost chair, which was one in a line of about twenty. Thankfully, they were all empty. I studied the wall in front of me as I waited. It was painted a clean white and had a blown-up magazine cover hung on it with a picture of George Clooney and the words "Chill Axel—The New Hollywood Star" in bold. I studied it, trying to think of something clever yet knowledgeable to say during the interview.

George Clooney really has stood the test of time. It's like his acting gets better with age, kind of like Chill Axel, I thought, wondering if that sounded like too much of an ego stroke. *Maybe I should start with a question. So, tell me what the magazine cover out in the lobby means to you and the company?* I thought, instantly feeling like that made me sound like the interviewer rather than the interviewee.

I was still lost in all my thoughts when the most crisp, kind voice said, "Mr. Fogerty."

I turned my head to the right, glancing over the row of translucent chairs to see Mr. Bickel standing there with a smile reminiscent of Ashton Kutcher, crooked yet over-confident. His hair was grey, but he didn't look old; the lines around his eyes making him look wise. He looked to be about forty, old enough to seem collected and worn in, but young enough to still have an ever-present cool vibe that spread to his inviting smile. He was immediately someone I admired, someone I wanted to be more like.

"Hi, Mr. Bickel," I said. "So, George Clooney?" I asked. "He only gets better with age."

"Glad you got the metaphor," Mr. Bickel said, looking back over his shoulder to reveal a wink as he led me down a wide hallway lined with giant open rooms. The air even felt different here, like it was filled with energizing molecules that stimulated the creative part of my brain. I felt excited, like I had the world at my fingertips.

I was abruptly brought back to reality when my phone started buzzing in my pocket.

Not now! I thought. Mr. Bickel didn't seem to notice as he continued to walk ahead of me. I quickly pulled it out of my pocket, just enough to see who was calling. It was Sanders. I hit the red "X" and then turned off my phone as nonchalantly as possible right before I heard Mr. Bickel say, "Here we are. Go ahead and have a seat."

It wasn't a ghost chair this time, but a plush leather chair that felt like a Tempur-Pedic mattress when I sat down. I felt a calmness rush over my body, as if the chair was telling me it was completely okay to be fully myself, to relax in knowing who I was. I took a deep breath as Mr. Bickel shut the door behind me.

"Clayton. I've been keeping my eye on your work for a while. In my position, I have to be innovative and always ahead of the curve. Your apps are consistently one and sometimes three steps in front of mine, conceptualizing what I wanted to do and putting it in an airtight capsule perfectly suitable for its targeted demographic. Tell me, how do you do that? What's your creative process?"

I felt the power of his words complimenting my work, validating my career. I smiled a genuine smile and began to answer his questions.

I walked out of the modern world of Chill Axel about an hour after I had entered it, feeling like I was already a part of it. I felt a sense of relief as I headed to lunch before going back to work. That's something I always admired about AnaScape. They had an open interview policy. AnaScape wants their employees to grow, so they allow two interviews a year, no questions asked, and the time is paid for, which is one of the reasons I gladly took the interview. My life has been with them for five years now. Did I really want to make a huge switch like trading in Steve Jobs for Bill Gates? I couldn't think of it like that. I had to view this as an opportunity to grow, no matter what the company was, or who my original loyalty belonged to. I had to have an open mind, and my initial thoughts were positive. The interview went great. Both Mr. Bickel and I felt like we had similar minds that built on one another. I started to weigh the pros and cons as I walked into the 8th Street Deli. I ordered and grabbed my phone from my pocket to check my emails. I forgot I'd turned it off. I had a missed call from Sanders—the one I declined earlier—and a text from her as well.

It read, I *went for a run today, but you probably already knew that.*

That's great! I don't know what you're insinuating, I replied, unsure if her text was angry or witty.

You mean you decided not to invade my thoughts today?

She was definitely angry, and she had the opal back, leaving me with no way to see her thoughts even if I wanted to, which validated the tone of her text. I started to call her, but she ignored it. I could tell it wasn't an accident by the way it cut off mid-ring. How could she be mad at me? When she left, I knew she was upset, but I could tell her deep feelings for me weren't going to let her stay that way. Her kiss gave that away every time. I figured she needed space, and then things would be fine. I wasn't going to let this stew. I was going to find her and confront her in person.

Twenty-Three

KELYNN HAD MADE it to work even after her taxing run. She was on her phone, bored at the front counter, the lunch rush already over. She looked up when she heard the loud footsteps of dress shoes coming through the door. It was Clay, who she was not used to seeing without his Chuck Taylors. "I'll take a latte with a sprinkle of cinnamon and a walk if you're up for it."

She looked up to meet his eyes. "Why are you here?" she asked, recovering quickly and putting on a mask of anger.

"I'm here for a coffee, and I wanted to see you."

"Clay, you asked me the other night if I'd run recently. I knew I'd never told you before."

"What?" Clay asked.

"Clay, stop pretending," she said, her eyes looking tired from thinking.

"Oh, in my truck. I guess you're right. I'm sorry. Sometimes it's hard to distinguish between what I've watched and what we've actually talked about."

"Oh," she said. His answer hurt her more than she expected as she grabbed a cup and began to write his order on the side of it.

"Hey . . . I'm so sorry. I know I can't take this back, but I want to try and fix things. Just tell me what to fix."

"I don't know. You pick. My heart or my mind?" she asked.

"Sanders. What's going on? I thought when you left last night we were on better terms," Clay said, grabbing her hand.

"Well, I don't know that I am," she said, letting his hand linger.

"I mean, I know you have to think things over and all, but . . ."

"Why are you dressed like that?" she asked, changing the subject.

"I had an interview today. Why did Indi say you might not be here much longer?"

"She told you that? Wait, when did you talk to Indi?"

"I was trying to track you down. I just so happened to try your house first."

She sighed, passing the cup down the line of orders. "I got an offer from Radical."

"That's amazing!" Clay said, squeezing her hand.

"Can we talk later? I have to work."

"Okay. Do you promise you'll answer my call?"

"Yeah," she said as if trying to convince herself.

"Can I just come over?" Clay asked.

"No," she said firmly.

"Okay. Well, I'll call you after work."

She played with his tie, not looking at his face. "Okay," she said, forcing herself to drop the silky fabric before her mind went places she wasn't ready for yet.

Clay left with his latte, and as Kel listened to the click of his shoes, they sounded heavier than when he walked in, like the soles had been filled with whole milk instead of the caffeinated drink in his hand. Kelynn watched him leave, but turned as he reached the door, so that if he looked back, she wouldn't be looking in his direction. She couldn't handle his eyes. His eyes always made everything else disappear. They made her not care about what he did, and she did care. He'd used her necklace against her.

He was manipulating you, she thought to herself, anger filling her, causing her jaw to clench.

He watched your personal dreams behind your back and didn't tell you. That's just as bad as lying to you. She nodded to herself.

Do not fall for him in those dress pants and tie and white button-down shirt that would be so easy to unbutton.

"Kel, snap out of it!" she yelled to herself under her breath as she switched places with Carter and began making drinks, the portion of her job where she could operate on autopilot.

Her mind began to weigh his side again as she worked. *Maybe it's not that bad. So, he watched your dreams behind your back. He just wanted to know you on a deeper level, but you weren't ready to let him into those thoughts yet. He would've known about them eventually. Is it bad that he knows now? From what he saw, he's probably scared he won't be in your future. In hindsight, this doesn't seem like it's something that should ruin the relationship, but then why do I feel so hurt?* Kelynn thought, juggling the good and bad about the situation.

"Kel, what do you think?" Carter asked.

"What do I think about what?" Kelynn asked, trying to sound like she hadn't been in her own head for the past half-hour.

"About Clay? You should totally let him come over tonight. He wants you. And if he wanted me, I'd jump on the opportunity. Literally," she added.

"Look, Carter, I'm not up for talking about this right now. We're kind of going through some stuff, and I just need to figure out how I feel about it all on my own before I let him and those tempting eyes anywhere near me."

"Hey, I hear ya. He's *so* tempting."

"Okay, okay. Back to work," Kelynn said, hoping the conversation would turn to something else. Carter was starting to make her feel uncomfortable. She could barely control her own thoughts and didn't want to know what was going through her fellow barista's mind about *her* boyfriend.

Wait, boyfriend? Kelynn thought.

She hadn't ever thought of him in those terms, but that's kind of what he was. She wondered if he thought that, too. She started wringing out a dirty rag, wishing she could simply squeeze out the parts of her life she didn't want to deal with.

Clay:

"KNOCK, KNOCK," I said as I entered Omi's room.

"Clayton, my boy!" Omi smiled, the wrinkles by her eyes creasing deeper. "And to what do I owe this honor?" she asked.

"Well, believe it or not, I need some advice."

Omi looked me up and down before she said, "Well, for starters, you need to eat more. You barely fill out your clothes anymore."

I laughed as she sat there with a serious expression, her hands clasped in her lap.

"No, Omi, I had something specific to talk to you about. Do you remember that girl we talked about last time?"

"I think so. Is she causing you problems?"

"More like I'm causing her problems. How do I explain this? I kind of went behind her back with something."

Omi studied me as I grabbed a chair next to hers, her eyes narrowing into a squint.

"I, uh, did it because I wanted to know more about her. I didn't realize it would hurt her."

"Clay, relationships are built on trust. Once you lose that trust, it's like living in a house with a foundation built over a sinkhole. Eventually it'll collapse."

"I know. I didn't realize at first that it would hurt her, and then the deeper I got into it, I didn't know how to tell her," I said, trying to be as vague as possible, so I didn't give my ninety-year-old grandmother a heart attack trying to explain that magic actually existed.

"You know, there was one time in our marriage when your grandfather lost my trust for a little while."

"Really?" I asked. "What'd Opi do?" I leaned in closer, dying to know about their marriage. Their love was the kind most people only experienced secondhand through movies.

"He went to work like every other day, but when he came home that night, he had a little black dachshund in his arms."

"Chase?" I asked, referring to the little dog I remembered playing with at their house when I was a kid.

"No, you never met this dog. He was from the early years of our marriage. Well, the whole reason he bought that dog was because he'd read my old letters to my best friend. I wrote about how I'd always wanted a little dachshund, along with many other personal details I never thought anyone else would read."

"So, he was doing something nice—something you always wanted?"

"Yes, but that was all tainted by how he did it," she said, playing with the fringe of the blanket wrapped around her. "Now, I eventually came around. I never punished the dog for it, that's for sure. I was in love with him from the minute I saw him in your Opi's arms."

"So, over time, you think she'll forgive me?" I asked, hopeful.

"It depends on what you did exactly, but it's possible," she said, pressing her lips together into a straight line.

"What made you trust Opi again?"

"Time," she said. "And lots of talking. It didn't hurt that the damn dog was so cute. It helped melt away my anger."

"How am I supposed to talk to her when she wants space?" I asked, sighing. I just wanted to know how to fix this so I could move on with Sanders.

"Give her the space. We don't say that so you'll pester us."

"Alright. Thanks, Omi."

"Now, tell me more about your job. How's that going?" Omi asked with an inquisitive expression.

I sat there catching her up on my life while she listened, never quick to interrupt. Sitting here with her reminded me of Monette and Sanders. How Sanders spent days here getting to know a stranger. I wanted to be like her, especially with someone I already knew. I had this feeling that Omi and I had just started on a journey of friendship, deeper than mere family ties, and I had Sanders to thank for it.

Twenty-Four

"I WAS HOPING this was the choice you would make. It will be a fairly easy transition. You already know the company, so directing people shouldn't be too difficult," Joe said confidently, shaking Kelynn's hand, welcoming her into her new role as Radical Entertainment's receptionist.

"Thank you, Joe. I'm excited to be here full-time where I really want to be."

"Good. And don't think just because your title is receptionist that we won't be giving you projects here and there to work on, okay? I see your potential, and it's much higher than this position."

"Thank you. I really do appreciate that. I want to be as involved as possible."

Kelynn turned to head towards her new "office" to start training with Andy. She had one week to learn as much as possible before Andy shipped off to New York to live out her dream. Even though this was a huge opportunity for growth, Kelynn couldn't help but feel envious of Andy and also a little sad to leave La Vita Dolce.

"Hey, rockstar!" Andy said as Kel walked up to the desk. The window at the back end of the fifth floor mimicked the size of the double glass doors, letting in a surplus of light, reassuring Kelynn that she would feel refreshed in this space, even if it was at a desk all day. She felt the largeness of the room, the openness, a metaphor for the new job and future possibilities it would bring.

"So, we'll start with the phone. This may seem super simple, but it's very important that calls get transferred to the right department, and sometimes it's tricky," Andy began. Kel's mind was muddied with the thought of Clay repetitively resurfacing.

Clay, Kelynn thought. *We were supposed to talk last night.*

She side-eyed her pocket, clicking the lock button on her phone to see if she'd missed his call. Her morning news briefing from *PopSugar* was the only thing on the screen.

He's over me, she thought.

She threw herself into training, giving it all she had so the tears wouldn't surface. At noon, Andy took her out to lunch. The two walked down the city streets to a Mediterranean café that sold gyros and falafels.

"I'm starving," Kelynn said, checking her watch.

"Lunch hour is great. It's nice to get out of the office. A lot of times, people will take you out," Andy said while poring over the menu.

"Really? Like who?" Kelynn asked, intrigued.

"It depends on the day and who you've been working with. I've had celebs take me out a few times, people from different departments. It just kind of varies."

"That's a nice perk," Kel said, feeling a little more excited.

"Yeah, you get to meet all kinds of people, and the more time you spend at reception, the more people will recognize and remember your face. They grow to rely on you. It's a great networking gig, honestly," she said, talking over the loud growling of her stomach.

"So, are you getting excited for New York?" Kelynn asked, hoping to live vicariously through her coworker for a few minutes.

"Yes and no. I mean, yes, it's a dream job, but I don't know much about New York. I don't know how to get around or where my favorite coffee shop will be. I'm wondering when the commute to and from work will start to feel familiar, ya know? I love being able to zone out while driving to work, but I'll be taking the subway. I'll have to be alert and make sure I get off at the right stop. It's a big adjustment. I know I can do it. It's terrifying, but a good terrifying, ya know?"

Kelynn bit into two French fries, their tips coated in ketchup. "Yeah, I guess I never thought about the little details that come with moving to a new place."

"It's a lot to think about," Andy said, taking a giant bite of her pita. Kelynn was unsure how she got such a big bite into a tiny, fast-moving mouth.

"You think you'll like this job?" Andy asked, taking another bite just as big.

"Yeah, I do. It's a good step for me."

"That didn't sound completely convincing," Andy said.

"Don't get me wrong. I'm so happy to finally have a full-time gig that I can rely on day in and day out, and I know I'll be learning so much about the company. I just think I'll miss the excitement of what the day used to bring. I never knew what department I'd be working in or what celebrities I might meet."

"You'll still meet them. They all have to check in with you and get badges for the day. You just won't be able to spend an entire day with them."

"I don't want to sound ungrateful. I just feel like I was in the action, and now I'm taking a step back in that area but a step forward in the working world. I feel kind of mixed."

"I did, too. I ended up loving it, though. I'm sure you will too, Kel. You can finally say this job is *yours*. You have an actual title and a very secure role, which is a must in the entertainment industry."

"You're right," Kel said, feeling a little lighter as she made her stomach heavier with two more French fries. "I wish we could do it together. You were always so fun to work with," Kel spoke up, her stifled tears threatening to reemerge.

"Hey, we've got another week. Don't say your goodbyes just yet," she said, looking past Kel out the window, fighting off her own tears. "Let's talk about something less sad," Andy said, taking a deep breath and fanning herself. "I don't want to mess up *my* makeup. We still have half a day of work left. Tell me about the guy you're seeing."

Caught off guard, Kelynn darted her eyes to the side. "Well, if you want me to do that, I'll really mess up my makeup," she said, her nostrils flaring, trying to suck in the air that suddenly felt thicker.

Twenty-Five

KELYNN GOT INTO her Jeep after her first day as an official full-time employee. She was beyond exhausted and her worn-in, leather seats felt like home.

She turned the key in the ignition, comforted by the purr of the engine as she shifted into reverse. She listened to her radio, hoping for a distraction from Clay. Ever since Andy asked about him, it was like she'd unlocked a code to a door that was keeping him contained in a room of her mind. She was supposed to be able to choose when he was allowed to be released, but it hit her harder than she expected today, and she couldn't shake the thought that he didn't call her. Maybe he wasn't the patient type. She wanted him, but the what ifs kept telling her otherwise.

What if he manipulates me into falling for him and then leaves me for someone else?

If he lied about this, what else is he willing to lie about?

What if we don't work out anyway? Then why should I waste my time on him now?

What if my future doesn't include him?

What if I lose my opal again? Can someone else see my dreams, too?

Kelynn began to feel herself falling into the blackness.

"I'm driving!" Kelynn yelled to herself, hoping her audible voice would snap her out of it.

The feeling subsided, but only slightly. She could feel it just under the surface, threatening to consume her any minute. Her eyes were deadlocked on the highway, each curve of the road keeping her alert enough to block out the haunting thoughts that so badly wanted to take over. She somewhat wanted to let them, to not worry about any of it for a little while, to sleep it off. However, she never felt rested after a blackout and was usually more confused than before.

Her eyes flashed from one lane to the next until she felt a buzzing in her pocket. She didn't have time to look at who was calling in fear that she would black out.

"Hello," she answered in a rushed tone.

"Hey, are we still on for dinner?" Indi asked, plates clanking in the background.

"Indi?"

"Yeah?" Indi drew out the word.

"Sorry, I didn't look at my phone before I answered. Listen, I need your help."

"What's going on?" Indi asked.

"I'm trying not to black out."

"Where are you?" Indi asked in a panicked voice.

"I'm driving."

"Kel, pull over!"

"No, really. I think I'll be okay. I'm almost home. I just need to focus on something to push the blackness away."

"Kel, you've never been able to fight them off before. What makes you think you can now?"

"I feel like I'm actually stronger than it for once. Can you please just distract me?"

"Kel, pull over," Indi said.

"Indi, please!" Kel begged.

"Okay. What sounds good for dinner?"

"I was thinking Tallulah's," Kel said, her eyes wide, still focused on the pavement in front of her.

"Oh, yes! We should start off with some hummus or maybe some acili ezme," Indi said, her voice heightened.

"What's acili ezme again? Turkish is a little foggy to me."

Indi explained, "Remember, it's like tomatoes and peppers and walnuts? You eat it with pita bread."

"Oh, yeah! I love that stuff. I'm actually starting to salivate," Kel said, laughing, releasing some of the tension built up in her shoulders from the drive.

"Kel?"

"I'm parked, Indi," Kel said, her voice much more relaxed. "I'm home. I'll feed Roscoe and then meet you there."

"Thank God you're okay. How's your head?"

"I have a mild headache, but nothing compared to normal. The blackness went away. All that food talk worked!" Kel said, feeling like she could conquer the world.

She wasn't used to being able to fight off a blackout, especially one that had progressed that far. They always, always consumed her like a wave that a surfer thinks they can tackle but plows them over the instant they try to ride it. She jump-kicked the air, reveling in her newfound strength.

Kelynn parked on the street next to the Turkish restaurant, her head feeling slightly underwater. It was as if she'd woken up from a blackout, already feeling the aftereffects. Her thoughts felt like walking through the ocean. She thought back to vacations, where she could see her feet through the water. It looked like it would be simple to move, but the water was always much harder to wade through than it appeared. That's how her thoughts felt—all jumbled up, barely out of reach, each one riding a different wave. She shifted the Jeep into park, noticing Indi's car was already parked a few spaces down.

Hopefully she has a table already, Kel thought, expecting some nourishment would alleviate some of the swimmy feeling.

She walked in searching for Indi and her long brunette hair that fell gracefully down her back in effortless curls. Kel's eyes waded through each table until they locked on her friend. There she was, standing next to a table rather than sitting at one.

That's odd, Kelynn thought.

As she began walking towards her, her viewpoint changed so she could see the others sitting at the table, including Gunner.

Shit, what was he doing here?

"Kelynn, hey. I was on the way to our table when I ran into Gunner."

"Hey, Gunner. Good to see you," Kelynn said, looking at him with what she hoped looked like shark eyes—dead, emotionless. She didn't want him to know she was hurt. He'd probably report back to Clay afterwards. That is, if they even talked about her. For all she knew, Clay kept everything about their relationship secret.

"Alright. We should probably head to our table now. I'm sure the waitress is wondering where we are," Indi said, politely smiling before walking down the steps and into another section of the restaurant.

Kelynn glared at her.

"What's wrong?" Indi asked, her defenses up.

"What was that about?"

"I passed by, and I couldn't just ignore him. Plus, we're still friends. He's actually super nice, Kel. You should get to know him."

"Well, maybe I won't have to now," Kel said in a snarky tone.

"Would you stop being so dramatic? You and Clay are going to work through this. It's just going to take time to build back up from whatever he did to ruin your trust. You both need time apart, and once you've cooled off, you'll realize that your feelings are too strong for him to not be together," Indi said, still unaware of the actual issue. She thought Clay had read Kel's diary—an excuse Kelynn used since she wasn't ready to deep dive into the opal magic again. She was still exhausted from trying to talk it through with Clay.

"It just threw me off that you were talking to him. I don't want Clay knowing where I am or if I look sad or happy or whatever."

"Kel, Gunner's a guy. He'll probably tell him that he saw you, but I'm sure that'll be the extent of it. Guys don't worry about the details like we do. I doubt he's going to tell Clay what you were wearing, and I know for a fact you'd want to know something like that if I saw Clay out somewhere."

"Okay, okay. I get it. I panicked."

"You're damn right! Now, let's get you a glass of champagne and me a bourbon."

"How do you drink that straight?" Kel laughed, trying to relax for Indi's sake. "So, how was work?" she asked, hoping to move the conversation off of herself as they moved to their table.

"Nope, no way. I've had my job for a year now. Nothing's changed. Tell me all about your day. Did you take it?"

Kel hesitated, knowing she'd lost the battle of control over the conversation. "I did."

"And? Tell me everything!" Indi said as she motioned for the waitress. She ordered drinks and an appetizer while the two got into Kel's fresh start.

"So, I know this subject was a little touchy the first time I brought it up, and we really don't have to talk about it, but I can't keep this from you."

"Okay . . ." Kel said, lifting her glass to her lips to take down another gulp before Indi spoke again.

"I was just talking with Gunner, as you know, and he texted me the other night about a camping trip."

"You're going camping? *You*, of all people?" Kel asked, almost spewing out her drink.

"I know I'm not the best at being outdoorsy, but it's a big group going, and I think it could be really fun. I didn't know if you and Clay were on speaking terms, so I'm inviting you."

"Clay's going?"

"Yeah, it's Clay, Gunner, Hastings, Lliam, Preston, Blakely, me, and I think a couple others. I don't know their names though."

"So my friend group and Clay's friend group are going camping together?"

"Basically. I'm sure he's waiting for you to call him before he invites you."

"He was supposed to call last night, but he didn't. I'll pass," Kel said, her lips a straight line.

Why is everything so bumpy lately? Kel thought as she looked at the intricate Turkish rug hanging on the wall behind Indi. She envied its soft surface and perfectly planned pattern, its complementary colors making perfect sense to anyone who glanced in its direction.

"Kel, just think it over, okay? You guys didn't break up. You just had a fight. One that's still going on, but that doesn't mean a trip would make it worse. I honestly think it's what you guys need."

"I can't trust him, Indi."

"Yes, you can. He just wanted to know more about you, Kel. It's honestly romantic how he genuinely cares. Don't lose that over something that scares you."

"I just need a little more time to think," Kel said, her expression softer, as though Indi had talked her a few steps back from the edge.

"Let's order some baklava to finish off your job celebration!" Indi said, raising her glass.

Twenty-Six

KELYNN STARTED OFF her Saturday feeling optimistic. It had been a long week, one that felt more like three weeks. She decided it was best to face what was going on in her head, so she began writing all of her thoughts down. She ripped out a sheet of paper from her notebook and wrote "Clay" in the center and circled it. She drew a web around him, attaching different thoughts to him, such as the opal necklace, her strong feelings for him, and her possible future with him. Then, she created another web, this time with the word "Entertainment Career" in the center with words like talent manager, A-list networking, and New York. Once she'd exhausted every scenario, she looked at both sheets side by side.

The one that had "Entertainment Career" in the center made so much more sense to her, most likely because it was centered around her and her wants. Her new job had finally given her some sort of clarity about what she wanted to do, and she hadn't realized it until now. Kelynn wanted to be a part of the action, a coordinator of some sort, maybe someone's right-hand man.

Then she looked at the paper that read "Clay." It was so messy, so complicated. The future was undefined with many more paths. It was overwhelming. It also shut down several possibilities that the other sheet offered, like being able to move at the drop of a hat or constantly travel for a job without worrying about someone else's schedule and life plans. She took a deep breath, staring back and forth at one, then the other. Even though Clay's seemed a lot harder and muddier, it was where her heart gravitated. There was no denying it. Even holding the two papers, she felt like her hand was magnetized to "Clay" and not "Entertainment Career."

Her phone buzzed. It was a text from Clay.

"So, he does exist," she said out loud to no one.

Sanders. I'll be out of town this weekend. I know you didn't ask to see me, but I just wanted you to know.

So, he's avoiding me further by going out of town. Who was he going with? A girl? An ex? She wasn't planning on seeing him anyway, but knowing it wasn't even an option triggered something. Before she knew it, her thoughts began to multiply. She felt like the twenty feet forward she had just taken were swept out from under her, and she was forced forty steps back.

Her breath quickened, her heart pounded, and her thoughts felt like they were crashing down, the weight of them making it harder for her to breathe. She tried to yell for Indi, but nothing would come out. She lay there looking up towards the ceiling, unable to grasp any sense of reality as the black wave overtook her, knocking her out cold.

Kel woke up, the sun shining in her windows, heating up her skin. She blinked a few times, feeling the itch of the carpet beneath her, realizing she had slept hard. Perfect little zigzags traced along her tanned skin from the pattern in the carpet as she slowly sat up.

"Good morning, Roscoe," she said to her pup as she reached for her phone, her head pounding.

Roscoe cocked his head at her, wondering whether it was time for a second breakfast.

"Oh, shit. It's three in the afternoon," she said after checking her phone, which revealed Clay's text she'd never responded to. She suddenly remembered the pieces of paper, the thoughts that she had finally laid out only to be jumbled up again when she received that text from Clay. She lay back down for a few minutes to make sure the blackness wouldn't overtake her again. She took a few slow deep breaths, her eyes closed, focusing on the air flowing in and out, her stomach rising and falling. Indi walked past her bedroom door on her way to take a much-needed shower. She was covered in mud.

"Kel? Everything okay?" she asked, peering in from behind the door frame.

"I thought I was conquering it," Kel said without opening her eyes.

"Conquering what?" Indi asked, inching closer to her.

"My blackouts. I had one today."

"Damn. I'm sorry, Kel. Are you sure you don't want to see a doctor again?"

"They're going to tell me what they've always told me. It's not something they can simply cure. It's not textbook."

"But what if you tried a different doctor, some sort of specialist or something?"

"They cost money, and my insurance isn't worth it."

"Kel, you get new insurance with your full-time job."

"Oh, that's right! I do!" Kel said, sitting up. "Whoa! Where have you been?" Kelynn asked, laughing at her friend's disheveled appearance.

"I may have gone hiking with a friend."

"Did you go down a mudslide, too?" she asked, still laughing.

"Maybe, but I'm glad you're at least feeling a little better. Why don't you give me a hug? You went through *so* much this morning," Indi said, stretching out her arms towards Kel.

"No! No! Get away! You better not get my bed dirty! I'll kill you, Indi!" she shrieked between gusts of laughter.

"Alright, alright. I'm going to go take a shower," Indi said, smiling and withdrawing her dirt-covered arms.

Twenty-Seven

TODAY WAS A new day, and one thought was clear. Kelynn needed to go back to the Villas Assisted Living Center. The days seemed to pass much slower when Kel wasn't talking to Clay. She felt like she had so much more time on her hands—time that she needed to fill with something to distract her. She had gotten past the mad feeling that kept boiling under her skin, threatening to make her explode on the next innocent passerby. She had now moved on to numbness. There was only one thing she did know—that she liked Clay more than she had thought she could ever like someone, but at the moment, she couldn't do anything about it, not with him out of town.

To push through, she focused her energy elsewhere. She'd been wrestling with the thought of going back to the assisted living center for a while and couldn't stand the weight it put on her. She just had to show up. Even if it was only for an hour, she had to go. Kel went to church that morning, like she did every Sunday. Simply being inside the walls of that building brought her spirits up. She felt centered as she left, headed to the place she once loved going. She showed up, feeling uneasy, as she took a deep breath and knocked on the front door.

"Well, hi, Ms. Sanders. It's been a little while since I've seen you." One of the nurses Kelynn regularly saw during her volunteer shift opened the door. "How are you?"

"I'm doing alright; better now that I'm back," Kelynn said.

"We're glad to have you. Do you have any requests for who you'd like to be paired up with?"

"I know Monette talked about a friend she had here. Do you know who that was?"

"Ah, that would be Miss Ferra. Right this way," the nurse said, walking to a room at the opposite end of the facility where Monette stayed.

Kelynn braced herself for the woman she was about to meet. She was nervous about starting a relationship with another resident.

"Knock, knock. Miss Ferra, I have a young lady here who would like to spend some time with you. Would you like to visit for a bit?"

"Oh, sure. That would be quite nice," she said in a voice that was perfectly weathered over the years. It had a nice, crisp tone, like she was once a singer who could hit deeper notes.

"Hi, Miss Ferra. I'm Kelynn," she said, shaking her hand.

Ferra invited her to sit down. The elderly woman explained how she had lost her husband, which was part of the reason she lived in the assisted living center. Kelynn asked about her family. Ferra started going down the family tree, naming this nephew and that daughter.

"And then there's my grandson, Clayton. He visits occasionally, but it's hard for him to get away from work."

"Clayton . . . Fogerty?" Kelynn asked, the puzzle pieces snapping together as the pictures on the dresser suddenly popped out to her, his face everywhere.

"Yes, dear. Do you know him?"

Her face turned red. "Yeah, he's a friend. I don't know why I didn't put it together."

"Not to worry. He's quite cute, isn't he?"

Kel smiled at the old woman's pride in her grandson.

Ferra continued, "He's a very nice boy. He has a good job and a big heart. Are you sure you're just friends? Clay's not one to keep females as friends."

"We may have gone out a few times."

"Once he gets back from Florida with his parents, I'm sure he'll tell me all about it."

Kelynn felt like she was learning things about Clay that he didn't want her to know, yet she wanted to know more. She wondered if that's how he felt after holding her opal.

Ferra continued, "His family heads to Miami almost every fall. They like a break from the chilly weather brought on by the mountains."

"We don't have to talk about him. Why don't we talk more about you? That's why I'm here, really. I want to know about your life, before Clay was even born."

"Well, alright then. We can do that, too. Let me just say one more thing about him. He's a really genuine man. I don't say that because he's my grandson or because I'm biased. I say that because I've seen how he is around all kinds of people and he's the same person time and time again. That's rare."

"You're right. That is rare. Most people adapt to different personalities. That's a very hard trait to keep—being yourself."

"That's Clayton," she said, shrugging her shoulders before diving into the details of her younger years.

Twenty-Eight

KELYNN COULD SENSE Indi's lack of interest in her ever-growing Clay story. She knew she was word-vomiting all of her thoughts onto her, except for the magic part, which she had yet to tell her. Kelynn decided it was time to go to someone else about him. She needed to talk about the opal, with someone other than Clay, to see if she was completely mental.

Hey, guys. Drinks tonight at Nightlight? I need a night out.

She sent the text to both Blakely and Preston.

YES! Finally, we get the fun Kel for a night! Preston responded.

Blakely texted back, *#pinkysout #GNO #letsdothis.*

It was official. They were all going out, and whether Kel was ready or not, she had to tell them what was going on. Indi was too close to her to separate reality from fiction. She needed people on the outside to be able to look at her situation and comment, mostly without bias.

She worked with Andy that day, handing out visitor passes, directing film crews where to go, and greeting potential clients. It was all about first impressions with this job. Kelynn could handle that, sporting her best smile. Andy showed her a few filing systems they had in place, and Kelynn busied herself with the giant pile of paperwork, hoping it would make the day fly by. She was unusually excited to go to Nightlife. It wasn't the bar she was thrilled about, but more so seeing her friends. Going to their "spot" would make things feel familiar, and with all the newness going on around her, she desperately needed familiar.

When the clock hit five, she rushed home to grab some dinner and freshen up. If she was going out, she was going to do it right. Roscoe watched her run her fingers through her beach-waved hair from the bed. He never liked it when she got ready to leave, and he could always tell. Kelynn put on a black strapless top and her go-to high-waisted black jeans. She finished off her look with a swipe of red lipstick and a spritz of Burberry perfume.

She turned to face Roscoe. "How do I look, Ro?"

Roscoe looked up at her without moving his head and let out a small sigh.

"Don't worry, Ross. I shouldn't be out too late. Just take a nice long nap, and I'll be back before ya know it!" she said, patting his head.

He rolled over hoping for a belly rub, but Kelynn couldn't afford to spend time lint-rolling dog hair off of her all-black outfit.

Kelynn could overhear her friends on the porch. She was about to open the door to join them, but when she heard them talking about her, she stopped.

"What do you think happened with Kel and Clay?" Blakely asked.

"Why do you think something happened?" Preston replied.

"I mean, we never go out with her anymore. All of a sudden, she wants to go drinking? That's not like her, not since college when she needed to blow off steam after big exams."

"That's true. I don't know. Maybe she had a night to herself, or maybe she actually missed us?" Preston said, shoving Blakely's shoulder as they stood at Kel's front door.

Kelynn answered the door just as they were about to knock.

"Were you watching for us?" Blakely asked.

"Yeah, and the Uber," Kelynn said, trying to brush off the comments they made, not knowing she could hear them.

"Aw, sweet! I was hoping you weren't the DD," Preston said excitedly.

"I couldn't be the only one not drinking, especially when I arranged this."

"Where's Indi?" Blakely asked.

"She had to work tonight," Kelynn said.

Preston looked Kel up and down. "Damn, Kel. When you want to go out, you really get into the spirit. I'm digging this look."

"Wow, I actually have your approval?" Kel asked, surprised at Preston's compliment.

"Hundred percent. A little slutty with a little class mixed together makes for the perfect *cocktail*," she laughed.

"I'm not looking for any tails tonight," Kelynn said, smiling at Preston's joke.

"Okay, okay," Preston said.

"Hey, by the way, how are you and Clay?" Blakely asked.

"Looks like the Uber's here," Kel said as the three girls piled into the back seat of a silver Honda Accord.

Once they arrived, they went down a side alley, the pavement feeling like home with each step. Blakely found the familiar metal door and turned the handle, leading the pack downstairs to whatever indie band was playing that night.

"So, our Uber driver was kind of cute," Blakely said once the bartender finished their drinks, sipping hers through the tiny mixing straw situated between two limes.

"Ew. No, he wasn't," Preston disagreed.

"Who are you comparing him to? Lliam?" Blakely pushed back.

"At least I have someone to fall back on," Preston argued.

"Okay. Enough, guys," Kelynn said, hoping to distract them. "I have something kind of crazy to talk about."

"Yes, please tell us about your crazy, insane sex life with Clay, because we need a good fantasy," Blakely said.

"What? That doesn't exist right now, and even if it did, I would not be telling you all the juicy details," Kelynn said.

"Wait. What isn't happening? Clay or your sex life?" Blakely asked, leaning closer.

"Either? Both?" Kel was annoyed. "I'm trying to tell you something important, and it involves Clay. Happy now?"

"Totally," Preston said, taking another drink.

"Just hear me out though, before you think I've gone off my rocker," Kelynn said.

"Who even says that anymore?" Blakely asked, squinting her eyes at Kel.

"Anyway . . ." Kel brushed off Blakely's critique, "The other night I went over to Clay's house and caught him . . ."

"Cheating on you?!" Preston asked. "I knew he was too good to be true."

"No, not cheating. He was holding . . . my opal necklace. You know the one my dad gave me?" She rubbed the gem for reference as Blakely and Preston nodded. "Well, while he was holding it, he was totally *out of it.*"

"What do you mean, out of it?" Blakely asked.

"He was . . . having a vision."

"What?" Preston looked confused.

"You guys can't tell anyone, but he explained it to me after I grabbed the necklace from him." Kel started to explain as both Blakely and Preston's eyebrows creased in confusion, their heads cocking to the side almost in unison like a dog hearing a whistle. "When he holds my necklace, he can see visions, or maybe dreams is a better word. They're all thoughts I've actually had, mostly about the future, that somehow transferred into the opal."

Both girls looked at each other and then back at Kel before bursting into laughter.

"Okay, Kel. That was a good one. What did you really catch him doing?" Preston asked, stirring her vodka tonic.

"I'm serious! When my dad gave it to me as a gift for my eighteenth birthday, he told me it came from my great-grandmother, who supposedly had it blessed by a Roma traveler. I know it sounds crazy, but I think it holds some Roma magic or something. Here, I'll prove it," Kel said, unclasping her necklace. "Which one of you wants to test it out?"

"Whatever. Just give it to me," Preston said, grabbing it from Kel.

Preston looked straight ahead, her eyes glazed over, gaining a distant quality. She sat that way for a few minutes, and then her body started to shake. It started at her shoulders and quivered down to her legs.

"She's having a seizure! What did you do?" Blakely screamed, terrified.

"I . . . I . . . I don't know," Kel said right before Preston burst into laughter, handing the necklace back to Kel.

"Aw, man, that was fun. I really had you going, didn't I?" Preston asked with tears streaming down her face from laughing so hard.

"Seriously, Preston. What the hell?" Kelynn took a swig of her drink to calm herself down.

"Blakely, I need you to hold it. Don't mess with me this time," Kelynn said, giving the two a scolding look.

"Okay, fine," Blakely said, taking the delicate necklace from Kel's hands.

"Kel, nothing is happening." She forcefully closed her eyes. "Honest. I don't see anything."

"Preston?" Kel said, turning to her friend who took the first turn.

"Sorry, Kel. It's just a necklace. I think Clay was lying to you to cover up something else."

"No, he wasn't, because . . . I saw it too, when I kissed him."

The two looked at her disbelieving, and then at each other for validation that neither of them thought Kel was speaking the truth.

"That's really weird. I wonder why it didn't work on you all," Kelynn said, holding the necklace for a minute before putting it back around her neck.

"What kind of dreams has he seen?" Blakely asked. "Ya know, if we're pretending this is real and all."

"They're all pretty personal, which is why we aren't on the best of terms currently. He should've told me."

"Okay, so let's say Clay has seen your thoughts about the future," Blakely said. "Don't you want him to know what you want? He basically has a key to see what you want without you having to tell him outright."

"That's a decent point," Kel said, moving on to her second vodka.

"Yeah, but he did go behind her back," Preston added. "I can't tell you how many times Lliam did that to me. He'd log onto my Instagram or Facebook and see what I was liking, look through my messages, and see who I followed."

"Kind of a different scenario, Pres. You cheated on him. Kind of a lot," Blakely said.

"He cheated on me, too!" Preston shot back.

"Not the point here, guys. I still don't know what to think about all of this," Kel said, rubbing her head.

"Do you love him?" Preston asked.

"I don't know. I really like him, but this has set us back a bit."

"How do you feel when he kisses you?" Blakely asked. "You can always tell your real feelings from a kiss."

"They're very strong," Kel said. "Like this vodka, which, speaking of, I need to dance. Now."

She stood up, annoyed with the conversation, and the music began to pound in her ears, shaking every sturdy thought that had taken root. They all began swimming again. She couldn't walk straight. The combination of the alcohol mixed with her jumbled thinking felt like she'd had ten drinks instead of two.

"Come on! It's been awhile since I've seen you drop it," Blakely said, grabbing Kel's hand.

Kel started to twist this way and that, but suddenly the crowd became too much. She didn't feel like she was moving freely anymore. "I . . . I need to sit down," Kelynn said, the room suddenly spinning. Her haunting thoughts were dulled by the alcohol but still present. She felt the blackness creep around the edges of her peripheral vision.

"Guys, I can't," Kel said, her eyes rolling backwards as her friends tried to catch her falling body before it hit the dance floor.

Twenty-Nine

HER EYES FLUTTERED open. All she could see was white—blindingly bright white. Looking from right to left, her head felt unusually heavy, too heavy to move.

"Good afternoon," a deep voice boomed from the left-hand side of the bed close to the doorway. His voice sounded muffled, like she was underwater and he was staring at her from above.

She blinked a few more times before his face shifted from blurry shapes to crystal clear.

"Dr. Roski?" Kelynn asked, recognition sinking in.

"Yes, Ms. Sanders. It's me. You blacked out again." He paused as if he was waiting for her to give some sort of response reflecting understanding, but Kelynn could barely shift in the bed let alone comprehend what was being said. "We tested your alcohol levels, but the amount in your system wouldn't have been enough to cause you to pass out. You rest now, but in a few I'm going to need you to tell me how many times this has happened recently and you've gone unchecked."

Kelynn stared blankly at the doctor. She couldn't remember how she got here, where Blakely and Preston were, what time it was, or what day it was for that matter. She closed her eyes, her head pounding from the blackout. She took several deep breaths and fell back into an unconscious state. After a few hours, she awoke, the night before coming back to her. She remembered how Blakely and Preston didn't see the opal visions like Clay could.

Was Clay making it all up? she wondered.

Kelynn shifted in the hospital bed to distract herself. She couldn't go down that road of endless possibilities and unknowns—not when she was recovering from a blackout.

"Ms. Sanders," Dr. Roski had come back into her room.

"Dr. Roski. You can call me Kelynn. I know it's been a while, but it's still me."

"My apologies, Kelynn. I didn't know how responsive you would be. Are you feeling more alert now?"

"Yes, can you please fill in the gaps for me?" she asked.

"Sure. What do you remember last?"

"I was dancing in a bar with my friends, or at least I was about to dance before everything went black."

"Apparently, your friends caught a taxi and brought you to the ER once that happened. After the ER doctors went through your medical file, they called me in." He paused to ensure she was following along. "Last time we talked, your blackouts were only happening on occasion, and you were taking medicine for them. That prescription expired quite some time ago, and according to your friends, this isn't the only time this has happened within the last few months."

"What did they tell you?" Kelynn asked, trying to focus.

"Your friends said it happened at a party in late August. They described the situation of finding you under a tree. Is that true?"

"Yes, that's true."

"Why didn't I get a call from you back then?"

"I guess, I didn't want to keep coming in, and then they started to go away for a bit."

"Oh, really? Did you change your diet or exercise habits, or would your stress levels have decreased for any reason?"

"No." Kelynn paused. "Dr. Roski, do you believe in forces between people?"

"I'm not sure what you mean," he said.

"Well, I met this guy, and when we look into each other's eyes, there is definitely some sort of magnet-like force connecting us. I can feel it and he can, too."

"Are you sure it's not love, and you're using this as a way to defer your feelings?" he asked, trying to swallow back a laugh.

"I really don't think so," she said. "Don't get me wrong, I have strong feelings for him, but there's more to it than that. When I started hanging out with him, my blackouts were pretty much non-existent."

"Maybe your stress levels were down because of him."

"Definitely not," Kelynn responded, her words coming out faster than her brain could process.

"Why, all of a sudden, have they started again?"

"I don't know, but I haven't seen him for almost two weeks."

"And how many times have you blacked out within that time?"

"Two, and there's the one that I fought off," she said, recalling each one.

"You were able to fight one off?"

"Yeah, I was focusing super hard on something simple to distract me. It prevented it from taking over my entire body. My thoughts were more like a string of scattered moments, like a constellation, rather than an all-encompassing thunderstorm."

"Well, Kelynn, I'm not sure about your theory, but we do need to do another EEG to test your brain cell activity now that you're fully awake. We tried to perform one when you came in, but you were quite unresponsive. Maybe we'll get a more precise assessment this time around."

Kelynn agreed to the test. She didn't think it would show them anything conducive since it hadn't in the past, but she respected Dr. Roski. He'd explained the necessity of an EEG in previous testing, specifically focusing on how it can pick up electrical impulses from various regions of the brain and reveal any abnormalities like brain tumors or disorders like epilepsy.

At this point, Kelynn wanted answers, but she had a feeling another test wouldn't show her the reaction Clay was causing.

Since Dr. Roski was a neurologist, she only had to wait an hour or so after the test to hear her results, which she used to take another nap.

"Find anything?" Kelynn asked, sitting up as Dr. Roski entered her hospital room holding a manila folder.

"Something minimal. Since this is now your third test, we were able to see your brain function a little more clearly and compare it to your previous ones. The test was able to detect increased electrical activity being conducted between the frontal and parietal lobes."

"What does that mean?"

"Both lobes are overactive at the same time. The frontal lobe, which is where problem-solving comes into play, and your parietal lobe, which controls your body awareness, both have high amounts of activity simultaneously. The combination of the overflow is what causes you to blackout. While we can see more of what's going on, there still isn't a simple antidote I can give you, but you do have options. One is to put you back on anti-anxiety meds to reduce the stress-filled thoughts."

"Okay," Kel said, taking in the new information.

"Another option is to find hobbies that allow you to express your frustration from problem-solving, such as kickboxing or running, or something that you find releases your built-up stress. Oh, and you might want to cut back on the caffeine."

She nodded, still absorbing his words.

"And apparently, we now have a third option."

"What's that?" she asked, hoping he had the magic answer at his fingertips.

"Keep seeing that young man. See if your blackouts continue to subside when you're with him. I'm a doctor, but I don't always have the answers. If you've found something, or in this case, some*one* who makes your life easier and reduces your symptoms, I say keep seeing him," he said, chuckling.

"You can't be serious," she said, shooting him an expression of disbelief.

"If it works, why not?" he asked, shrugging his shoulders. "I want you to make a follow-up appointment with me for sometime in the next couple of weeks."

"I will," she said. "Am I free to go?"

"Yes, Kelynn. Just head to the nurses' station to the right, and they'll get you checked out. It was good to see you. Please take care of yourself."

"Thank you," she said, gathering her things someone had placed in a chair beside the bed.

She picked up her phone to find over forty texts from Blakely and Preston combined wanting to make sure she was recovering okay. Instead of responding to them, she called Indi to come pick her up.

Clay.

"HEY, CAN I come in for a bit?" Sanders asked, standing on my doorstep.

"Yeah, of course." The words came out of my mouth, but when I heard them, I couldn't believe them. She was *here*, and she wanted to talk to me. The freeze-out was over.

She walked past me and sat down on the couch, staring straight ahead as if she were afraid to speak.

"I . . . I don't know where to start exactly," Sanders said this while adjusting her rings, as if moving one of them would give her the words to say.

"Then, can I?" I asked as I shut the door, hoping she would give me a chance to tell her what I'd been thinking.

She glanced to her left and looked into my eyes. She nodded and then shifted back to staring at her hands.

"Why didn't you call?" she asked right before I was about to start talking.

I sat in front of her on the floor and took her hands in mine.

"Sanders, I felt like you didn't want me to, not really, and I already had that trip planned with my parents. I figured I'd let you breathe, but this time away from you has been really eye-opening." I saw her take a deep breath, her eyebrows pulled together, I assumed in anticipation. "It was really rough. I missed the hell out of you," I said, squeezing her hands tighter. She let out a sigh and her lips formed a small creased smile. "I don't know what you're about to tell me, but if you're going to break up with me, you need to know a few things first. One, when I'm around you, it's like the muddy waters of my life are made clear, and I can see the fish swimming around—all their colors, shapes, sizes, and movements. It's like I can hear you encouraging me, or telling me what move to make before you even open your mouth. You know that interview I had?"

"With Chill Axel?" she answered.

I nodded. "They offered me the job."

"Clay, that's great! Why didn't you tell me?"

"I still haven't given them an answer because when you're out of the picture, it's like I can't function as well. It's almost as if I can see shadows of fish, but not the actual colors and details of their scales, so I can't know what to do or where to go. I feel like I can't see five feet in front of me to make a decision unless you're by my side, and I didn't realize that until I left. It also hit me that you're the reason I even felt inspired to look for another job. Well, you and my Omi. Either way, you have been a part of this process from the start, and I needed you close to figure out how to finish it, but not just for that"

Sanders was silent. Her hands rested in mine, but her eyes looked past me. Her face was now a blank slate. She had been giving me all the signs before that she was into me, but now I wasn't sure what she was about to tell me. Now I was the one holding my breath and creasing my forehead as her eyes moved from behind me to my eyes. I could feel the wavelength of electricity connecting us.

"I have a lot I want to say, and it may take me longer to get it out, but my thoughts are kind of everywhere."

"That's fair," I said, hanging on to every word.

"I don't like feeling dependent on anyone," she started, "and I'm not the type of person to openly admit my flaws or weaknesses to someone I'm seeing. But I think you're in my life for a reason, which terrifies and excites me at the same time."

My heart was pounding the more she talked.

"While you were gone, I went to my doctor. Well, I was taken to him, actually."

"What do you mean by *taken* to him? Someone forced you to go?"

"I blacked out twice while I was away from you. The second time, I was at a bar with Blakely and Preston. They took me to the hospital."

"Oh, shit. Why didn't you call me, Sanders?"

"Clay, I didn't know where I stood on things. That's partially why I was having the blackouts. There were so many 'what if' scenarios running through my brain that it crashed on me like an overloaded computer."

"How are you feeling now?" I asked, rubbing the palms of her hands.

"I feel better. I'm still not super clear on everything, but I'm alright."

"What did the doctor say?"

"Damn it, Clay. I'm trying to tell you!" she said, her voice sounding like it was laced with a small dose of sarcasm.

I couldn't help but let out a small laugh. "I'm sorry. I just want to know everything. Take your time," I said, shifting closer, her feet resting on my thighs.

"The doctor did an EEG test of my brain. Basically, I have an overwhelming amount of activity in two of my lobes, so they overflow into one another, causing me to blackout. I have too many thoughts, and my brain can't physically process all of them, so it moves them to places they aren't meant to go, in order for me to function."

I looked at her, concerned.

"Is it curable?" I asked sheepishly, hoping I wouldn't disturb her train of thought.

"No, I can take anti-anxiety meds, and it's recommended that I take up a hobby to help me reduce stress and release endorphins. Oh, and apparently I should cut back on the coffee, which shouldn't be too hard now that I'm no longer a barista."

Sanders stopped to look at me. I could tell she was hiding a smile, but I was unsure why. Nothing she was saying was great news or of much help for her.

"But I talked to the doctor and he pretty much prescribed me . . . you."

"What does that mean?" I asked, inching closer to her.

"I told him that the more I hang out with you, the less frequent and more manageable my blackouts become. He recommended that I continue to be around you," she said, rolling her eyes even though I could tell she believed what she was saying. I sat there dying to talk, but I could tell she wasn't finished.

"Clay, about my feelings." She paused. "I like you a lot. I have very strong feelings for you, and . . . I want to be with you." I let out a sigh of relief. "When I look at the future with all my career goals, it makes at least a little more sense, and the path is mostly straight, but when I look at it with you involved, all of the unknowns multiply by, like, a thousand. It scares me, but I know it's what I want. It's what makes me happier. I'm still walking through muddy waters, too. When I'm with you, they're clearer, but being with you also makes them messy in a way I didn't expect, but a beautiful mess," she said, waiting for my response. I bit my lip just in case she wasn't done talking. "I missed you. I'm done now," she said as she smiled and put her hands on the back of my head, rubbing her fingers through my hair. "Has anyone ever told you how amazingly attractive you are?" she asked, moving her hands to my beard.

I watched her watching me, the look in her eyes reflecting exactly how I felt about her. I closed the gap between her and I and kissed her, still kneeling on the ground in front of her. She kissed me back, igniting the fire I had so desperately missed while we were apart.

This is what kissing should always be like, I thought as her lips moved with mine, her tongue like a sparkler, setting ablaze all the passion that existed in my veins.

Sanders pulled back. "Clay, I really missed you."

"I missed you way more," I said, my nose scrunched against hers as I leaned in again and kissed her once more.

She pulled me close for a hug while she sat on my lap, feeling like she was a koala, and I was the tree. I stood, picking her up, and laid her down on the couch, brushing my fingers over her long sun-bleached hair. "So, tell me," I said.

"What?" she asked, facing me.

"What bar did you go to?"

She laughed, and we spent the next hour telling each other about the past two weeks. We were playing catch-up while making out between stories. I loved hearing her voice, her laugh, and the way she described things, but also the way her lips felt. I wanted to listen to her and kiss her at the same time, which was impossible. She barely told me about one of her days before we were tangled up kissing again.

"Do you know what you're going to choose?" Sanders asked in reference to my Chill Axel interview.

"They gave me a generous offer, but the thought of leaving AnaScape is like an out-of-body experience. It's all I know, and I feel comfortable there. Going to Chill Axel is the complete opposite. Everything and everyone would be new, and I wouldn't have a groove when I first got there. It would take time for it to feel like my home."

"*You're* not comfortable, but I chose you," Sanders said while playing footsie with me. "I chose the scarier option because I think without you, I'm not fully who I want to be."

"You make a valid point," I said, staring at her deep green eyes, her freckles that danced across her nose onto her cheeks, and her petite teeth lined with light pink lips. "You scare me, too," I said, taking her in.

She smiled, stroking the opal before she kissed me again, causing a vision to take us both to a hotel by a beach where we were lying in a bed. She stopped kissing me and dropped the opal as her cheeks turned an embarrassed shade of red.

Clay.

I HELD HER hand in my right and Willie's leash in the left. The four of us were walking towards my favorite beaten trail. We almost felt like a family—Sanders, Roscoe, Willie, and me. It was about time our dogs met, and I figured hiking would be a great bonding experience for all of us. I led the way up the side of the mountain, the dirt beneath my feet feeling like home. I could follow this trail in my sleep. There was a time when I would come here every single day after work, back when I started at AnaScape. It allowed me to clear my head. Any stress or anxiety from the day was released here. This place also sparked a lot of creativity I could take into work the next day. Many of the apps I've developed started right here on this mountain. Taking Sanders here felt personal, like showing someone something you've worked on for a long time. Even if it isn't finished yet, you hope it's brilliant, but you're unsure until someone else says so, too.

"Clay!" Sanders hollered from behind me, further down the hill. I had to let go of her hand when Willie pulled me towards a squirrel. "Wait up!"

"Sorry, I kind of spaced out. You know when you drive to work and zone out because your body knows the way?"

"You know this place *that* well?" she asked, sounding shocked and a little out of breath.

"I've come here at least fifty times. It's kind of therapeutic."

"Yeah, it's gorgeous," Kel said, peering between the leaves of the trees at the rays of sun shining through.

"It's great in winter months like this because it's just cool enough that it's refreshing after a hard climb."

"Come on, Roscoe," she said, tugging on the leash.

"Is Roscoe used to climbing?" I asked, a little worried since we were only about five minutes into the forty-five-minute hike. "I probably should have asked that before we started."

"He's used to walks, but he loves to smell everything. I'm sure the farther we go, he'll get tired of doing anything but walking."

"We're about fifteen minutes out from a really cool lookout point where we can stop and let him rest for a bit."

She pulled her puffer jacket tighter around her face as she finally succeeded at grabbing Roscoe's attention. We kept going, moving forward. She copied each step I took, avoiding rocks and placing her feet between tree roots as I did. It was cute. She trusted me. We walked uphill, both quiet, lost in our own thoughts. It was nice to be together but not needing to fill the open space with words.

"Here we are," I said as we approached my favorite rock. My seat was practically imprinted in it.

"Oh my gosh, Clay. This is . . . perfect," she said, taking heavy breaths between words.

"I love it. It's not too steep, so Roscoe should be okay near the edge. It's almost like stairs all the way down with how the rocks lay, so no fear of falling."

"Thank God. Come on, Roscoe. Let's get some water," she said, the two sitting side-by-side.

"I've never shared this spot with anyone. This has been my little secret for years."

She smiled as she drank from her CamelBak straw. She leaned in and kissed me.

"This is nice. I never take time to just sit and be," Sanders said, kicking her legs as they dangled over the side. "We should do this more often."

"I have to ask you something," I said, a little uneasy about how she'd feel.

"What's up?" she asked, leaning back on her hands and taking in the profile of the spine of the mountains stacked in the distance.

"Has Indi talked to you about the camping trip coming up?"

"Oh, yeah. I was kind of pissed about it, but that was when you and I weren't talking."

"How do you feel now?"

"A little better," she said, smiling but not facing me. She had one dimple that appeared whenever she smiled so big that it spread to her eyes. I loved that little dimple. It was a dead giveaway of how happy she actually was.

"Well, I, for one, would really like it if you came with us," I said, gliding my hand over my mouth and letting it rest on my beard, nervous of her answer.

"I'll think it over," she said. "It's just with my new job, I'm not sure I want to go away for a weekend instead of relaxing."

"This *will* be relaxing."

"Yeah, but Hastings will be there. That doesn't sound super relaxing."

"He used to be chill. He's always been a douche when it comes to girls, but he had some redeeming qualities back in college. He was actually a good friend back then."

"What the hell happened to him?" Sanders asked.

"Life kinda hit him hard. His dad passed away a year or so ago, and he hasn't had a steady job since."

"That's tough," she said, staring off into the distance.

"Just think it over. I would really like to spend the weekend with you and all of our friends. We haven't all hung out yet."

"Except for at your party, but I don't remember much of that," she said, laughing.

"By the way, speaking of the trip, how much has Indi told you about her and Gunner?" I asked, standing up and brushing the dirt from my pants.

"We talked a couple times. Last I heard, they were just friends," Sanders said.

"Well, I hope that's not true for his sake."

"Wait, why?" Sanders asked, snapping her head in my direction.

"He's really into her. They actually went hiking the other day, but no worries it wasn't on our trail," I said, the words coming out before I could stop them. It felt right to claim something as "ours," but I wasn't sure Sanders would agree.

"So that's who she went hiking with! She told me they agreed they were better as friends."

Thank God, she didn't even notice my comment about the trail, I thought, continuing to shift the focus to another couple.

"Maybe you should check on that, because Gunner is one to kiss and tell, and he's definitely told me."

"I guess that's kind of cute," she said, surprising me.

"You're cool with it?"

"Yeah, I wasn't at first because you were really new to me, and it felt like she was invading my territory. I'm not good at sharing." She paused. "That's the first time I've ever admitted that out loud," she said, straining to pull Roscoe up the trail as we continued on.

"Whoa. Good to know," I said.

"What is?" she asked, catching up to me.

"That you're protective of me and maybe kind of jealous?" I said, winking at her.

"Okay. Maybe the first part of that is true, but . . ." She finished her thought by shoving me.

"Hey, watch it!" I said laughing, "Don't make me lose my balance or I might fall and take Willie with me!"

She smirked as I regained my footing. "So this is officially *our* trail?" she asked. "I kind of like that."

Thirty

"KELYNN CHANEY SANDERS, I cannot believe you told Preston and Blakely before ME!" Indi yelled.

"Indi, you don't understand. I knew they wouldn't care whether it was true or not, whereas you would have gone down a rabbit hole of research. I needed unbiased, uninvested opinions. I'm sorry," Kelynn said, her hands up, as if proving she was unarmed would calm her roommate.

"You're damn right I'm going down a rabbit hole of research. This isn't some normal thing. You can't just tell me some psychic nomad gave your family a magic necklace. That shit isn't normal," she rebutted, her voice unwavering at its high volume. "I can't believe I fell for that crap about Clay finding your diary. I should've known better. You haven't had a diary since high school!"

"I know. I really can't believe I pulled that off. But if you really want to dig deeper, I'd be happy to know more about it honestly. All I know is that it works with Clay." She paused, releasing a breath as she saw Indi's shoulders relax, even if only slightly. "I still feel weird about it, but somewhat relieved that you all know. Now, I don't have to hold this secret in all the time."

"Okay. There's just one more thing I need to know," Indi said, her flushed cheeks slowly returning to their normal color.

"Anything," Kelynn said.

"I need to know if it works on me," Indi said, extending her hand.

"Right now? We need to be leaving," Kelynn said.

"I don't care. If you're really my best friend, I need to know."

"Fine. I get it," Kelynn said, shaking her head as she unclasped her necklace. The gemstone slid into Indi's palm. She rolled it around in her hand, watching the light dance through its facets. She took in a sharp breath and looked up at Kelynn.

"Damn. It doesn't work on me," she said, disappointed.

"You're still my best friend," Kelynn said, reassuringly. "I'm sorry I never told you. I just didn't want one more person to think I was crazy. Especially you."

"I don't think you're crazy—maybe a bit more spiritual than I thought. I'm still going to do some mad research, but for now I believe you," Indi said.

Kelynn slung her duffel bag over her shoulder. "You ready?"

"Totally. I'm so glad you're going," Indi said, dragging her bag behind her down the stairs, making a thud with each step.

"Me, too. I've decided to have an open mind about everyone going. Even couples."

"What's that supposed to mean?" she asked.

"Indi, I know you're seeing Gunner," Kelynn said just as Indi hit the bottom of the stairs.

"What? That's crazy. I told you we're just friends."

"Indi, it's okay. Clay told me, and I want you to know, I'm fine with it. I mean, it's kind of weird. We like guys who are best friends, but it could be kinda fun."

"Really?!" Indi yelled, hugging Kel. "Thank goodness you're chill about it now. I can finally tell you all about him."

"Deal," Kel said. "But let's talk in the car. Clay's already waiting out front."

"Looks like we're the last ones," Clay said, shifting gears to park in front of three big blue tents with a fire burning in the center.

"They've already set it all up!" Kel said, excited. "I feel kind of bad we took a detour. We should've helped."

"You worry too much," Clay said, reaching across her to open her door and then hopping out to grab Indi's. "This is a vacation. Everyone else was probably just excited to get the tents up. Let's go explore!" Clay said, walking around to the bed of the truck where his and Gunner's duffels lay.

Kel felt a little uneasy. Even though she'd met Clay's friends, she didn't really *know* them. Walking into this trip felt like a statement, like she was declaring that she was here to stay—that Clay was now a part of her story, too, not just theirs. A small swarm of toxic butterflies invaded her stomach, making her fearful of their opinions. She didn't want to invade anyone's space or make Clay's friends feel threatened. Kel needed to start off on the right foot, but showing up last made her stomach jump into her throat, causing their arrival to feel tainted already.

"What happened? You guys get lost?" Lliam asked, coming out of the woods with Preston.

"We made a coffee stop," Clay said.

"Preston, why do you have leaves in your hair?" Kelynn asked, walking towards the campsite.

"We just finished a grueling hike," she said, quickly running her fingers through her hair.

"Yeah, okay. We'll go with that," Kel said, smiling and grabbing her duffel from Clay.

"Where's everyone sleeping?" she asked.

"Well, we figured we'd do a guys and girls tent, and then anyone who wants to sleep in couples can use the other tent. I'll be waiting, ladies," Hastings said, opening the zippered door of the coed tent.

"Gross," Preston said, moving closer to Lliam.

"Oh, please," he said, putting distance between them. "You went out with him."

"Lliam, I already explained that to you."

"Yeah, it was to make me jealous, but we both know that didn't mean you had to sleep with him."

"I didn't!" Preston said, shoving him backwards. He stuck his arm out just in time to catch himself on a nearby tree.

"That's not what *he* said," Lliam said, pointing to the tent Hastings had just gone into.

"And you believe him over me?" she asked, her voice growing louder. "Hastings, of all people!"

"Let's hope she didn't wake any sleeping bears," Clay whispered to Kel.

"Yeah, seriously," she said, laughing. "I'm gonna start prepping for dinner." Kelynn grabbed a few bags of groceries from one of the tents and headed for the picnic tables set up just far enough away from the fire.

"Right behind ya!" Clay said, grabbing a cooler.

Kel chopped up some potatoes while Clay put hot dogs on sticks. The rest of the crew made their way over to the firepit. For the moment, everyone seemed calm, like nature had finally sunken in enough to draw them together, away from the stress back home. Indi got up, leaving her blanket with Gunner and went into one of the tents.

"Where ya goin'?" Gunner asked.

She didn't respond to him but emerged dragging a cooler. "It's five o'clock!" she said, pushing the top open to expose a case of beer.

"Alright! Let's get this camping trip officially started," Gunner said, getting up to help her.

Hastings pulled out a guitar and started strumming. Kelynn took a few sips of her beer as they took turns roasting hot dogs over the fire. She grabbed a couple slices of bread and toasted them, adding cheese after they were nice and burnt for a makeshift grilled cheese. Just as she took her first bite, Hastings started to play "Green Eyes" by Coldplay. Her dad used to play her that song when she was younger. She felt like it was written for her and her very own green eyes. She sat there eating her fireside dinner and listening to his voice carry each lyric delicately. His whole mood seemed to have shifted. He was softer. She loved watching people get lost in their craft, but she didn't realize Hastings was an actual human that could feel anything but lust. He finished the song with his eyes still locked on the sky.

"So, you're more than just a DJ," Kelynn said, looking over at his direction, half of her grilled cheese resting in her right hand.

"I guess," he said, his head still turned upward. "I just prefer DJing to this," he said. "Unless I'm camping. It's really the only occasion I bring out Ole Betsy."

"That's your guitar's name?" Kelynn asked.

"Yeah, she's been around for a long time. She's been passed down through generations of my family," he said, finally turning to face her.

His eyes looked kinder, like Ole Betsy had taken Hastings's terrible qualities and drowned them in the nearby lake.

"How come you only play in the . . . " she paused, looking around her, "middle of nowhere?"

He chuckled. "It's too personal. When I DJ, I still lose myself in the music, but no one cares that I'm playing it. They like the songs they know. When it's only me singing and playing guitar, I'm giving a piece of myself to whoever listens. I can't do that in public. That's not who I am."

"I think it is who you are, and you shouldn't be afraid to show it," she said, smiling.

"Well, forget it. I'm not soft. This shit helps me when I'm secluded. No girls are gonna shake their asses to that," he said, taking a swig of beer before burping.

"And now we're back to the real Hastings," she said blankly as she got up to move across the fire where Clay was sitting.

"Hey, babe," he said, mid-conversation with Lliam.

"So, you think you're gonna take it?" Lliam asked.

"I'm leaning in that direction. Still trying to figure it all out," Clay said about his job offer from Chill Axel.

"You're set either way. You have a great job now, but that one sounds great, too," Lliam said, moving his hands up and down like he was weighing something in each one.

"Yeah, but that makes it that much harder. I have to decide between two great places. Why can't one be shitty?" Clay said.

"Sometimes you just have to leap. Take the pressure off of yourself and freefall. You'll grow no matter what choice you make," Kel said.

Clay wrapped his arm around her and pulled her close, kissing the side of her head.

"Did you get cold over there by Hastings or what?" Clay asked, looking in his direction as he put his guitar back in its case.

"Yeah, you could say that," she said, frustrated that the minute Hastings showed a more vulnerable side, he immediately shut down and reverted back to his douchebag nature.

"I'm gonna head to bed," Kel said, kissing Clay.

"Alright, I get the hint," Lliam said, moving across the circle towards Preston, who had conveniently moved towards Hastings.

"You cool if I stay up a bit longer?" Clay asked.

"Yeah, of course. Hang with your friends. Just don't go chasing down any bears."

He laughed. "Not tonight," he said, snuggling her close enough that she could feel his rib cage move with each chuckle.

"I'll be in the tent in a few," he said.

"Oh . . . I was kind of planning on staying in the girls' tent," she said, distancing herself from him.

"Oh. That's cool, too," he said, a hint of disappointment lining his voice. "I'll come say goodnight in a few," Clay said, rubbing his hands together in front of the fire.

Thirty-One

KELYNN SQUIRMED IN her sleeping bag trying to shift her body downward to keep as warm as possible. She had two blankets on top of her—one inside the sleeping bag and one on the outside. The night was definitely colder than any of them had expected. She could hear the crickets and cicadas chirping in the background alongside the occasional hooting of a distant owl. She took five deep breaths, trying to relax her tense body that was betraying her.

One inhale, one exhale. Two inhale, two exhale. Three inhale, three exhale.

Before she got to the fourth inhale, she heard a noise. Someone was walking outside the tent. Clay had told her good night hours ago. As far as she knew, everyone was asleep. The steps walked around the entire circumference of the tent. She shriveled up into a tiny ball when they were closest to her. As they reached the front, she could hear the zipper beginning to pull. Whoever it was, was coming inside. Kel slowly moved her arm out of the warmth of the sleeping bag and reached behind her head, searching for her metal water bottle. She blindly moved her hand all around, first thumbing her bathroom bag, then her duffel, until finally she felt the cool exterior of the jug. She wrapped her hand around it and pulled it back into her sleeping bag, her back facing the opening of the tent. Kel's breath started to quicken as the zipper noise continued. Whoever it was, was purposefully trying to stay quiet. The noise stopped. She heard footsteps but was in disbelief at the sound that followed. They were zipping it shut again just as slowly. If someone tried to hurt her or her friends, this wasn't going to be a quick getaway. Her heart beat so loudly, she confused it with the pounding feet coming towards her. She held her breath and shut her eyes as tight as she could. Kel started to pray out of fear when a hand touched her shoulder.

She gripped the water bottle lid tight ready to swing when she heard, "Sanders, you awake?"

She let out her held breath in a panic, whipping around to see Clay.

"Whoa. Light sleeper?" he asked.

"Clay! What are you doing here?! I thought you were some creep!" she said, revealing her hidden water bottle.

"Damn, I'm sorry!" he whispered. "I was trying not to wake you, but I couldn't sleep. Gunner is snoring, and it's freezing in there. I thought maybe you were cold, too."

"I am, but I'm also firing mad now, too!" she whisper-yelled. "You scared the shit out of me!"

Clay laughed quietly. "Let me make it up to you," he said, sitting down next to her.

"Fine. Come make me warm," she said, unzipping her sleeping bag.

Clay accepted her invitation and climbed inside the sleeping bag that was barely big enough with both of them turning sideways to fit. She turned to face him, burying her face in his chest.

"Sanders," he said. "I can feel your heart. It's racing."

"Yeah, you freaked me out," she said, looking away from him.

"You sure that's it?" he asked, pulling her chin up.

She nodded, moving closer to him, their lips touching. He wrapped his arms around her, cradling the back of her head with one while the other covered the perimeter of her back.

She could feel the heat emanating from his body. She finally started to feel warm, but was nowhere close to sleeping. She felt fully alive, like Clay had set her free. She wanted him—every part of him. He kissed her harder. She knew he wanted her, too. Time didn't exist when their lips were locked. The only way to start time again was to stop kissing, which Clay did as soon as he heard Blakely rustling in her sleeping bag.

"Do you think we woke her?" he asked, his body frozen.

"No, she's probably just moving in her sleep," Kelynn said, kissing him again. He climbed on top of her, using his arms to hold himself up, so he didn't crush her. He kissed her again and again, their tongues connecting, setting off another shower of fireworks.

He stopped to look at her. "Ya know something? I like you in the moonlight. You look so beautiful," he said before closing his eyes to kiss her again.

"Clay, I like you," she said before he kissed her again. "A lot."

"Sanders, I like you more than that," he said, his hand moving to her hip.

"I have to tell you something," she said, moving his hand back up to her face, cradling it against her cheek.

"Tell me anything," he said.

"Ever since I first saw you, I've noticed the connection between us . . . . and I don't just mean romantically." She was so close to Clay she barely had to whisper for him to hear her. "It feels stronger than that, like my very biological makeup is attracted to yours. Like who we are at our cores is linked."

"I would be lying if I said I hadn't noticed it, too—that electric wave when I look into your eyes," Clay said. "I like it, though. It's like something bigger than us is pulling me towards you, pushing us together."

"Exactly, but I think there's something else to it. Remember how the doctor said I should keep hanging out with you?"

"Like I'm your personal prescription?" Clay joked.

Kel pushed him back, barely moving him since he was trapped in the same sleeping bag as her. "I'm serious."

"Sorry, I'm listening. Go on," Clay said, smiling at her.

"I think … I think you're my catalyst."

Clay opened his mouth as if to say something but stayed silent, confusion dancing across his eyebrows.

"When you're in my life, things are easier. I don't blackout. I can see my future clearer and more than that, my present. I like feeling like I'm standing on solid ground, and I think it's partially you that makes that possible." She stopped to catch her breath from talking so fast. "It's like you propel me forward. You cause this reaction that helps me see things in plain sight for what they are without fear diluting them."

"Does this mean you want me around forever?" Clay asked.

"It means when you are around, you open me up to the beauty of this life, and I'm scared that if you're not around, I won't be able to find it again."

"We can figure it out together," Clay said, laying a light kiss on her lips. "I'm not going anywhere," he said, trying to understand the weight of what she said.

"Clay, will you do something for me?" Kelynn asked after a minute of silence. Clay looked at her expectantly. "Will you hold my opal? I want to feel a release again."

"Of course," Clay said, moving his hand up from inside the tightly packed sleeping bag and finding the tiny gem in the dark. He went into a daze, the magic taking over. Kel let him watch for a few minutes before taking the necklace back from him.

"Tell me what you saw," she said, excited this time.

He told her how he went into a world with puppies everywhere. They were trapped under tree roots in the woods. He was surrounded by other people, all wearing matching shirts with "Wildlife Rescue" printed on them.

"It was my job—to save animals. I watched as leaves fell from the trees and turned into sand, creating the beach under my feet. Then, I was helping seagulls from an oil spill as they squawked around me, filling the air with the sound of flapping wings. It felt so real. It's such an unbelievable rush every time one of these dreams ends," he said, sighing.

Kelynn could see his eyes sparkle in the moonlight. She felt the electricity as she looked into them while they lay in the tent underneath the star-filled sky, knowing he was meant for her.

Thirty-Two

THE NEXT MORNING, Kelynn woke up to find Indi and Blakely towering over her. Their arms were crossed, and she could tell they were holding back laughter especially with Blakely's chin quivering, clearly having a hard time keeping up the act.

"What's going on?" Kel asked, squinting, her eyes not ready for the sunshine pouring through the open tent door.

"You let an intruder into the girls' tent!" Indi said, her eyes motioning to Clay, who was asleep behind her in her sleeping bag.

"Guys, *he* is the one who came in here. I didn't ask him to!" she said, throwing her thumb up behind her in his direction.

"Well, you're the one who let him stay!" Blakely said.

"I'm sorry," Kelynn whispered. "Nothing happened," she said, pulling out one of her legs fully clothed in layers down to the socks.

"That doesn't prove anything!" Indi said, starting to laugh, her parental act not lasting long.

"We could have woken up to the two of you doing who knows what!" Blakely said, laughing alongside Indi.

"But you didn't, and *we* didn't!" Kelynn reiterated, motioning towards Clay. "Neither of us could sleep from the cold, so we just pooled our resources."

Indi raised an eyebrow, and Blakely smirked.

"Ew! Not like that!" Kelynn whisper-yelled. "Guys, go on. I don't want him to wake up the same way I did!" she said, smiling at her friends.

The two rolled their eyes and left the tent to start breakfast. The aroma of fresh coffee lured everyone else out of bed.

"Looks like the happy couples need extra sleep from all their hard work last night," Hastings said to the rest of the gang as they emerged from the tents.

"Hastings, not now," Blakely said, shooting him a look.

"What?" Hastings said, throwing up his arms.

"It's too early for your thoughts to be put into the universe," Blakely said, running a brush through her knotted hair before giving up and throwing on a beanie.

Breakfast consisted of eggs and bacon, and Indi poured coffee into thermoses. The winter air felt extra crisp this morning as stocking caps sat cozily on each of their heads.

"I have a proposal," Hastings announced.

They all turned to look at him, most of their eyes still heavy with sleep.

"We should go on a scavenger hunt. We split into teams, make a list of stuff to find in the woods, and whoever gets back here first with everything on the list wins."

"That actually sounds kind of fun," Kelynn said as she sipped her black coffee.

"There's a twist," Hastings said. "Every time you find one of the things on your list, everyone on your team has to drink. It makes it more challenging," he said with a smirk of pride across his square jaw.

Preston laughed. "Sure, this *does* sound fun. I'm down."

The rest of them looked at each other, nodding in agreement.

"Alright. Let's come up with a list," Clay said, rubbing his hands together and smiling at Hastings with a "game on" look in his eye.

Thirty-Three

THEY PLAYED ROCK, paper, scissors, breaking them up into two groups. Team One consisted of Blakely, Indi, Clay, and Hastings. That left team two with Gunner, Kelynn, Preston, and Lliam.

Clay fist bumped Kelynn right before Hastings yelled, "And, go!" as they took off in opposite directions with their teams into the woods.

Team two passed through several tree canopies, almost shivering in unison.

"Does everyone have a beer?" Lliam asked.

Each person responded with some form of yes, signifying they were ready to play. Clay took hold of team one's list, skimming it to calculate how far they actually had to go to find the things they needed to win.

"We need toilet paper from the bathrooms," Gunner said to his team, pointing in the direction of the camp's restrooms.

"Let's go!" Kelynn yelled, her competitiveness surfacing. She loved games, especially ones where someone had to lose. She felt the adrenaline pumping through her blood and broke out into a jog.

"We might as well stay warm while we play," she said, running through the trail, her inner compass telling her where to turn. She was too excited to think about being separated from Clay and the fact that he hadn't shared how he felt about being her catalyst.

Lliam caught up with Kel, leaving Preston—who was dragging her feet—behind with Gunner. The rest of the team waited while Kel ran inside as fast as she could to snag a piece of toilet paper. She came out with an entire roll.

"Got it! Everyone, drink!" she said, feeling a rush as she popped the cap off her beer and took a long swig.

"Geez, Kel! Take small sips, or you know you won't be able to make it to the end," Preston said laughing as she took an even longer drink from her own bottle.

Kel looked at the rest of the team and shrugged. "Okay, Gunner. What's next?"

"We need a leaf that has clearly been chewed on by a caterpillar."

"What the hell?" Lliam asked. The four of them shuffled through the leaves at their feet until Gunner found a yellow leaf with little circular bites taken out of it.

"Guys, look!" Gunner shouted, spotting a squirrel. "We need a picture of a squirrel. Who has their phone?" he asked. Preston snapped the picture right before the little guy ran off deeper into the woods.

"Did you get it?" Kel yelled.

"Yeah," Preston said at a normal decibel. "But I might be deaf now," she said, covering her ears. "Can everyone drink except Kel?" she asked, rolling her eyes but smiling at the same time.

"We gotta play by the rules," Gunner said, smiling at Kel. "Just take a baby sip, okay?"

Kel nodded, eyeing them mischievously, but obeyed Gunner's request and tipped the bottle back slightly, taking in a small taste. They moved further through the trail looking for their next item, an empty can or bottle of some sort that couldn't be the brand of beer they brought. This had to be Indi's contribution to the list. She was all about preserving Mother Nature, or what was left of her. Gunner hung back to make sure Kelynn didn't lag behind since she was practically sporting a name tag that read "Lightweight."

"Are you alright?" Gunner asked, trying to match the speed of her steps.

"Yeah, I'm great," she said, holding a thumbs up and winking. "Ya know, we should probably get to know each other better. You're my boyfriend's best friend," she said, slightly slurring her words.

"That's true, and I'm dating *your* best friend," he said, trying to hold back his laughter. Kelynn tripped over a tree root, and he instinctively grabbed her elbow. "You got it?" he asked, lifting her back up.

"Yeah, did you see that step? It came out of nowhere. I thought dirt paths were supposed to be stepless."

"Right. We've got to catch back up with the group," Gunner said, looking ahead to see them all stopped and looking back at them.

"It'll be a little bit, guys," Gunner yelled, motioning them forward.

"You know, I don't even know your last name," Kelynn said, holding onto his arm.

"Here. Why don't we lock arms? If you trip, I'll automatically catch you," he said, intertwining his arm around hers. "And it's Chapman," he added.

"Chapman," she repeated. "Sounds very formal. Can I call you Chappy? I like that better."

"Sure," Gunner said, smiling as the two weaved in and out, dodging holes and stepping over roots.

They finally made it back to the group to find Preston and Lliam making out behind a tree and giggling.

"Uh, guys. We made it," Gunner said, clearing his throat.

"We were just passing the time," Lliam said, taking Preston's hand and walking back to the trail.

"Looks like we only need one more item," Gunner said, looking over the list for what felt like the millionth time.

"What is it?" Preston asked, wiping her lips.

"It might be hard to find," he said with hesitation.

"We have to snap a picture of a woodpecker, owl, or bear."

"That's the most random combination of animals," Kelynn said, looking up towards the sky, hoping to see an owl sitting on a nearby branch.

"We also have to be super quiet to find any of those," Lliam said, eyeing Kelynn.

"Why are you looking at me?" Kelynn asked, her volume causing a flock of birds to take off from a tree above.

Lliam pressed his lips together in frustration as Kel proved his point without even trying.

"Okay. Let's head back the way we came. If we see one, we're more likely to beat the other team back to the campsite," Gunner said, already walking in that direction.

"Shhh!" Lliam put his finger to his lips in an effort to silence the group. "Do you hear that?" he whispered.

"Woodpecker," Gunner said, cocking his head to the left, where the noise came from.

The guys climbed into the woods off the path while the girls hung back, popping two more beers. Kelynn was paying more attention to the guys than to Preston, as she watched their heads turn towards the sky in search of the bird.

"It's up there!" Lliam said, craning his neck upward as they stood directly under the tree where the woodpecker tapped repeatedly.

"Give me your phone," Gunner said.

"I don't have mine," Lliam said.

"Well, shit, I don't have mine either."

"Girls!" Lliam tried to whisper-yell through the trees. He could see them laughing and drinking. He waved his arms around, but no luck.

Gunner made a bird call, which somehow caught their attention.

"We need a phone," Gunner mouthed the words, holding his hand up to his ear with his thumb pointing towards the back of his head and his pinky outstretched next to his mouth.

Preston squinted her eyes, trying to make out what Gunner was saying. "They need a phone. Oh my gosh. They're so dumb," Preston said, searching her backpack for hers.

"I've got mine, too," Kelynn said, reaching into her fanny pack. She waded through the woods, trying to tiptoe on the crunchy leaves.

"You got it," Gunner whispered. "Nice and slow," he said, putting up both of his hands.

Kelynn stretched out her arm, but she failed to see the stick directly in front of her left foot. She tripped, falling into Gunner, who successfully caught her but not without a tiny yelp escaping Kel's throat.

"Shit!" she whispered. "I'm sorry."

"It's okay," Gunner said, checking Kelynn's ankle.

"Look, guys! It's still there," Lliam said, craning his neck again at the woodpecker, who was no longer pecking, but still locked onto the cedar's trunk.

Gunner held up the phone and snapped a picture just before it took off.

"Nice timing," Kel said, smiling at the two guys she now considered friends.

"Okay. Let's hurry back!" Lliam said, using his full voice so Preston could hear him, too.

"Onward!" Kelynn yelled, her beer sloshing in one hand while she held the other out for balance, jumping over tree stumps and running through the trail back to the camp.

"I think I hear someone," Lliam said, quieting his steps.

"That's them!" Preston yelled. "Haul ass!" she said, breaking out into a sprint, hoping to make it back to the firepit before the other team.

Led by Kel, they rushed through the trees into the clearing. They could see the tents, the firepit scent filling their nostrils.

Just as they made a dash for it, Clay jumped out from behind Indi, making one last sprint for the fire. Kelynn's momentum was more powerful than she realized as she crashed into Clay, beer spewing everywhere. The teams broke out in laughter as Kel and Clay sat on the ground, trying to make sense of what happened.

"So, who got here first?" Hastings asked, drinking his unspilled Corona.

"It looked like a *smack*-dab tie to me," Gunner said, laughing.

"Let's see who got the most stuff," Indi said, pulling items out of her pack.

The teams counted everything, coming up even. Team one was ruled the winner, though, since Gunner's picture of the woodpecker looked more like a smudgy shadow on a tree than a bird.

"Man, I thought we had 'em," Kelynn said. "Technically, it was a tie."

"You're so competitive," Gunner extended his closed hand for a fist bump.

"At times," Kel said, accepting the invite, their knuckles colliding. "Is anyone sober?" she asked, loud enough for the whole group to hear her.

"I am," Clay said.

"Yeah, me, too," Gunner agreed.

"Who's ready to head back?" Kelynn asked, tired of her toes feeling numb and finding leaves in her hair.

"I can drive, too," Blakely shouted as she threw her duffel onto her back.

"Perfect," Clay said. "Why don't we head back and stop by Clunkerton's before going home?"

Everyone nodded in agreement, ready for civilization and a proper warm meal.

On the way home, Kel rode shotgun with Clay driving and Hastings in the backseat, who was shockingly silent most of the drive. They listened to music, the heat blasting.

As Kelynn reached for Clay's free hand, she said, "I had a good time. Thanks for inviting me."

"Anytime," he said. "Sorry we weren't on the same team."

"I actually had a lot of fun with Gunner."

"Really? He can be pretty quiet," Clay said.

"Well, the beers got me talking which got him talking."

"Good," he said, laughing.

Kelynn peeked into the side view mirror to see Hastings sleeping in the backseat.

"Is he out?" Clay asked.

"Cold," Kel said.

"Perfect. I want to talk more about this catalyst theory."

Kelynn felt butterflies shoot up in her stomach. "It's not a theory, Clay. I know it. I think that's why you're the only person who's able to see my thoughts in the opal."

"How do you know I'm the only one who can do that?"

"I tested it on some other people," Kelynn said.

"Hold up. You told someone else? Did they think you were insane?"

"Maybe a little, but they held my necklace, Clay, and nothing happened."

"Now that I think about it, Gunner has held it, too. He took it from me when I was holding it one time, and he wasn't fazed at all, but he doesn't know why I was holding it. But who did *you* tell?" he asked.

"Blakely and Preston. Oh, and Indi too, but I thought maybe it was just girls who couldn't see them, so I had one of my male coworkers hold it. I didn't tell him about the visions. I just acted like I had my hands full and needed help with something."

"That's so wild," he said, rubbing his chin. "So, how exactly am I your catalyst? I need to know more."

"I looked it up and it's really sciency," she said, realizing the beer hadn't quite worked its way out of her system.

Clay chuckled. "Okay. I can't wait for this super-scientific definition."

"I'll try my best. Okay, a catalyst is kind of like a liquid or some substance that creates a chemical reaction, but it isn't permanently affected by that reaction," she said, pausing before continuing. "I didn't realize that a human could take the place of this *substance*."

"So, if I'm the substance in this scenario, I make the chemical reaction happen, which, in our case, is the elimination of your blackouts?"

"Yes, but not just the elimination. You also uncomplicate things in my head, making my dreams clearer and morphing them into a bigger and better picture than they ever were on my own. You push me forward to where I want to be."

"But part of that definition isn't true for us," Clay said.

"What do you mean?" Kel asked, playing with her hands, his words making her uneasy.

"In your definition, the substance doesn't undergo change, but I have. I feel the same way. I've never suffered from blackouts, but when I'm with you I'm a better me, a more confident me. It's like I feel you believing in me without you saying a word."

"But I *need* you for me to be able to feel this way. You don't need me," she said. "I didn't even know this Kel existed, a more confident and steady Kel."

"You mean drunk Kel?" he asked, grabbing her hand and laughing.

"No, I knew *that* Kel existed a long time ago. She's a hell of a good time. But really, I always thought I'd have to choose between a career and a relationship, but I feel like with you, they go hand in hand. When I'm with you, I'm able to make progress," she said, squeezing his hand. Kelynn thought about how every word she'd said to him felt not only true, but somehow factual. Clay *was* her catalyst. She needed him for her life to react, to grow, to spark passion. While that gave her a sense of peace, feeling as though they were meant to cross paths, she couldn't fully accept the thought of being dependent on a man, even if that man was Clay. The air suddenly felt thicker in the car, causing Kelynn's stomach to drop and her mind to rebel against her own theory.

Clay

I PULLED UP to Clunkerton's ready to be around other people. Being in the woods was a solid detox, but after a while, I longed to be back in the city, where the busyness could distract me from the fact that I was falling in love. I've known for some time now that's what was happening between me and Sanders, but when she told me I was her catalyst, it felt like I hit the ground face first. My entire being took a deep dive into the pit of . . . I can't believe I'm actually thinking this word, but love. This—oh man—*this* was an intense love, with Sanders as my gravity, and I, her catalyst. I opened the door as our whole camping crew walked in. The bar was buzzing tonight, and thankfully a table was open. We were all ready for hot food and cold drinks.

"Hey, Kel!"

"Hey, Ferdinand." Sanders waved her arm as she peeled off her down puffer coat.

I couldn't blame him for noticing her. Her presence captured the entire room. Her smile invited you in, her teeth beaming with confidence. The blonde tips of her hair swaying back and forth on her back was enough to distract anyone. She turned to look at me, but I felt like she was moving in slow motion. Her eyelashes bounced with each blink of those deep-green eyes. She winked at me before grabbing a seat in a booth, where she ended up sandwiched between Hastings and me.

"So, did you like the trip?" Hastings asked.

"Yes," I overheard her say. "It was actually a pretty good time . . . even with you there." Hastings rolled his eyes and pulled out his phone. "In all seriousness, I feel like I got to see some of the real you while we were out in the woods and that Hastings is more than tolerable," she said.

He nodded, smiling at her. I was relieved they were somewhat getting along.

"You're my boyfriend's friend, and if he sees something in you, then I want to see that in you, too."

"Alright, alright," Hastings said, seeming uncomfortable with Sanders's sincerity. "Let's work on that with some more beer," he said, waving Ferdinand over to our table. "A round of Heinekens, good sir," Hastings said, sounding obnoxious as he yelled over the other loud tables. "In honor of all of our new friendships!" he finished, practically sticking out his tongue.

I wrapped my arm around Sanders, pulling her closer to me. Someone brought up college, distracting me from Hastings.

"Oh my gosh! Kelynn, do you remember that one girl who somehow got into your dorm room and slept in your bed?" Blakely asked.

"Yes!" Sanders yelled. "That was so insane. Like, how?"

They burst out laughing. Everyone appeared to be at ease now that they were back home. It was official. My girlfriend was becoming part of the group. At that moment, the door opened and a gust of wind grabbed my attention as I turned my head in response to the cool air. I needed a minute to wrap my head around it all.

"I'll be right back," I said, tapping Sanders's back and squeezing my way out of the tight booth.

Thirty-Four

KELYNN WATCHED HIM walk outside, a little confused.

"Anyone want to sing karaoke?" she asked, hoping to turn her attention back to the fun they'd been having moments before.

Indi followed Kel to the secret room except there wasn't karaoke. Instead, a DJ was set up in place of the usual handheld microphone lying on the stage. Kel headed to the dance floor, the beer begging her body to move. Indi followed suit as they moved deeper into the thick of the crowd. The room smelled of sweat and booze. They made it close to the middle where no one cared about anyone watching. Kelynn was getting warm dancing in her beanie and flannel. Without missing a beat, she unbuttoned her shirt, leaving only a crop top underneath. She tied it around her waist and shimmied her hands around the curves of her body.

"Hey! There you guys are!" Indi yelled as Hastings and the rest of the group walked into the bookshelf passageway.

Kel moved her hips left and right, her body naturally gliding to every rhythm the DJ played. Suddenly, a hand was around her waist, and a sturdy body was behind her, moving her body along his. She quickly turned around to see Hastings lewdly smiling down at her.

"Hastings, what the hell?!" Kelynn yelled.

"What? I thought we were having fun?" he defended.

"No! How many times do I have to tell you to back off? I'm with Clay!"

"Dude, you're so dumb! Why do you even care about him? Don't you know your entire relationship is based on a bet?" Hastings yelled over the music.

"What?" Kelynn shouted as she tried to put space between them, her ears ringing as Hastings's words came out in slow motion.

"Back when you and I went out, he bet me he could actually do better than me and get you on a second date," Hastings responded, smiling, seemingly finding enjoyment in sharing the dreadful news.

"Screw you!" Kelynn yelled back, shoving him as hard as she could, but he merely took a slight step backwards to regain his balance.

She stormed out of the crowd, confused by Hastings's comment.

Why would Clay make a bet about me? she wondered, feeling shaky, hoping Hastings was lying, but the look in his eyes revealed at least a small amount of truth.

Kelynn, dripping in sweat, reached for the door, the backside of the bookshelf. She shoved her way through and glanced at the booth, hoping Clay wasn't there. All she wanted was air, but Hastings's words stole every ounce of oxygen she had in her lungs.

Clay.

I SAW SANDERS out of the corner of my eye, her face red with tears falling down her cheeks.

"Sanders?" I yelled from the side of the building. "What's going on?"

She turned to face me.

"Explain it to me!" she said through quivering breaths. "Explain how our whole relationship was a bet!"

"Whoa, what?" I asked, looking at her anger-stricken face. "Sanders," I said, slowly walking towards her, afraid if I moved too fast she might run.

"Is it true?" she asked, looking at her feet, shivering.

"No, our relationship is based on real, genuine feelings. What changed since I walked outside?"

"Hastings made a move on me, and I yelled at him. He told me I shouldn't even care about you because our entire relationship was based on a bet."

"Damn it, Hastings. Why does he always have to get in the middle of stuff?" I asked aloud, putting two-and-two together. "When you went out with Hastings, Lliam asked me to break up the date because he thought Hastings was lying and that he was actually taking out Preston," I started to explain. "Lliam had me spy on you guys to make sure it wasn't her. Hastings found out and said I owed him. So he bet me $100 I couldn't make it to a second date with you."

"So, you saw me there?" Sanders asked, turning to me, making my stomach feel like a weight had just been thrown into it.

"Yes."

"Wait. I think I remember seeing you. You were standing outside the restaurant, walking back and forth on the sidewalk."

"I didn't know if you saw me," I said. "That's why I never mentioned it. I felt the connection between us that night, even from a distance, but you were with my friend and I had no idea who you were."

"I felt something, too. Why didn't you tell me once we started dating?"

"I don't know. I didn't think it was important. Our relationship was not based on a bet. I would've asked you out regardless. I felt something real with you outside of anything between Hastings and me."

She sighed, looking up at the sky, her tears practically freezing solid on her face.

"Sanders. Look at me," I said.

She shook her head, leaning against the side of the building, her breath uneven.

"Please," I said, pleading with her.

She turned only her head towards me, the rest of her body frozen against the brick wall.

"Sanders, none of that stuff matters. I didn't lie to you or leave that information out on purpose. I was excited to get to know you, no matter where I first saw you or who you dated first. Sanders," I caught my own breath, "I love you."

For a minute, I couldn't breathe. It was as if time had stopped. I couldn't see anything but her. She looked back at me, her eyes red and swollen from crying, but she didn't say a word. A new flow of tears masked her face with a fresh stream. She looked away from me and back at the sky for a minute before picking herself up from the wall and walking towards me.

"I can't trust you," was all she said as she walked past me back to the bar, leaving me alone in the dark, my heart feeling as though it would never beat a steady rhythm again—empty like the beer cans scattered around my feet.

Thirty-Five

KELYNN COULD FEEL the engine of the plane rumbling, vibrating underneath the aisle beneath her feet as she made her way to her seat. The passengers along either side seemed uninterested in the upcoming flight. Kelynn couldn't be more excited about her destination. She was finally taking control of her life without relying on anyone. She needed to make a future for herself, so she reached out to Andy to find an executive who she could speak with about a multimedia coordinator opening. It was official—Kelynn was headed to New York to interview for a company she'd admired from afar, The Vine. It was a media distribution company dealing with record labels, film companies, and practically every other entertainment asset that piqued Kel's interest. She squeezed her arms closer to her chest, trying to maneuver her luggage down the line without bumping into the other passengers whose shoulders brushed against her as she walked past.

"Seat 42E," she said quietly to herself, scanning the aisles for her number. Kelynn kept walking farther back, slight claustrophobia kicking in.

"Ah, finally," she said, smiling at an empty row and taking the window seat.

She used the last few minutes to scroll through Instagram before the flight attendant came on the loudspeaker. Switching to airplane mode, she put her earbuds in and zoned out to her favorite travel playlist as they ascended. She stared at the clouds mere inches from her nose while she thought about the bigger meaning of life. She tried to make shapes out of the puffs of clouds they were flying in line with, but they looked more like cotton candy than anything else. When at eye level, the magic of the clouds was almost ruined like going to Disneyworld and meeting Mickey Mouse only to see human eyes inside the mesh parts of the costume. Kelynn pondered this for a while, realizing that's how she felt about Clay. She thought he was this amazing character, but when she saw the person underneath, that person was a complete liar. Her anger had dwindled to a burning candle, rather than a raging wildfire, but she was left with a deep cut that ran from the pit of her stomach all the way up through the center of her heart.

Surprisingly, being away from Clay for a couple of weeks hadn't caused any blackouts. Maybe he wasn't her catalyst after all, or maybe she felt so numb that no amount of thoughts could penetrate the barrier of wounds and scars surrounding every lobe of her brain. "Space Oddity" began to play in her earbuds, a song she and Clay used to listen to while driving around Chapel Hill. She sat there in the pain for a few minutes, her instincts telling her to press skip, but she couldn't bring herself to rush past the song. Kel touched her lips, transported to a time when Clay wrapped his arms around her at a bar, then to his couch, where he made her feel safe and scared at the same time, then to dinner, then to the tent on their camping trip. She relived every kiss while the song played, letting herself feel what she'd been blocking. Her heart was slowly cracking open. A tear slipped out of the corner of her eye, making its way down her cheek before she wiped it away. She needed to feel this, just for a moment, the song bringing it all back. She loved Clay. Why didn't she say it back to him? She asked herself that question over and over, but she knew what she said in that moment was just as true as her love for him. There were pieces of him she couldn't trust. She laid her head back against the seat, turned up the volume on her phone as high as it would go, and closed her eyes.

"Attention." Kelynn jolted awake, confused about where she was before realizing she was still on the plane taking her to New York. Anxious butterflies awoke in her stomach. "We are preparing for landing. Please buckle your seatbelts. Thanks for a smooth flight," the pilot said over the intercom.

She looked out the window, finally able to see land again—land completely covered by tall buildings and hundreds of cars. The bustling below excited her, filling her head with all the possibilities of becoming a part of this city. Kelynn laid her head back against the chair as the plane made a bumpy landing.

Thirty-Six

"THANK YOU," KELYNN said to the taxi driver as he let her out at her hotel. He didn't respond but got out and helped her with her bags before speeding off into the ever-present city traffic.

Kelynn walked up the stairs of the hotel entrance pulling her luggage behind her, ready to settle in for the next few days. She headed for the elevators after receiving her room key and pressed the button for the twenty-second floor. She couldn't wait to see the view. Kel felt like her heart was soaring with each floor as the elevator beeped its way up. She opened the door to her room, feeling exhausted from the variety of emotions bouncing around in her head. As she began to unpack and rearrange the contents of her suitcase before lying on the bed for a nice nap, she mentally sank back into numbness.

Hey, did you make it yet? her text from Andy read.

Yes, I'm so exhausted. Taking a nap. Want to grab dinner? Kelynn replied.

I wish I could, but I'm going out with a few people from the crew tonight. Grab coffee tomorrow? Andy texted back.

Sounds perfect, Kelynn answered, relieved that Andy wasn't available. She needed to rest and prep for her interview. She was hoping to venture to a few other businesses to hand out her résumé while she was in town, maybe with a recommendation from Andy, but she needed to map out where she was going and arrange it around her interview. She set her phone on the bedside table and climbed into the hotel bed that felt like a cloud. She took a deep breath, trying to release the thoughts that came to her in the clouds a few hours prior. Kel imagined a different thought flying out with each exhale. It didn't take long for her to fall into a deep sleep, finding comfort in a new place, far away from the pain, while also far away from part of her heart—a big part of her heart, she was starting to realize.

Kelynn woke up the next morning feeling energized. Even with a nap, she slept well after a solo dinner. Her first stop was the interview with The Vine. She thought this would be her best shot to transition from one multimedia company to another. Kelynn went with a black skirt, small heels that laced up her legs, and a tucked-in black sweater. The less color, the better, in her opinion. She wanted to make more of an impression than her clothes. Her resumé and portfolio rested under one arm, a water bottle in the other. The subway routes were so confusing, but Kel came prepared. She mapped it out the week prior the best she could down to the minute, so she would be early. She felt like all of her thoughts were organized perfectly until her phone rang with the name Hastings popping up on the screen.

"Hello?" Kelynn answered cautiously.

The other line was awkwardly silent for a moment until Hastings finally responded with, "Hey, we need to talk."

"Listen, I don't have a lot of time. I have a big day ahead of me."

"I need you to know what happened with Clay after the night we went out," he insisted.

"Okay," she said, suddenly unable to think of another excuse.

"He didn't take the money. Even though he won the bet, he didn't care about it. He only cared about you."

Kelynn was silent.

"He loves you. I've never seen him like this. The bet wasn't serious. It wasn't even about you, really," Hastings said. "He won't talk to me right now, and I can't lose him. He's like a brother. Would you just think about talking to him?" Hastings continued to talk, trying to convince her to his version of that night.

"Thank you," Kelynn interrupted, "for calling and telling me this, but I really have to go now."

The subway train was crowded with people heading to work, people who looked like they were along for the ride, tourists with cameras slung around their necks, and everyone in between. She tried to picture herself as one of the locals sitting and reading on their commute to work, getting lost in a book before reality hit. A noise coming from someone's phone brought her back to the present just in time for her to get off at the next stop. Her heart raced as she held her portfolio tightly under her arm.

The train came to a halt as Kelynn took a deep breath repeatedly reminding herself that she was brilliant, that she exuded confidence, and that, ultimately, she could do this. She stepped off the subway and made her way out of the underground world and into the sunshine of the day.

Walking down the crowded street made her feel alive, like she was part of the buzzing community of people making big things happen in almost every industry imaginable. The doors to the office where her interview was about to happen were solid glass and heavy. Kel would have to increase her weightlifting to at least twenty pounds per arm if she wanted to open those doors every day without throwing her back out. She walked up to the receptionist who seemed relaxed, wearing a concert T-shirt and black jeans. Suddenly, Kelynn felt incredibly overdressed.

Better to be overdressed than under, she told herself trying to calm her nerves.

"Hi. Are you here for an interview?" the receptionist asked, doing a once-over of Kelynn's getup.

"Yes, with Ms. Wittacker," Kelynn answered, trying to appear confident.

"She'll be down in just a minute. Feel free to help yourself to our assortment of bagels and fruits while you wait," the receptionist motioned to a glass table that looked heavier than the doors, covered with a wide variety of donuts, bagels, and muffins, and to top it all off, a basket brimming with a plethora of fruits.

"Great, thanks." Kelynn's stomach growled just looking at it, but she was sure the tiniest piece of food would get stuck in her teeth, so she sat in the chair farthest away from the elegant breakfast buffet.

"Ms. Sanders," a voice said, coming from the set of glass doors that separated the reception area from the rest of the office.

Clay.

"INDI, YOU HAVE to tell me where she is," I said. By the look on her face, I was coming off a little too intense. I knew my hair looked like it hadn't been washed, let alone combed in a week since I always ran my hands through my hair when I was stressed. It was most likely sticking straight up—adding to my desperate, certifiable appearance with part of my button-down shirt hanging outside of my pants, untucked, and my beard needed a trim, but I didn't care. I needed answers.

"That beard must be a record. Are you in some sort of . . . *bet*?" Her words pricked me, and I assumed so on purpose.

"I know you're protecting her and you think I'm this horrible person, but I'm scared for her."

"Why?" Indi rolled her eyes at me.

"What about her blackouts? What if she passes out somewhere and none of us can find her?"

"She has been doing really well with that. Clay, she doesn't need you anymore."

"I don't buy it. I don't care if she needs me. I need her. I lo—" I stopped talking when Indi turned towards me, looking enraged, her eyebrows raised.

"Don't say it, Clayton. You've lied to her more than once. I would have run away a lot sooner than she did. You're lucky she stuck around this long."

"Indi, please. Put yourself in my shoes. Imagine Gunner leaving you, not responding to you, not giving you a chance to explain anything." Finally, I felt like I had gotten to her.

"She's not here," Indi said, her voice the slightest bit softer.

"Indi, I'm begging you," I said, touching her arm. She didn't shove me away but instead turned towards me. I think she could finally see the weight of my despair.

"She's in New York," she said.

"New York?!" I repeated in disbelief. "Where in New York?"

"She's staying in Times Square at a Hilton."

"That's all I needed. Thank you," I said, squeezing her arm gently.

"Good luck, Clay," Indi said, her face blank as she watched me leave her house.

My feet were moving faster than I thought possible—dodging a suitcase here, sliding past a group of people there, and squeezing in and out of every crowded section of the airport to make it to my gate. Sweat poured down my face. The back of my shirt stuck to me under my backpack. I didn't care. I would shower when I got there. I just had to *get* there. I sprinted up to the gate, stopping as the last person boarded, my broken breaths threatening to burst my lungs. The attendant looked at me like I was a normal customer, probably dealing with people like me daily.

"Hello, sir. You're just in time for our last flight to New York."

I nodded, unable to make a sound that wasn't laced with gusts of air as she scanned my ticket. I was on my way, one slowed step after another, making my way towards Sanders.

Thirty-Seven

"I'M SURE IT went better than you think, Kel," Andy said, sipping her cappuccino.

"She was just so intimidating. I feel like I stumbled all over myself. I couldn't get out of my own head enough to clearly talk about my own head."

Andy laughed while crossing her legs. "That's how I usually feel, too, but I think they like it when you're nervous. It shows that you actually care."

"I guess," Kel said, scanning the pretentious café menu. "How long did it take you to get used to this type of coffee?" she asked, attempting to decipher the flowery language.

"Once I find a favorite, I stick with it. I stopped trying to blindly guess from that bullshit menu months ago."

"They even have Kopi Luwak!" Kelynn said.

"Oh my gosh! You promised me a cup, remember?" Andy asked, laughing.

"Holy crap! It's $35 for a six ounces!"

"Legit, holy crap," Andy said, making them both laugh.

"I've missed you," Kel said, taking her menu to the register to finally place an order.

She walked back to the table carrying a simple latte. Andy smiled at the predictability of her friend.

"How have things been since you moved here?" Kelynn asked, her cup meeting her lips.

"Things have been hard, like *really* hard. It's a great job, and I'm learning every day, but I'm worn out constantly. My body is trying to adjust to all the changes, and it's not as fast as my mind."

"Yeah, I get that. You feel the physical exhaustion earlier in the day, but your mind keeps grinding, and then you dream about it all at night when you're supposed to relax. At least that's how I've been functioning."

"Yes!" Andy said. "I had a dream the other night I was on a shoot and couldn't move my arms. The director, production manager, and stagehands were all yelling at me to go get stuff. I would run and come back empty-handed! Anything I tried to grab would fall straight to the ground. It was the weirdest sensation," Andy said in one breath.

Kel shook her head. "How's the subway?"

"That's the easiest thing to conquer here," Andy said. "It took me about two weeks to understand how it worked. Knowing which cardinal direction you're traveling helps immensely. I don't travel too far from where I work and live, unless it's to explore, so I feel pretty solid about that," she said. "Where are we going today? I can't remember."

"Viacom, Sony Music, several other record labels, a couple film companies . . ."

Kelynn stopped going through her list as she watched Andy's disoriented expression. "Um, Kel, do you have 'Share My Location' enabled for Clay on your phone?"

"Oh yeah. We set that up as a joke on the camping trip. Why?"

"Because it looks like someone may have followed you here," she said, her eyes glued to the window, recognizing Clay from his social media.

Kelynn looked over her shoulder and saw Clay pacing directly outside the coffee shop.

"How the hell . . ." Kelynn slowly sputtered, suddenly on her feet and moving towards the door. She didn't feel like she was in control of her body, convinced her eyes were lying to her.

She threw open the door, a mixture of anger and pain stinging the back of her eyes and surfacing at the back of her throat. Before she could open her mouth, he turned to face her. His expression was soft, like a hurt puppy. To Kelynn's surprise, when he looked into her eyes, some of her anger subsided.

"Sanders, don't walk away from me," Clay said, bridging the gap between them. "I didn't come here to ruin your trip or drag you back home. If this is what you want, that's fine, but I couldn't stay in Chapel Hill knowing that if someone offered you something worthwhile, you might leave without ever hearing me out."

Kelynn stood there for a minute, still in disbelief that he was *here*. Clay was in New York, standing on the same street as her, staring into her eyes, the magnetic wave igniting now stronger than ever.

"You don't have to explain," Kelynn said, trying to sound calm.

"No, you don't understand . . ."

Kelynn cut him off. "Hastings called me. He told me everything."

"What? When? Since when do you trust his word over mine?" Clay asked, some of Kel's anger transferring to him.

"This morning, he called before my first interview. I didn't want to believe him, but from the things he was saying about you, I knew he wasn't lying. He made me promise not to tell anyone."

"What did he say?" Clay asked, but it sounded almost like begging.

"Why don't we go inside and talk over coffee. Mine's currently getting cold," she said, turning her back and heading inside. Clay lingered outside for a minute longer before joining her, looking speechless as he rubbed his beard in confusion.

Clay.

"SO, HASTINGS CALLED you out of the blue?" I asked while taking the seat across from Sanders as Andy eyed me from a table behind her.

"Yeah, it was pretty bad timing. He called right before I had to leave for my interview. He said he knew I wasn't speaking to you, and he didn't want to lose you as a friend," she said, her eyes glued to mine. "He explained the bet to me, how it was his idea. He told me that you refused the money after our second date, and how he was more mad that you agreed to ruin his date than anything." She smirked.

"I was protecting another friend," I said, trying to defend myself.

"I know that now, too. He said you talked to him that night after I left Clunkerton's. He described how angry you were at yourself and at him," she said, looking down, thumbing the rim of her coffee mug. "I still need to hear a couple things directly from you, though—like how we never met before this when Lliam and Preston have been a thing for years."

"Sanders, what Hastings said is true. I'm in love with you. I would've never made that bet had I known it was you it'd affect. I shouldn't have done it no matter who it was about, but I especially hate myself for doing it to you."

Sanders studied me. I felt like every word I said was under evaluation. I was more nervous now than in my interview with Chill Axel.

"And I think you'll agree with me on this, but like you, I tried to stay as far away from the Lliam and Preston drama as I could. This instance aside, of course. But I'm honestly glad I got involved this one time because it led me to you." I sat in silence, rubbing my beard, waiting for her to respond, hoping she believed the truths that escaped my lips.

"I know I've lied to you in the past—" I started to say, but she reached her hand out for mine, causing me to stop.

"Thank you. That's all I needed," she said, wiping a tear that had escaped and was making headway down her cheek. "I made a mistake, too—coming here. I should've stayed. I should've heard you out. You know my past and how people have lied to me and even left me for the sheer possibility of money. I couldn't handle it from you, too."

I moved to the chair beside her. I held her hands, touching each tiny finger that fit so perfectly next to each of mine. She calmed down, her breathing finding a normal rhythm again, and a small smile started to form.

"Do you want to explore the city with me?" she asked.

"Yes, one hundred times, yes. But what about Andy?"

"I'll talk to her."

"Okay. I'll be outside. Take your time. Tell Andy I said hi. From the looks of it, she could kill me any second." I nodded in Andy's direction before taking my coffee and heading out into the chilly spring day New York was offering.

Who knew today would turn out so much better than I'd thought? I was ready to get on bended knee to explain why my life was pointless without Sanders in it. For once, I actually owed Hastings. The door opened with Sanders behind it. She was holding a bag of bagels and two coffees.

"Give me one minute. I saw someone on the way here. He reminds me of Roger," She walked to the end of the street to a corner where a man sat in a lump covered in tattered blankets. I watched as she handed him the food and coffee. He shook her hand, and with that, she started walking back towards me.

"You ready?" Sanders asked. I was more sure of my answer than anything else in the world.

Thirty-Eight

KELYNN WALKED SLOWLY out of the Viacom office, scanning the street before locking eyes with Clay, who was waiting patiently a few sidewalk paces down.

"How'd it go?" he asked, pulling his denim jacket closer together as a breeze brushed past.

"They took my resumé, so that's better than most, I guess. They could have thrown it away as soon as I left, though."

"You did all you can do right now. You even applied online beforehand. Making a personal pitstop to show them how committed you are is rare. I'm sure they noticed that. Who knows? Maybe they have offices all over the country, too. Like with Chill Axel, they have small offices in most decent-sized cities."

"Yeah, you're pretty lucky with jobs in Chapel Hill," she said, letting out a sigh of frustration. "Wait! You just said Chill Axel. Did you take the job?"

"Yeah, I did. I accepted it the day after we got back from camping. Anytime we talked about it, I just felt your energy pushing me towards it."

"That's amazing!" she said, hugging him. "Well, between Radical and this trip, I've finally figured one thing out."

"Oh, yeah? What's that?" Clay asked.

"I know I want to work in entertainment. I want to focus my career on that; not singing, or writing books, or anything else you've seen. I think going for one dream will help me, and this one is a big one."

"That's great, Sanders. I'm here for it, for you."

"Thank you," she said, watching Clay's eyes reflect the city lights. "Do you have a place to stay tonight?"

"No, actually. I hadn't figured that part of my plan out, yet."

"You can stay with me," Kelynn said, turning the corner headed to their next résumé drop-off location.

"What?" Clay asked, trying to catch up to her.

"What? I don't want you to waste your money on a hotel room when you weren't even planning on spending money on a plane ticket. Plus, I already have one."

"You sure?" Clay asked, still a little shocked.

She turned to face him, stopping him in his tracks, and smiled without showing her teeth. "Yes, I'm sure," she said, looking deep into his eyes before planting her lips on his. Clay kissed her back, wrapping his arms around her. It was then she knew she had forgiven Clay. She loved him, even if she couldn't tell him yet. Her motto, "You can't force love," came to mind. It was true. From day one, when he was standing on the sidewalk in front of the Lantern, something that felt otherworldly just clicked. It had never been about forcing feelings but more so trying to stop them from growing out of her control.

Clay stopped to look at her. "I missed you, Sanders," he said, kissing her again.

"I missed you more," Kelynn said, grabbing his hand.

She led them down a few more blocks before leaving Clay outside once again. She stayed longer at this one, patiently waiting for the receptionist to hang up the phone and acknowledge her presence. It was finally Kelynn's turn, but when she handed in her resumé, the receptionist threw it in a pile of at least thirty others. Her heart sank as she turned to leave, trying to convince herself this trip wasn't a mistake.

"Okay. No more," Kelynn said, joining Clay outside.

"You sure?" Clay asked.

"Yeah, I'm exhausted, and I don't even know if I want to live in New York anymore."

"Why not?" Clay asked, puzzled.

"I think I'd be more successful in a smaller city—one that doesn't have five million people fighting over the same job," she said.

"You know what would cheer you up?"

"What?" she asked, her face not nearly as hopeful as Clay's.

"Let's go find Greenwich Village. You know, the setting of *Friends*?"

"That sounds amazing. Let's go!" she said, her entire mood instantly lifted.

Clay smiled as they fist bumped. "Come on. We should grab food around there, too."

"Welcome to my humble abode," Kelynn said, swinging the hotel room door open. They had finished dinner and were both worn out from traveling.

Clay laughed. "It's nice. How long have you lived here?"

"About six months," Kelynn said, playing along.

"Yeah? It's got a great view of the city."

"It can be pretty noisy, though," Kelynn said, taking Clay's baseball hat and turning it backwards before placing it on her own head.

"Oh, I bet," he said, wrapping his arms around her waist as they both looked out the window. "At least it blocks out noisy neighbors." Clay kissed her cheek and slowly moved down her neck, following the arc of it as she leaned her head back into him.

"I don't want to leave," Kel whispered, turning around to see his face.

"We don't have to yet," Clay said, holding her face in his hands as his lips met hers.

He walked her backwards until the backs of her legs hit the side of the bed. She sat down as Clay moved forward, all the while not letting his lips leave hers. They were weaving in and out, the heat building with each kiss. He kissed her neck, her shoulders, her ear, while running his hands through her hair. She started to pull her shirt up, but Clay stopped her halfway.

"What's wrong?" Kelynn asked, self-conscious.

"I don't want to push you," Clay said, his eyes glued to her exposed stomach.

"You're not," Kelynn said, pulling him back down into a kiss.

"I think we should wait," he said, stopping her again.

She looked at him, trying to force reason back into her brain. "You're probably right," Kelynn said, letting out a sigh.

"I just want this to be perfect. I want you to fully trust me before anything else happens."

"I'm getting there," Kelynn said, smiling, pulling him down again for one more kiss.

"Yeah, but you're not fully there," Clay said, smiling back at her, before pulling her shirt back down.

He got up and started to make a bed on the floor of the hotel room with an extra blanket and pillow from the closet.

"Clay, you don't have to do *that*," Kelynn said, sitting up on the bed.

"Yes, I do, Sanders," he said. "I do if we're not going to do that," he said, giving her a look that made her want him even more.

Kelynn blushed, taking a deep breath. "Well, can we at least stay up and talk for a bit?" she asked, not wanting to sleep.

"Yeah, I'd like that," Clay said, taking a seat on the ground.

Her voice got quiet, almost fragile. "Thank you for finding me."

"Of course."

"I don't just mean here in New York. You found the real me buried underneath all my thoughts, and . . . you brought me out of the dark."

Clay smiled up at her as he kissed her hand.

"Clay, will you do it again?" she asked, holding onto his hand a little longer before releasing it.

"Do what?" he asked.

"Hold my opal."

Clay got up from his makeshift bed and sat next to her. He touched just above her heart. Before he was fully ready, his surroundings changed. Her heart felt lighter as she looked at him after taking the opal back.

He explained to Kelynn what he saw, how he was sitting in a shared workspace, the exposed brick walls making him feel inspired for some reason.

"I opened a laptop to find an unread email from someone named James Bennet. The subject line read, *Article Submission: Trick Yourself into Therapy while Traveling*. I clicked it to see the body of the email, which so kindly relayed the message that my twenty-third submission was a winner. I was being published in *The New York Times*, or rather, *you* were."

She looked at him with a dopey smile. He kissed her forehead before returning to the floor to sleep.

"Goodnight, Sanders," he said, taking a deep breath from the rush of the opal's powers.

She let out a sigh, a shred of peace consuming her. "Goodnight, Fogerty."

Thirty-Nine

CLAY STOOD IN line for Starbucks at the John F. Kennedy Airport, thumbing through his emails. Kelynn figured he was trying to pass the time before the perfectly bitter aroma of coffee hit his taste buds. She knew exhaustion ruled over his body from traveling less than twenty-four hours ago.

"Uh, I'm getting a call, and it's from a New York number," Kelynn said, jolting Clay out of his sleepy state.

"Go answer it. I'll handle the coffee."

Kelynn smiled with excitement, biting her lip in expectation.

"Hello?" she answered, trying to sound as professional as she could with one word.

"Hi, is this Ms. Sanders?"

"Yes, it is," she said, holding her breath in anticipation.

"This is Jule Gen. I'm calling you because I came across your résumé and wanted to reach out to you with an opportunity. It's not in New York, but I think it fits your skill set." Kelynn listened intently as Jule explained a possible position. She hung up the phone, staring at the screen in disbelief.

"Who was it?" Clay asked from a distance as Kelynn walked back.

"It was someone from Viacom. Remember when we dropped my résumé off there?"

"Yeah, what'd she say? Are you moving to New York?"

"No, but she knows someone back in Raleigh who works for a media relations company. They mainly do marketing for other companies like Viacom—essentially entertainment agencies that need support for internal branding and with executing award shows and events! It's also an easy commute from Chapel Hill." She felt a wave of relief. She didn't travel all the way to New York for nothing. She thought she'd have to choose between Clay and a career. Her heart had already chosen Clay, but she didn't realize she could have both, melding all of her loves together. She knew there had been a plan for her all along, even though it looked different than she'd imagined. Suddenly, Chapel Hill had a ring to it, it hadn't before. Who knew the little town had so much to offer.

"Sanders, that's amazing!" Clay put down the coffee, picked up Kelynn, and spun her around.

He came to a stop and kissed her. "I'm so proud of you."

Kelynn looked around, still giggling. "Clay, people are starting to stare."

"I don't care, Sanders. Not one bit."

As he put her down, she knew she had to tell him she loved him, that she still believed he was her catalyst, and that without him, none of this would have happened.

"Hey, Clay," she said before she could think twice.

He turned to face her while he picked up their coffees.

"Yeah?"

"I love you," she said, barely recognizing the words as they left her lips.

He smiled at her, watching her eyes connected to his.

"I know," he said, an expression of relief across his face.

He hugged her with his one free hand, lingering there for a while longer before kissing her head. "I love you so much," he said.

He handed her the latte he'd ordered for her as they walked through the airport to their gate. They moved in silence—the only sound was the suitcases, reassuring them that they were on the same path and that no matter where life took them, there would always be two sets of wheels rolling alongside them.

Forty

THE JOLT OF the airplane's wheels connecting with the pavement below shook Kelynn awake. Her head had been resting comfortably on Clay's shoulder. She felt completely at ease with him. There was a tiny wet spot on his T-shirt where she must've drooled in her sleep.

Her cheeks flushed, and she quickly turned to look out the small oval window when Clay grabbed her hand. "Hey."

Her eyebrows raised in anticipation of what he was going to say next.

"I had a great time with you, Sanders," he said, closing the gap between their lips.

It sent a rage of sparks through Kelynn as she kissed him again and again until the plane stopped. The other passengers made their way down the aisle, grabbing luggage from the overhead bins and filing out of the metal tube. Kelynn didn't want to leave. This whole trip had solidified who she saw herself becoming, who she saw *them* becoming. Clay gazed into her eyes and then tapped her leg in a *Hey, c'mon* manner. He quickly grabbed their luggage and carried both bags off the plane.

"Want me to drive you home? You can sleep on the way," Clay suggested.

"No, I drove here, and I definitely do not want to pay for an extra day of parking," Kelynn said, feeling frustrated that they had to separate. "Trust me. Your offer is quite enticing."

A half-smile formed across Clay's face as he pulled her close and kissed her again. He didn't let go, but kissed her forehead, breathing her in.

"I'll see you soon," he said matter-of-factly. "I'm glad you're back. And I don't just mean back in town."

Kelynn took in a sharp breath. Leaving him now in the airport parking garage felt so monumental. She was irrationally afraid that something else would threaten their relationship and she would never see him again when she would most likely see him tomorrow.

"I'll see you soon," she finally uttered after what felt like twenty minutes of taking him in—his warm, deep-colored flannel, his flawless burly beard, his blue-grey eyes looking so deeply into what felt like her soul in its entirety.

"I love you," Clay said, his back turned as he walked towards the opposite end of the parking garage.

"I love you!" Kelynn shouted back. Clay shot a wink back at her over his shoulder.

I really do love you—more than I ever thought possible. Why does it feel like part of my heart is walking away right now? Brush it off, Kel. You need sleep, she thought, feeling lovesick and exhausted. If she hadn't been sure before, she knew now. Clay was her catalyst, the otherworldly force that somehow moved her forward. She also knew she didn't need him. She'd lived on this Earth long enough without him. But being with him made it better, and she wanted it that way. Even if she reached all her aspirations on her own and beat her medical condition, she would have lost the one person who made her experience a love she didn't know could exist. She wanted her catalyst, an interdependent reaction.

Clay.

THE DAY AFTER we got back from New York, I woke up on a high. Sanders had left me without warning. I thought I'd lost her—that she didn't want me in her life—when she knew we were the one thing we each needed. And now we were together. I woke up to Willie licking my face, ready for breakfast. Who gets that excited every day for the same damn meal? I looked outside at the sunshine and felt like it was casting a bright light on everything in my life.

Sanders. My warm bed. Coffee. Sanders. The Blue Ridge Mountains. Sanders. My new job. Sanders. Sanders. Sanders. I had to see her, but I had to do something much more important first.

I grabbed my keys off the kitchen table and headed into town. I parked outside of a little run-down-looking antique store. As I walked in, I inhaled deeply, a musty scent filling the air.

"Can I help you?" a frail woman asked me, breaking my train of thought.

I asked to see their ring selection.

"What exactly are you searching for?" the Scavenger Antiques store clerk asked, looking at me over bifocals that barely rested on the end of her nose.

I replied, "Something almost magical," as the woman furrowed her brow in confusion.

Sanders was going to meet me at our spot, my favorite overlook in the mountains. As soon as I saw her turn the bend in the trail, she took off running.

As she jumped into my arms, wrapping her legs around me, I whispered into the tangles of her hair, "I missed you." I could tell by the look on her face those words meant more than simply ten letters put together.

"I missed you more," she replied.

"Not possible," I said, fumbling through my pocket.

"I have some news," she said. "I got the job in Raleigh! They called me this morning and asked me to jump on a video call for an interview and offered it on the spot."

"Sanders, congratulations! You're so cool! This is going to be a life-changing adventure for you—for us," I said, pulling her in close.

As I released my embrace, I pulled out a small triangle-shaped box from my coat pocket.

"What's this?" Sanders asked, backing away.

"No worries. I know we're taking things slow, but I want you to have this," I said, opening the lid.

She gasped and then giggled. "An opal. How'd you know?"

"I know it's not fair what I saw with your necklace, but I'm hoping somehow this has magical powers that let you see inside of *my* head, so you can see how much I love you and how much I want to have a future with you. Sanders . . ." I stopped myself. "Kelynn, this is a promise ring—a promise to you that I want to be in your world forever, and that I want you to invade my world, every inch of it."

"My catalyst," Sanders said, holding out her left hand. "Thank you for not proposing."

I kissed her, smelling her sweet scent, feeling her hair brush against my face in the wind so close to me. I looked into her evergreen eyes. "You know, Sanders, you're a real cute catalyst for me, too."

 Nat Bickel

We sat down, taking in the mountainscape, picturing the future while the opal hugged her finger, beaming with the afterglow of the sun at the end of a long rainstorm.

Acknowledgments

Thank you, God, for my love of writing. The magical earth you created gives me daily inspiration.

Jacob, I don't know where I'd be without you. You give me the courage to continue to write in new ways about hard things and break through my own barriers. Thank you for loving me like no other human ever could and inspiring me to be the best Nat. Thank you for your kind heart and gentle spirit.

My OG Fam—Mom, Dad, and Ryan—I'm grateful for your surprised reaction each and every time to dive into one of my stories. Your encouragement has made me believe in my gift and continue to share it.

To my best friend, Gwen, I can't thank you enough for crafting the most beautiful cover design. You broke through my limited vision and created a treasure.

Bob Staley, thank you for being a dedicated pen pal and a model of what a genuine caring person looks like in my early years. I owe it to you for lighting the spark to even think of writing a book. You asked me to write one quickly before your time ran out, and while I didn't get to accomplish that task, I know one day I'll get to tell you all about this journey.

Monette Short, I'm beyond grateful for our laughter and how you helped me not take myself so seriously. You always welcomed me and made me feel like a true friend.

To S.E. Hinton, the author of *The Outsiders*—when my freshman year in high school kicked off by reading a book written by someone my age, a fire started within my heart. Thank you for being the igniting element that got my creative juices flowing and for putting the YA genre on the map.

Thanks to Ben Stiller for his performance in *The Secret Life of Walter Mitty*. That movie inspired me to do big things beyond myself with the soundtrack becoming my theme music during the majority of my writing sessions.

To Jimmy Fallon, for letting Kelynn on your show and for always having a genuine interest in others' talents. I hope one day you'll let me on stage to talk about mine.

I want to thank the Lonely Island, for just bein' ya.

Thanks to Miley Cyrus, for creating music so raw with your beautifully-crafted vocal chords and for being an all around caring human who outpours love.

To Greta Gerwig, who wrote the screenplay for the 2019 adaptation of *Little Women* by Louisa May Alcott. The scene where Jo March gets to watch the first physical copy of her book come to life helped me keep pushing. I wanted that same feeling. Walking out of that theater gave me a rejuvenated spirit towards finishing my own novel.

To my beta readers, Elizabeth, Gracie, Josie, and Presley, thank you for your genuine feedback and fangirl moments. You made me believe in myself and made me feel truly seen through my words.

To my editors, Nicole Frail, Kim Robertson, Kathy Anderkin, Lynne Murphy, Andy Pecore, and Zachary Robertson, thank you for your patience. Thank you for being my personal cheerleading squad. All of you made this book even more special, making my message more refined. I needed your variety of perspectives in order to succeed. You cannot truly know the extent of my immense gratitude for your hours of hard work.

Lastly, thank you to all the family and friends who encouraged me to keep writing, who checked in to see how the book was coming. You made me believe in myself and in this novel. Thank you for that rare level of benevolence.